THE SUMMERS

THE SUMMERS

RONYA OTHMANN

Translated by Gary Schmidt

THE UNIVERSITY OF WISCONSIN PRESS

Publication of this book has been made possible, in part,
through support from the Brittingham Trust.

The University of Wisconsin Press
728 State Street, Suite 443
Madison, Wisconsin 53706
uwpress.wisc.edu

Gray's Inn House, 127 Clerkenwell Road
London EC1R 5DB, United Kingdom
eurospanbookstore.com

Printed in the United States of America
This book may be available in a digital edition.

Library of Congress Cataloging-in-Publication Data

Names: Othmann, Ronya, 1993– author. | Schmidt, Gary, 1967– translator.
Title: The summers / Ronya Othmann ; translated by Gary Schmidt.
Other titles: Sommer. English
Description: Madison, Wisconsin : The University of Wisconsin Press, 2023. |
Originally published by Carl Hanser Verlag under the title Die Sommer.
Identifiers: LCCN 2022028870 | ISBN 9780299341046 (paperback)
Subjects: LCSH: Families—Germany—Fiction. | Families—Syria—Fiction. |
Yezidis—Fiction. | Syria—History—Civil War, 2011—Fiction. |
LCGFT: Fiction. | Novels.
Classification: LCC PT2715.T46 S6613 2023 | DDC 833/.92—dc23/eng/20220822
LC record available at https://lccn.loc.gov/2022028870

Ji bo bavê min, ji bo malbata min, ji bi xwişkên min.

Berxwedan jîyane.

TRANSLATOR'S PREFACE

In order to foreground and respect the Kurdish-speaking communities represented by Ronya Othmann, we have decided to use the spellings of Kurdish names in the Hawar alphabet in which the Kurmanji dialect is written, an extended version of the Latin alphabet that includes the additional characters ç, ê, î, ş, û. For example, instead of the anglicized Qamishli for the city in Syria, we use Qamişlo. Arabic place-names are only used in the translation when they appear in the original, for example to emphasize the forced renaming of communities and erasure of the Kurdish language. In addition, special characters not used in English are retained when referencing Kurdish words, for example in the name of the protagonist's aunts Evîn and Havîn. Eszter Spät's *The Yezidis* (London: Saqi, 2005) has been consulted for the glossary.

THE SUMMERS

On the main road there was a sign with flaking letters that formed the name: Tel Khatoun. The sign was cockeyed, perhaps because of the wind. Just a few meters past it, a narrow gravel lane branched off from the main road. It led past garden fences into the village. The village used to have a different name. It had only been called Tel Khatoun since the time when all other villages and cities in the region had also been given new names.

It was just one of many villages between Tirbespî and Rmelan. One that nobody just wandered into. One you only went to if you knew the people who lived there.

Leyla could walk down the lane to the village in her mind: ten steps from Tel Khatoun's metal sign to where the lane branched off, then fifteen steps to her grandparents' garden, and then, between her grandparents' garden and their neighbors' garden three hundred steps on the gravel lane, where most of the time the chickens were already coming toward you, and then past the left side of the fountain to her grandparents' house.

Her grandparents' house stood at the entrance to the village, its garden poking into the landscape like a long green tongue. If you walked past the olive trees, orange trees, flower beds, and tobacco plants as far as the rear wire fence, you could look back to the main road you had come from. All around were fields, and beyond the fields a mountain range rose in the distance, the Turkish border.

If Leyla had not known what was happening on that border, she might have thought the mountains were beautiful.

The house was made from the same clay as the landscape, even having the same color. Admittedly, Leyla had only been to the village in the summer. From her father she knew that in springtime the country was covered in green, there were far more plants blooming, and the ground was damp and clumpy. The grass only faded over the course of the summer months under the hot sun, the heat desiccating the earth and the wind pushing more and more dust before it. Every year, the more the summer advanced, the more desolate the landscape became.

Leyla had spent entire days lying on the thin foam mats in the house, staring at the ceiling. The ceiling beams were thick tree trunks whose boughs had been cut and their bark shaved off. Above the beams was the vaulted straw, and above that the roof was sealed with a layer of clay so that no rain could seep in. The windows were small and deep, the walls thick in order to keep out the summer heat and winter cold. There were only two narrow doors. The metal one led to the courtyard and the street, the wooden one to the garden out back.

Many years ago, all the village men had gathered to build the house. They had fired bricks out of clay, then hauled and stacked them. They worked for three days until the house was finished.

Chickens lived in the courtyard next to the house, as in all the village courtyards. Their droppings lay sprinkled everywhere on the dusty ground. Two lofts stood there on tall, narrow metal feet; those were the summer beds. In the winter they slept on the wool mattresses and rugs inside the house.

The house was not large, just two rooms and a small corridor. There was no furniture, just pillows on the floor with holes in their covers and thin mattresses. The walls were painted white, but the paint was flaking off, revealing a mixture of clay and straw that had been smeared over the fired bricks. Hanging from the ceiling in the middle of both rooms were large fans that spun incessantly throughout the summer.

On my grandparents' property there were smaller houses not meant to be lived in. The kitchen and shower were in one of them, in another the pantry. There was a hut for the chicken, another one for the bees, and in one of the summers sometime later on there was even an outhouse.

The village was as flat as the landscape surrounding it. Only in the village center was there a hill, for the dead. It wasn't really a hill but more of a small mound. Leyla wondered if this hill had been constructed by people or if the people had chosen it in order to build their village around it. Or if it had slowly grown up, swelling from generations of the dead that had been buried there over the course of centuries. For there were such hills in other villages too.

Grandmother called dying the day you changed your clothes. Leyla imagined all the dying people being handed freshly washed clothing made of coarse material the color of the earth.

~

Her grandmother's phrase about the day you changed your clothes popped into her mind again suddenly as she walked down the empty street. It wasn't raining, but the air was damp.

The arrival board at the streetcar stop showed five minutes. Besides her, there were three men waiting. One sat on the bench and typed something into his phone. The other was wearing an orange safety vest and held a steaming cup of coffee in his hand. The third just stood there, smoked, and stared into space. They didn't even turn their heads when Leyla joined them. The minutes on the destination board fell from five to four, from four to three, three to two, two to one. Then the streetcar arrived.

Leyla put on her backpack again.

You always tell a story from its end, she thought. Even if you start with the beginning.

[1]

Every summer they flew to the country where her father had grown up. The country had two names. One of them could be found on maps, globes, and official documents.

The family used the other one.

Both names could be assigned their respective territory. If you laid these territories on top of one another, they overlapped.

One of the countries was Syria, the Syrian Arab Republic. The other one was Kurdistan, their country. Kurdistan was located inside the Syrian Arab Republic but extended beyond its borders. It had no officially recognized frontiers. Her father said they were the rightful owners of the land but in spite of that were only tolerated, and often not even that.

Later, Leyla would look in vain for Kurdistan in the school atlas. The Europeans are to blame, her father said and cracked a sunflower seed between his teeth. To be more precise: France and Great Britain, when they divided it up among themselves on the drawing board with a pencil and a ruler one hundred years ago. Since then, our country extends across four states.

You must not tell anyone the name of the country, her father said. When someone asks you where we are going then you'll tell them: to your grandparents' house.

The journey to her grandparents' country was long. They always had to change planes at several airports. Sometimes, they only had a layover of a few hours, sometimes a whole day or longer. Leyla didn't mind; on the contrary, she would have liked to stay longer at the airports. She loved the orderly, air-conditioned waiting rooms; the transit area with its duty-free shops, where you could buy expensive perfumes, expensive makeup, and expensive alcohol; the long corridors that hundreds of people walked through daily without leaving behind a trace, from all corners of the globe to all corners of the globe. Leyla loved that everybody here was equally a stranger to everyone else: the personnel to the passengers, the passengers to each other, in a certain sense even the airports to their surroundings. When they finally arrived and a hot wind blew in their faces as they climbed out of the plane—how Leyla loved that moment! Every time, she stopped for a few seconds on the gangway, inhaling deeply and gazing into the landscape. She would have stayed longer up there if the passengers behind her had not pushed her and had her mother not grabbed her by the arm and pulled her forward.

Palm trees behind the runway, the dry earth. The big glass facade with its star-shaped ornaments, the smooth tile floor. The life-sized gold-framed portraits of the president and the presidential father, was that in Aleppo or Damascus? She couldn't remember. Nowadays, the only flights left were domestic, if there were any at all, for they had fought at the airports too. Military planes had taken off and landed there; she had seen the pictures on television but didn't want to think about them. Back then, when traveling every summer vacation to her grandparents' house, they had no inkling of all that. Or did they? She suddenly remembered the men at the airports, all of them in the secret service, her father said, with their pleated pants, ironed shirts, and slicked-back hair. Her father bribed the agents so they would stop asking questions and let the family pass. Back then she had not understood why her father had silently pushed bottles of whiskey across the table and slipped the agents lighters and flashlights. They expected this kind of payment, a fee that was neither demanded verbally nor put down on paper but that everyone knew they had to pay to be let through. So that they don't give us any trouble, her father said.

Leyla didn't pay much attention to the agents or her father's bribes. He spoke Arabic with them, and Leyla did not understand Arabic. She was busy adjusting her new dress and hopping across the shiny tiles in her black shoes with the white ribbons. Whoever touched the cracks was dead, the game she always played when they traveled, impatient for the journey to continue.

With her new little patent-leather shoes, her white stockings trimmed with lace netting, the hem of her new dress swaying, with its white polka dots and lace collar, Leyla felt like a princess, too beautiful for the dusty village. Once they arrived, she was sent first by her grandmother to change clothes before being allowed to play with her cousins.

Her father had bought her the dress, in Qamişlo. She liked best of all to go shopping with him, or with her aunt. Her mother had never bought her a dress like that. She would have said, what do you want with that? It's made of plastic. It will get dirty right away. It doesn't keep you warm. You will only sweat in it. It's not practical. Things always had to be practical for her mother, which had to do with her job: she was a nurse. And in the hospital, everything was practical, from the work clothes, beds, and hand disinfectants to the building itself. Practical carried the same weight as reasonable. Whether something was practical or not counted far more than if it was pretty. But the things her mother thought were practical Leyla thought were ugly. The one thing ruled out the other, she thought. Either you shivered or you sweated, either you could move freely or you were pretty. You couldn't have everything at the same time.

~

Nobody was pretty, neither in her mother's family nor her father's. Or maybe just barely her maternal great-grandmother and her sisters in the Black Forest family when they were young women. Leyla liked looking at the old sepia photographs of them. The sisters had been washerwomen, with high cheekbones and a feverish glow in their eyes, a weak smile on their lips.

She herself often stood in front of the mirror in the bathroom and tried to imitate that smile. But no matter how hard she tried, it ended up as a grimace.

After the last war in Germany, they had eaten a lot in her mother's family, in the fifties and sixties. In Leyla's parents' kitchen there was a cookbook that her mother's Black Forest grandmother had given her as a wedding present. Leyla could not remember her mother ever cooking anything from that cookbook. Written in her Black Forest grandmother's neat handwriting on the green lines of the book it said, My favorite recipes: *maultaschen, schupfnudeln* and head cheese, Landjäger sausage, cold cuts, beef brisket in horseradish sauce, vanilla wedges, pancakes, pudding.

Her mother's family had never been able to get rid of their obesity. Her elderly relatives suffered from diabetes, dying from heart attacks or strokes. When they were younger, they tried one diet after the other but finally gave up and bought only loose clothing. Her mother was the exception, having broken with her family's traditions. And still she was not beautiful, Leyla thought. She always had the same functional haircut, never used makeup or nail polish, wore her white smock in the hospital and similar practical clothes at home, only in color.

In her father's family everyone worked in the fields, or in Germany on construction sites, or, if they had managed to get ahead, in their own kebab shops. Her father's relatives had chapped hands, bent backs, and haggard faces. They smoked almost without exception, smoked at home, smoked on the way to work, smoked on their breaks. Their bodies were their tools, which would soon show signs of wear and tear. They put their hands on their hips, rubbed their shoulders with their fists, said their backs were hurting them. Their feet hurt nonstop from standing so much.

The workplace accidents were worse. Or what had happened to Uncle Nûrî, a story told over and over again in her family as soon as the topic of work came up. Back then, Uncle Nûrî worked in road construction. A backbreaking job, her father said. It was autumn and her uncle caught a cold. A harmless cold, so he thought. It will pass. But it didn't.

Tomorrow I will go to the doctor, her uncle had said to his wife. And again the next day he would say, tomorrow I really will go to the doctor. But instead of going to the doctor he just kept going to work.

At some point in time Leyla had gone with her parents to Hanover to visit Uncle Nûrî in the hospital. He was already in a coma by then. A cold, the doctors said. A cold that her uncle had carried around for so long that it had traveled to his brain and caused meningitis.

It took a few days for her uncle to wake up from the coma and a few months before he was released from the hospital, but he never got well again. Uncle Nûrî forgot, and forgetting is the worst of all, said her father. Uncle Nûrî couldn't remember that he had already eaten lunch an hour afterward.

~

When her father came home from work, he always came through the door silently, unlike her mother, who called out loudly *I'm back* every time. He had the dust from the construction site in his hair, on his skin, in his clothes. He showered and changed before sitting down exhausted at the kitchen table to eat hastily.

After eating he went into the living room and turned on the television. He watched the evening news in three different languages. He'd say: Leyla, get me the sunflower seeds from the kitchen. Leyla, get me a glass of water. And Leyla went in the kitchen, fetched the sunflower seeds and the glass of water, and was allowed to join her father in front of the TV until she got tired, fell asleep, and her mother carried her to bed. For a while, her mother had tried to impose a strict bedtime, like in the hospital, where there were clear rules about visiting hours and quiet hours began at nine o'clock. Her mother loved clear-cut rules. When her mother was on the nightshift, Leyla could eat as many sweets as she wanted. Her father also let her drink cola, bought her a kebab and chicken nuggets. When her mother wasn't home, Leyla fell asleep in front of the television.

But on some evenings her father stayed longer at the kitchen table. He'd reach for the bag with the salted sunflower seeds, crack them between his teeth, spit out the shells on the table. The shells piled up while her father spoke.

He drew little crosses on a paper napkin with a ballpoint pen.

The crosses are mines, her father would say. There was, he'd say, always just one meter between one death and another. All deaths together formed a square pattern. Whoever was sure of his steps could fool death. Whoever stepped in the wrong place, however, lost an arm, a leg, or his life.

Her father said that people often crossed the border at night. They had family and friends on the other side, and they traded. The border was close. If a mine blew up, they heard it in the village.

There were mines for people and mines for tanks, her father would say. The ones for tanks looked like plastic plates. Once my neighbor found such a plate. He thought, you can always use something like that, as a watering bowl for the chicken for example. He was lucky: he only lost one hand.

Leyla thought about how in the summer she used to run out into the fields. True, her father had said that the mines had been removed years ago, but what if, she thought, they had forgotten just one single mine?

～

It was as if her father had a book in his head that he just had to open, Leyla thought. She would just have to say the right word while he was still sitting at the kitchen table, before he got up to go in the living room, and her father would already be laughing, reaching for the bag of sunflower seeds, starting to tell his story.

Tell me the story of Aziz and the chickens, Leyla said.

Not today, said her father. I am so tired from work.

Please, said Leyla. Just the one.

Her father sighed. Well, okay, just the one, but no more after that and I'm going to make it quick.

Only a few people in the village could speak Arabic, her father began, standing up to pour himself a glass of water before sitting down again. Even if he said he would be brief, Leyla knew that it could take longer.

Actually, only the younger people could speak Arabic, her father said, the ones who had gone to school. And our neighbor Aziz, like my parents, had never gone to school.

Like my father, he also had a small radio, one that ran on batteries that he took into the fields or, like my father, onto the roof, because the reception there was the best.

Every few days he called me to come over so that I could translate the evening news for him. He told his wife to bring me some tea and *kûlîçe* because he knew how much I liked to eat her cookies. I was always willing to translate in exchange for *kûlîçe*.

It was late summer of 1973. I was twelve years old and was already going to school in town. After school I would play the *saz* and dream of studying one day in Damascus or Aleppo. There was a war going on between Israel and Syria.

The Jews are barbaric, my Arabic teacher at school had said. They murder children. Back then that didn't interest me, for I had never encountered a Jew. True, there was a Jewish family in Qamişlo, but I did not associate them with the Jews that my teacher kept talking about all the time. The Jews in Qamişlo—they were the Azra family. To this day they are still spice traders there. You know them, Leyla: we shop at their store when we are in Qamişlo. There was nothing special about the Azra family. Their spices tasted the same as all the others.

The situation was tense, even I could sense that. That's why Aziz wanted me to come over every evening to translate the news. As if he could gain control over the situation by doing so, he sat like a possessed man in front of the radio without a break, never turning it off. I had to translate.

After a few days I didn't feel like doing it anymore.

We were on vacation from school, and my friends met every afternoon behind the school to play soccer, staying until sundown.

And yet I sat with Aziz in front of the radio. The newscaster on the radio talked and talked. The regime was so certain of victory you would have thought the war had been won long ago. That annoyed me. And Aziz annoyed me too, the way he just kept sitting there in front of his radio, fidgety and frightened like a child. I didn't even think about it when I translated the news that Israel had just invaded Syria.

Aziz dropped the prayer chain from his hand, whose pearls he had just been pushing back and forth between his fingers. It was too late.

What will happen now? he asked and looked at me aghast.

Wait! Be quiet, they are still talking! I have to concentrate, I said.

I couldn't think of anything to say.

Aziz got impatient: Come on, tell me what they are saying!

In the meantime, the newscaster had come to the weather forecast.

They are already in Damascus, I said. On the way, they confiscated the sheep of seventeen shepherds.

Aziz looked at me, horrified. What now? he asked.

What now? I repeated.

What are the Jews doing with the sheep?

What do I know? What do you think they would do with the sheep? Eat them, I suppose.

That doesn't sound good, said Aziz.

I came again the next evening. Aziz's wife brought tea and cookies. Aziz turned on his radio.

The Israelis are now in Homs.

The next day I said they were now in Aleppo. They are taking the most direct route toward us. Tomorrow they will be in Raqqa and the day after tomorrow in Hasakah.

Hasakah, Aziz repeated with panic in his voice. Then they are already almost here!

I nodded. Everywhere they go they are taking sheep, goats, cows, and donkeys.

What about my chickens? Aziz asked in great agitation. Do you think they'll take my chickens away from me?

Of course, I said. They will take *all* of your chickens away from you.

When I came the next evening to translate, Aziz was not at home. Even in the courtyard it was strangely still. But from the garden came noises and loud yelling. I went around back and there was a huge pool of blood on the ground. Everywhere there were heads of chickens, feathers, and, in the midst of it all, Aziz's wife with the butcher knife and the children, who were running around trying to catch the last living chickens. In the middle of all the chaos was Aziz, who greeted me grimly and clutched another chicken.

What's going on here? I asked, although I knew exactly what was going on. Aziz, are those all your chickens?

He nodded. Come over tomorrow for dinner, he said.

But you haven't slaughtered all your chickens? I asked, seeing what I had caused.

Of course, he said. Better we eat them than the enemy get hold of them!

Three days later, I happened to be in the living room when I saw Aziz cutting across the yard toward our house. He had both hands balled up into fists. I could tell by the way he was walking that he was furious. He yelled my name. Silo, where are you? he screamed. Come out! I'll rip your head off like I did to my chickens!

I jumped back from the window, left the house through the back door, climbed over the garden fence, and ran across the fields to the neighboring village, where I visited a friend, staying overnight, hoping that by the next day Aziz would calm down.

~

Her mother came home early from work. She had taken the afternoon off to pick up Leyla at school, and they rode downtown together. Leyla was not in the mood to traipse through department stores and supermarkets, like they did every summer before traveling, in search of *reasonable gifts*, as her mother called them. Leyla constantly lagged behind, lingering in front of the lingerie, which she found strange, or the high-heeled shoes, until her mother pulled her along: Don't break anything, then we'll have to pay for that too!

They went first to Karstadt, then to smaller clothing stores, buying cardigans, T-shirts, and sweatshirts, then made their way to Kaufhof and finally to Veneto. There, Leyla got to have two scoops of ice cream for having courageously stuck it out, as her mother said. They purchased the things they were still missing in the supermarkets around the corner from where they lived, depending on what was on sale in each of them. They bought everything they had been asked to buy over the course of the year in telephone conversations: oily ointments for cracked feet, medicines, cameras, blenders, and those electric toothbrushes advertised on German television commercials you could see even in the village via satellite disk. Everybody in the village always knew what you could get in German department stores: sweets and toys for children, leggings for the babies that had been born during the year and were proudly held up to the camera for the videotapes sent to Germany.

The requests changed over time. One year vitamin pills were in high demand in the village, another year it was iron pills. Sometimes you'd hear that Xalil's wife was given a microwave this year by her brother in Germany, and sometimes I'd hear from Kawa that we could buy hand blenders here.

Her grandparents' requests were the most modest. Her father always had to ask several times and every time they both said they needed nothing. We are not coming with nothing, father said, and then at some point grandfather would respond that he needed a hat to protect him from the sun and grandmother needed a new pocketknife.

And as the very last thing, Leyla's parents bought the bottles of whiskey, the flashing lighters, and the perfume to bribe the agents.

At home, mother stuffed everything into suitcases and shopping bags, adding the clothes that Leyla had outgrown over the course of the year. There was hardly any room left for books, just enough for one or two. Take one that you can read several times, her father said. Leyla could not decide, laying out all her books on the floor in front of her and grabbing one without looking at it. *A Little Princess.*

Luggage was restricted to twenty kilos per passenger. If it went over a little, Syrian air could be persuaded, but books were heavy. Leyla calculated how many pages per day she would have. The days in the village were long, and the midday heat was oppressive. Every family withdrew into its house, lay under the fans, and slept. There was nothing to do and Leyla was bored. Only with books could she fill the long midday hours.

Because she read so much, the village people said she was a serious girl. Even her cousin Zozan thought she was precocious and arrogant. At least it seemed that way to Leyla, but maybe Zozan was just envious. Leyla was the only child in the village who owned books.

Years later she wondered why she and Zozan had never been friends. Everything pointed in that direction. They were almost the same age, two cousins who spent every summer with each other.

Books were not the only thing that separated Leyla from the other children. There was also the way she stumbled when she was out in the village with Zozan. She didn't know where the ditches were and where you had to jump while running and playing catch. The other children knew every ditch that the wastewater ran through, the open sewers of the village, invisible from spring on, when the grass had grown tall. They all just took these in one leap without even thinking about it. Their feet knew the way at night too, in the dark, when the power went out and Leyla found herself over and over falling into the mire, ashamed. Zozan said Leyla had no eyes in her head and told everyone in the village about it, whether they wanted to hear it or not. The oh-so-smart cousin from Germany. Almanya, as she called her, actually fell into the filthy slime!

And there were also the missing words when she spoke and her pronunciation, the fact that she couldn't roll her *r*'s the way everyone else did. She sounded so silly that Zozan mimicked her when she brought Leyla along to meet her friends, for her grandmother had told Zozan, take Leyla along, but Zozan only did it grudgingly, thinking Leyla wouldn't understand them. Leyla stood next to Zozan and their friends and felt like a mute dog just trotting behind them. At some point she quit speaking unless somebody spoke to her first.

Zozan was two years younger but knew better about everything. When Leyla did the laundry in the big tin tub in the yard, Zozan took the bar of soap out of her hand and said, Not that way, you do it like this! When Leyla made tea, Zozan said, You are letting it steep way too long. When Leyla cut up cucumbers for the salad, the pieces were too large; when she rolled grape leaves they fell apart when they were cooked; when she looked after her little cousin, who was still a baby at that time, he immediately started crying.

Except for Zozan, everyone was friendly to her, more than friendly. Whenever her second or third cousins, her countless real aunts, aunts by marriage, and sisters and cousins of the aunts by marriage arrived from town for a visit, they heaped compliments and gifts on Leyla. They hung plastic bracelets on her, chains, flower- or butterfly-shaped barrettes, and glittering scarves that they wore on their arms and necks and in their hair, simply taking them off to thrust on Leyla. Leyla was always embarrassed by all that; she felt bad when people were so generous to her.

Bah! said Zozan. They only do that because your father gives them money. If he didn't, they'd starve. He paid Bêrîvan's grandfather's doctor bill and gave Kawa money for the migrant smugglers so he could go to Germany.

Maybe Zozan had been right, Leyla thought later on. She too had been arrogant and a smart aleck, at least just as much as Zozan. She had looked down on everyone because her English was better than Zozan's smattering of village school English, had always smirked at her for constantly envisioning her wedding, which dress she would wear, which hairstyle she would have, how beautiful her makeup would be. I, Leyla said one summer to Zozan, have other goals in my life besides finding a husband, having seven children, and baking bread. How holier-than-thou she had been back then. Marrying, having children, that was all Zozan could allow herself to dream of. She couldn't compete with Leyla's English, polished by tutors, or with the plans Leyla's father had for her: diploma, college, medical school or law school.

But Zozan had also often braided her hair, Leyla remembered. She sat quietly while Zozan combed and worked her hair, humming softly. Once when she asked Zozan where she had learned so many types of braids, she said she had made them all up herself. Once, during one of the final summers, she told Leyla she'd really like to be a hairstylist, that was her secret. She put flowers from the garden in Leyla's hair and talked about how she would one day open up her own hair salon in al-Qahtaniya. And Leyla was ashamed. She was ashamed of the way she, the only child from Almanya, had come to the village every summer, carefully climbed out of the car in her patent-leather shoes and fresh dress, and teetered over the dusty earth toward the others like a princess on a state visit.

The most conspicuous thing about Leyla, however, was her mother, who was so different from all the other village mothers; she smelled different, talked differently, even looked different with her shoulder-length light-brown hair always tied back, *because it was practical*, as she said, and she never wore skirts like the other village women. She spoke Arabic and Kurdish, since before marrying she had worked as a nurse for an aid organization and been sent first to Lebanon for an extended stay and later to Iran and then Iraq. There, during the Anfal campaign, Saddam Hussein's genocide against the Kurds, she had tended to Kurdish refugees and learned a kind of makeshift Kurdish that was different from the Kurdish spoken in the village, making her seem even stranger in the eyes of the villagers. And then there was the fact that she was quiet and never gossiped, and never ever talked about the things she had seen in Iraq.

Your mother is a spy, Zozan had once said. Who says that? asked Leyla. The village says it, Zozan replied.

Once, when the authorities had refused to issue her father a special visa that he could use to enter and leave the country freely and Leyla was too little to travel on her own, her mother decided to come along. She packed a suitcase like one she had used for her earlier deployments full of medicine, bandages, sterile pads, and immunizations.

After a few days, the first village women already turned up. They said they had heard there was a nurse there from Almanya. Her mother learned quickly. New words from the village soon got mixed in with her makeshift Iraqi Kurdish: she now said *eat*, *drink*, *tired*, *pain*, *children*, and *tomatoes* in the village dialect, supplementing this with the broken Arabic she had learned in Lebanon and at the adult education center in Germany. Her linguistic potpourri was as practical as a mobile hospital that one simply plopped down in the landscape: it worked despite something being missing every time you turned around, and everything had to go quickly, leaving no time to exchange pleasantries or platitudes. In time, her mother got used to the village and the village got used to her. Later, during those summers her mother was there, the village women still said she was a spy, but one who knew how to give injections.

~

Her grandfather sat most of the time on a rug, where he slept, rolled cigarettes, smoked, and ate salted sunflower seeds. You could always find him wherever the family happened to be; he hobbled around with his cane, his can of tobacco, and the chain with the big round pearls that he always pushed back and forth between his fingers while talking or just sitting there, while the others carried the pillows, rug, and mat behind him, from the house to the garden or into the yard and back again.

He always had the same clothes on, şal û şapik, like most of the old men of the village wore, a loose pair of pants and shirt in brown, olive, or gray tones, sewn for him by Leyla's grandmother, the pants having a wide, meter-long cloth scarf wrapped around his waist. He always wore a hat and had his wooden cane with him. His eyes were cloudy. To Leyla, it looked like someone had poured milk over his eyeballs. She thought it was because of the milk that her grandfather was blind: he couldn't see through it. His eyes had not always had that murky color. Her grandmother said that they used to be dark brown, the color of walnuts, almost black.

Nobody, not even he himself, knew exactly how old he was. Just as her grandmother didn't know how old she was, no more than all the other old people in the village. For a long time, Leyla had thought her grandfather was the oldest person in the world. He remembered things that had happened a hundred, two hundred years ago. He could tell stories about wars and battles, about Mem and Zîn, as if he had been there himself. He simply must have been there when all that happened, he knew it so well. The story of Mem and Zîn was the saddest story Leyla had ever heard. Mem, a court scribe from the Alan family, and Princess Zîn from the Botan family fell in love. They wanted to marry, but a conspiracy thwarted their plans. Bakir, an evil man, killed Mem. When Zîn learned of Mem's death, she collapsed at his grave and died as well. But that wasn't the end of the story: the people quickly got wind of Mem and Zîn's death and, becoming enraged, they killed the evil Bakir, who had to suffer the humiliation of being buried under Mem and Zîn's feet. But a thornbush nourished by Bakir's blood grew out of him. The roots of the thornbush dug so deep into the earth and pushed so mightily between the graves of Mem and Zîn that even in death the two remained separated.

~

Sometimes Leyla's grandfather received a visit from a friend whose name she could later no longer remember. In her family, they had simply called him the Armenian. He came to the village and stayed for tea, or for a few days. The Armenian had grown up in the same region as her grandfather, Beşiri it was called, near Batman. Leyla didn't know whether they had known each other back then or if their families had just been connected in some way.

The Armenian had other acquaintances in the village who also invited him to visit. But his real reason for coming was to visit her grandfather. They would sit for hours in the yard or the living room, smoking, drinking tea, and eating fruit that Zozan, Leyla, or her grandmother served them, and sometimes Leyla sat with them. As long as she sat still, she was allowed to stay, and her grandfather and the Armenian paid no more attention to her. They were completely absorbed in comparing their memories, talking about families, villages, and names that Leyla had never heard before. The Armenian was a few years younger than her grandfather. Today, Leyla knew that both her grandfather and the Armenian could only have known those names, families, and villages from stories, for all had already long since vanished when the two were born. Years later in college, Leyla read 1915, 1916, and suddenly she had dates for what the two had always talked about.

Her grandfather told stories about the Armenians who had been their neighbors in the village and others who had lived in the nearby hamlets, in Kurukanah and Maribe, and in the nearest towns, in Kars, Diyarbakir, Van, who had been craftsmen, had built stoves, the Tigran family, the Gasparyan family, the Gagarjah family, or were their names different? But they had been cabinetmakers, and the such-and-such family, blacksmiths. Some were farmers and kept cattle just like her grandfather's family. It had been a good region for agriculture; the soil near the Tigris was fertile. Up until the day, her grandfather said, when the soldiers came to the villages and towns. It was summer, and they came on horses. Their horses' hooves struck the ground dully, raising dust. The soldiers rounded up the families. Only a few were able to hide, for example Mrs. Sona, whom even Leyla's father could remember well as an old woman years later. Up until her death she returned again and again to the village to visit her family, as she said: mother, father, sisters and brothers, although not her biological mother, her biological father, her biological sisters and brothers. When she was a little girl, they had dressed her in Yazidi clothes, long, wide pants under the skirt, a white headscarf, and concealed her from the soldiers as the daughter of a Yazidi family. Mrs. Sona stayed with this family until she married, having no other place to return to, for all the others had been driven into the huge graves that they had been forced to dig for themselves in the hundred-degree heat of high summer under the soldiers' surveillance. To this day, nothing grows there, her grandfather said, because the soil is soaked in blood. And others, he said, died in the Syrian desert, or in the Tigris River, where the soldiers used their sabers to hack off the hands of all those who clung desperately to the shrubs and tufts of grass so that they would not be swept away by the current.

It was from a village in this region that the singer Karapetê Xaço came, whose songs her grandfather sometimes listened to with the Armenian, her grandfather singing along. Karapetê Xaço's village in the province of Batman was called Bileyder. Besides him only one brother and two sisters survived; Xaço was fifteen years old at the time. He joined the French Foreign Legion, stayed there for the next fifteen years, married a woman from Qamişlo, and ultimately moved with his family to Yerevan. He was one of the best *dengbêj* that had ever lived. Every day at quarter to four in the afternoon and at quarter to nine, grandfather said, I climbed onto the roof, after we had finally bought a radio, a small portable one with batteries— Nûrî bought it for me—I climbed onto the roof because the reception was best there and listened to the Kurdish broadcast from Radio Yerevan. Twice a day for half an hour. That's where I heard Xaço's voice again and again. He died poor, grandfather said. I sing for forty million Kurds; forty million Kurds cannot feed me, he is reported to have said. His voice, like a nightingale, have you ever heard anything so beautiful, Leyla? her grandfather asked, and the Armenian and her grandfather looked at her.

~

It was hard for him to walk. He only managed a few steps bent over forward while leaning on his cane. With his other hand he felt for the wall or the shoulders of his children and grandchildren, seeking support. Once he found it, he grabbed hold with his trembling hand, his white knuckles bulging.

He was always calling for her grandmother when he needed something or if he was just bored. And Leyla believed he was often bored, for he could barely walk and was blind. Leyla had never known him differently.

But earlier, her grandmother said, he was always as busy as she was, in the field, with the animals, with the tea and tobacco that he had brought over to Turkey to sell. Since her grandfather had gone blind and lame, her father said, her grandmother worked twice as hard. Or even three times as hard, because Grandfather constantly needed her help, not even being able to dress himself anymore.

Leyla, go sit with your grandfather, her father told her, it makes him happy when you are with him. And Leyla liked to sit with her grandfather, but after a while she always got bored and she started to scratch open her mosquito bites or pick off the lint from the carpet. Grandfather reached for his tobacco. I can't find my tobacco, Leyla, have you seen my tobacco? He reached for his cup, the cup was empty: Leyla, can you bring me some water? I'm thirsty.

Leyla fetched him some water and sat down with him again. He reached his hand out to feel her hair: Zozan? No, it's you, Leyla. Grandfather could tell his two granddaughters apart by the length of their braids.

He began to talk about his daughter-in-law Havîn, she was so lazy. She is always so lazy. Can you explain to me why she is so lazy, Leyla? Just one day after Memo married her, I said we should send her back, she's not worth the bride-price. Havîn was one of his favorite topics, her grand-father never tired of telling stories about everything she had done wrong. Her kûlîçe don't taste good, said her grandfather, in the rare case that she actually bakes, which she seldom does because she is so lazy. But they just don't taste good. Which he didn't understand because baking kûlîçe really was not hard. Even Zozan could do it better than her mother.

Leyla believed that ranting was her grandfather's favorite pastime, mostly about people that she did not know. The one or the other suppos-edly lied, this one or that one was two-faced, Grandfather said. Leyla, you agree with me, don't you? And Leyla would nod to herself and loudly say yes, although she didn't know who her grandfather was talking about.

He constantly called for her grandmother. Most of the time she came right away, but sometimes, when she was busy or just didn't feel like it, she pretended not to hear him. She just walked right past him when he called for her: Hawa! Hawa! She would walk straight across the yard, looking over and beyond him, and in his blindness he didn't notice. Sometimes Leyla found that so funny that she couldn't help laughing and her grandfather was furious. What's so funny? Stop laughing!

Every morning at sunrise, while everyone else was still sleeping, her grandmother got up and said her morning prayers. Leyla was awakened by her soft voice. It took a moment for her to realize what her grandmother was doing. She was the only one in the family who prayed. Leyla had never seen anyone pray before. She was fascinated.

When he was a child, her grandfather had also prayed, her grandmother said when Leyla asked her. But then his two sisters died suddenly of senseless childhood illnesses. God gives life and he takes it back again, her grandmother said. From then on, her grandfather was an only child. And about God he could only curse.

Two beautiful sisters I had, with long black hair and delicate faces, he would shout. Why couldn't God have left me at least one single sister?

Since God was not a good topic for her grandfather, her grandmother was in charge of all familial religious obligations. She fasted, cooked for holy days and served the shaykhs, *pîrs*, and *qewals* when they came to visit. On Wednesdays she did not wash. Many years ago, she had even gone on a pilgrimage to Lalish with her youngest son, Memo, although she otherwise never left the village. She taught her children and grandchildren to sing the hymn of Sherfedîn and not to swear or spit on the floor and never to wear the color blue.

After her morning prayers, which she said while still seated on the bed, she got up carefully in order not to wake her sleeping grandchildren, climbed down the ladder to the yard from the loft, and went to feed the chickens, prepare breakfast, make tea, water the garden, bake bread, pull weeds, transplant beds, sow seeds, harvest, fix the fence. If it got hot, she went into the house and darned, made lunch, ate, and slept until it got cooler again. Then she'd go back outside, fill the water canister in the kitchen, pick grapes, sort out the overripe ones for the raki, thread okra onto yarn, hang it to dry in the pantry, and tend to the bees. In between she made tea for the neighbors who came to visit, brought food and water to Leyla's grandfather, washed him, and watched the grandchildren. She consoled them when they were crying after hurting themselves, covered them up with a blanket so that they didn't get chilled when they fell asleep under the fan, pulled Mîran and Roda apart when they had gotten into a fight, and rocked little Roda in her arms until he fell asleep.

While she did this, Leyla and Zozan were always at her side, as if they were her left and right hands. If visitors came and she wanted to bring them fruit and tea, she thrust Roda into Leyla's arms. But just as soon as her grandmother left the room, the infant opened his toothless mouth and started wailing. His face turned red, his eyes watered, and no matter what Leyla did, whether she patted his back, tried to distract him by making faces, rocked him in her arms, he didn't stop crying. He screamed so loudly that Leyla was frightened, wondering what she had done wrong. Had she accidentally hurt him, or could he, just a baby, not stand her either? Close to tears herself, she gave up and carried the infant into the kitchen, where he immediately calmed down once he was in his grandmother's arms.

In one of the later summers, her grandmother suddenly fell ill and collapsed. Leyla was coming back from playing soccer with Mîran, Welat, and Roda and found her lying in the living room. Aunt Pero and Uncle Memo were sitting next to her. Aunt Pero checked her pulse and laid her hand on her forehead. Leyla got scared when she saw her grandmother like that and started to cry. Her grandmother lay there motionless with her eyes closed, her hand limp in Leyla's aunt's other hand. Leyla, go over to Zozan's, her aunt said. But Leyla didn't want to go. She sat down.

At some point her grandmother opened her eyes again. Nothing, Aunt Pero said, can kill Grandmother that fast. But Leyla was inconsolable. Even if her grandmother wasn't dying now, one day she would. She had never thought about it, but suddenly it was obvious to her. Her grandmother was old. One day she would just not be there anymore.

Her grandmother remained lying on the floor. Her aunt poured lukewarm tea into her mouth. I'm dizzy, her grandmother said softly. Her circulation was going crazy. Her voice sounded weak, as if it came from far away. She turned her head away and stared at the wall, as if the mere act of seeing took a toll on her. Finally, she closed her eyes again, but she didn't sleep. Leyla sat next to her and watched her chest rise and fall gently. I can't get up, her grandmother said. Her aunt brought a bowl of chicken soup. I'm not hungry, said her grandmother.

Because her grandmother was sick, everything in the household immediately fell apart. Nobody could remember where to find anything in the pantry. Aunt Havîn searched for a while but then gave up and just put out bread, oil, and za'atar on the tray. She said that would have to suffice and sat back down in front of the television to keep watching her Egyptian soap opera.

The grandchildren started quarreling and got into a fight in the yard. Uncle Memo had driven to town with her father to get medicine. The onions stayed out in the sun too long and dried up. A chicken got run over by a car. Two turkeys got lost in the fields, and Leyla and Zozan ran after them trying to catch them, which was no easy matter, since Leyla was afraid of turkeys and ran away as soon as they came close to her. On top of that,

Leyla was afraid of the snakes that might be anywhere in the fields; she didn't know whether to watch out for them first or for the turkeys. At some point Zozan screamed at her to pull herself together, the turkeys weren't going to kill her.

Leyla ran home crying. She was dizzy from the heat; she had to sit down and drink some water. But not for too long, since Zozan was waiting outside. Leyla went to look for Mîran, Welat, and Roda to go with her into the fields, to Zozan and the turkeys. Finally, they all came back to the house, scratched up and exhausted. Uncle Memo and her father were finally back from town. We can't manage on our own, Leyla said.

For three days they ate yogurt and bread that diminished and dried out day by day. They urgently needed to bake but without her grandmother's direction they didn't know how to begin. Her father fed the chickens and watered the garden, but then people came to visit and everything fell apart again. In the garden, the fruit fell from the trees, and the birds pecked the grapes apart. Twice a day Aunt Pero came from next door, looked in on Leyla's grandmother, and tried to take care of the most important chores with Zozan. She prepared the bread dough with Leyla and Zozan and lit the oven. It's good when you both learn to do that on your own, she said. Then she went back to take care of her own household, garden, and three children.

It continued like that for a week or two until her grandmother felt better again and could give instructions from her sickbed. Hardly was she back on her feet when she was already grinding grain, baking bread, tending to the garden, and making tea.

～

Aunt Havîn had been little help when her grandmother was sick, Leyla thought. She was just as dependent as Leyla and Zozan on Grandmother's direction. Her grandmother said Aunt Havîn wasn't used to working, having grown up in town. Grandfather said she was just lazy.

Her mother, Zozan had told her, was born in July. That's why they had named her Havîn: summer.

Aunt Havîn had gone to school in town up to the ninth grade. When she turned eighteen, Uncle Memo borrowed money from Leyla's father in Germany to pay the bride-price. In that way, he and Havîn were able to get married and she moved to the village to join him and his parents. The two of them had a big wedding. Hundreds of guests came, a *zurna* player, a drummer, Garachi, and the people danced for three days and three nights. Zozan and Leyla often watched the wedding video. Aunt Havîn gazed at the floor. Her lips were painted bright red with a dark red border, as was the fashion then, with false eyelashes and her face made up to be pale white. She didn't smile the way Leyla and Zozan imagined princesses would, in her bulky white dress with lots of net lace and sparkling sequins, her jet-black hair pinned up. Her tresses, fixed with hairspray, fell into her face, and not even a windstorm could have messed them up.

The Havîn that Leyla knew was a sluggish, bloated woman who had borne five children, complained about calluses on her feet, and spent the days watching her beloved Egyptian television series. These were romances, about men who were doctors and women who wore elegant clothes and looked beautiful even when they cried, which happened often. Havîn discussed these from beginning to end with her sisters and sisters-in-law when they came from town to visit.

Her grandmother said that the first harvest in the field had been a shock for Aunt Havîn.

When she arrived, she had absolutely no idea how to grind grain, slaughter chickens when it was time, or plant tomatoes. Once she left a whole sack of garlic in the sun and it all dried out. She and Uncle Memo had been married three weeks when Grandfather said: We'll send her back, she isn't worth the bride-price. Her grandfather told that story over and over and then counted the women in the village that his son could have married instead of her. Those women would have been used to the hard work in the fields. That would have worked out better, he said. But young people aren't reasonable anymore, they watched too many movies. His own parents, after all, had decided for him. Parents knew what was best for their children. A daughter-in-law had to get along not just with the son but also with the whole family. But Memo didn't want to listen to me, Grandfather said, sighing.

Only after her fifth child did Havîn start taking the pill. Leyla knew that, because her mother was supposed to bring her the pill one summer. Her mother was also supposed to put her aunt at ease. People told me, Aunt Havîn said, that you can never have children again once you take the pill. If I had known that's not true, then of course I would have taken it earlier.

~

Her sisters and sisters-in-law came every few weeks to visit. They had running water in their houses and apartments in town, no water tanks over the bathroom and kitchen that had to be filled up every morning before you could shower or wash dishes, which meant the water in summer was always too warm or, in the early morning winter, much too cold. The sisters and sisters-in-law had toilets and tiled bathrooms. Since they didn't have to work in the fields, they also had enough time to clean their houses; their floors were shiny and there weren't chicken droppings lying around everywhere like in the village. They could wear blouses every day and skirts that didn't get filthy from the dust or mud, sandals with thin straps made for paved streets and asphalt, too good for the clay ground in the village.

Leyla saw Aunt Havîn in genuine high spirits only when those visitors were there from town and all the women were standing in the kitchen, Aunt Evîn smoking, Aunt Rengîn with her baby in her arms, and Havîn between them, showing off her new kitchen gadgets. That's a blender, Havîn said proudly and took it out of the box. It was still shiny.

All brand new, she said. The blender is good when you want to make baby food. The sisters and sisters-in-law nodded approvingly. Can I try it? Aunt Rengîn asked, and thrust her baby into Aunt Evîn's arms.

Aunt Havîn put tea on. She was almost like a young girl in those moments, thought Leyla, who was sitting on the counter next to the sink and had been silent for so long that she'd been forgotten. Aunt Havîn seemed young when Aunt Rengîn and Aunt Evîn were there for a visit.

Come on, give me a cigarette, Evîn, Aunt Havîn said.

You don't smoke, Evîn answered, laughing.

Yes, I do! Just give me one, Havîn said, or are you stingy?

But your husband would object to your smoking, Aunt Evîn said, raising her freshly plucked eyebrows scoffingly.

My husband has nothing to say about it, Aunt Havîn said, and even if he did, he's just afraid that I'll smoke all his cigarettes. Man, Evîn, let me give it a try!

~

Aunt Evîn took out her pack of Marlboros, pulled out a cigarette, and gave it to Aunt Havîn.

Lighter, demanded Aunt Havîn.

As you wish. Aunt Evîn gave it to her, but Aunt Havîn fumbled with it and had to light the cigarette several times because it kept going out. Aunt Rengîn stood next to her and laughed so hard that the tea splashed out of the glass in her right hand.

Aunt Havîn inhaled dramatically and immediately started to cough. The women burst into laughter and Aunt Havîn, her eyes still watering from coughing, laughed along with them.

Although she had married into a village family, her relatives from Almanya at least compensated for something. Perhaps that even made the chicken droppings bearable, thought Leyla. After these visits, Aunt Havîn was usually in a good mood for a few hours. She stroked Leyla's hair, and Leyla could almost put up with her in those moments. But it didn't last very long, only until her grandmother called for Havîn to come into the garden or her grandfather started ranting for her not to sit around so lazily, reminding Havîn where she actually was: in a village where nothing ever happened except that for at least five hours daily the power went out. Then Aunt Havîn would again fall into her usual sluggishness and retreat to the television or take a nap, hoping that she'd at least be left in peace if she could never undo her self-chosen misfortune.

~

The days passed by like the chickens that strutted around in the yard, calm and unperturbed. Nothing happened, and soon Leyla no longer knew what day of the week it was or when Aunt Rengîn and Aunt Evîn had come from town to visit, perhaps four or five or six days ago? The more the days blended together and the less Leyla was able to tell how long she had been in the village, the more anxious she became. Whether seated for lunch or watering the garden in the late afternoon, Leyla imagined that a catastrophe was impending. She knew that catastrophes did not always announce themselves. Catastrophes could arrive suddenly, as one did many years ago when Grandmother's father had been lying in the shade of a tree taking a nap and men came and killed him. She knew that what her grandmother called *ferman* never announced itself.

Leyla imagined the world would soon be destroyed by a flood or an earthquake, as it was at the time of the Great Flood. Her grandmother had told her about the hill near Shaykhan where, in ancient times, out of all the people of the world only one old woman and a cow were able to save themselves. When the flood came, thought Leyla, if she had an airplane and could save just one single person, or two other people, or three, four, ten, twenty . . . in any case, if not everyone could survive, who should be the one she should take with her in her airplane? Who should be chosen? And then she was ashamed for these thoughts. Who was she to make decisions about the life and death of her people, God?

She sat in the sun and wrote the names of those to be rescued from death on the ground with a twig.

She erased the names, raising dust. She drew meaningless patterns. At midday, when everyone was sleeping, she jumped barefoot from one shadow to the next. Once, when she missed her mark and landed in a patch of sun, she had to be quick, for the ground was smoldering. She imagined she was walking on lava.

Her grandmother, thought Leyla. Her grandmother would be the first one she let into her airplane.

~

Of all Aunt Havîn's sisters and sisters-in-law, she liked Aunt Evîn the most. The people in the village said that Havîn would be the prettier one if she didn't always make such a face and that Aunt Evîn was the smarter of the two sisters. Leyla believed that Aunt Evîn was what the people called a phenomenon. She had a large nose, a deep voice, a resounding laugh. Whenever she spoke, she did it loudly and emphatically. She couldn't be overlooked. She commented on everything, but Leyla did not have the feeling that anyone was bothered by that; on the contrary, people seemed to value her opinion. When Aunt Evîn was visiting in the village, all the children wanted to be her friend; indeed, everyone wanted to be liked by her. If she bestowed her attention on someone, it was a kind of accolade.

The reason for this was that Aunt Evîn was grown up, but grown up differently than their parents and grandparents. At the same time, she had an undefined youth to her, appearing more carefree than the others. She laughed a lot, told jokes, and yet everyone respected her. Perhaps this was because she was unmarried and had been taking care of her ailing mother for many years. Leyla remembered how often, when they had been visiting her in town, Aunt Evîn had jumped up midsentence because her mother was calling for her because she was thirsty or in pain or had to go to the bathroom. Her mother could not even go to the bathroom by herself.

Leyla did not know what kind of a sickness Aunt Evîn's mother suffered from. Maybe she had not been told or had simply forgotten it. Most of the time, Evîn's mother lay in her sickbed sleeping. If she called for Aunt Evîn in a thin voice, she did it so softly that Leyla could barely hear it. But Aunt Evîn always heard, no matter how quiet she called. My mother, she would say, getting up abruptly.

Sometimes during their visits, when Leyla's father said, Come on, go say hello to her, Evîn's mother would talk to her. But never for long, for Leyla believed that even the shortest conversation would overtax her. Aunt Evîn's mother spoke in a weak voice, and at the end of every sentence it threatened to fail, so that Leyla had difficulty understanding her. Aunt Evîn's mother saw Leyla's baffled face and repeated her sentences until Leyla looked even more confused, and her mother repeated them over and over until her voice was no more than a croak that turned into a choking cough. Then Leyla was overcome by panic, the poor woman was just about to suffocate because Leyla had not understood her sentences and the next time Leyla nodded eagerly even though she once again did not understand a single word of what Aunt Evîn's mother was saying.

That really is a lot of work you have with your mother, isn't it? Leyla once asked, but Aunt Evîn shrugged her shoulders, a bit surprised about Leyla's stupid question. What else was she supposed to do with her mother than give her food and take care of her?

Is it true, Leyla, that in Almanya there are houses where you take your parents when they are old and sick? asked Aunt Evîn during a different visit.

Later, after Aunt Evîn's mother had died, she took care of her father, who was unable to get over the death of his wife and lost all of his strength. After her oldest brother married, she took care of his children, who grew up in her household. And then all of a sudden, she turned twenty-five years old. When Leyla heard that, she could not believe it. Never had she connected Aunt Evîn to any kind of age. As absurd as it appeared to her in retrospect, she had never thought that Aunt Evîn could age like any other human being. To Leyla, Aunt Evîn still appeared to be so young that she never even comprehended that the little wrinkles that appeared on her face over the years, multiplying and getting larger, were the result of aging. For Leyla they were laugh lines. And when one summer gray strands popped up in Aunt Evîn's dark-brown hair, Leyla did not notice them right away because Aunt Evîn had presumably pulled out the few little gray hairs before anyone could see them. Shortly thereafter, Evîn started coloring her hair, and Leyla quickly got used to her hair being a shade darker and soon didn't even notice it anymore.

The people in the village said that at twenty-five Evîn wouldn't be able to find a husband anymore. In the best case a widower, if she was lucky.

But Leyla could not imagine that Evîn would seriously be on the look-out for a widower. She seemed always to be too busy for that.

Whenever they visited Evîn in town, she made kebabs and french fries for them, and there was Pepsi and 7 Up to drink. She strolled with Leyla and Zozan to the main street where the shops were and bought them an ice cream. Afterward, she showed Leyla the books she had had to read for her diploma in English that she kept on a shelf in her bedroom: Charles Dickens's *A Christmas Carol*, Charlotte Brontë's *Jane Eyre* in excerpts. Shyness suddenly overcame Leyla. Alone with Evîn in her room, where there was only a bed and a wardrobe next to it with Aunt Evîn's and Aunt Rengîn's clothes, a mirror on the wall, beneath it a small shelf with a pack of cigarettes and a little bottle of nail polish, Leyla did not know what to say. So it was here in this room that Aunt Evîn slept, at least in the winter; in the summer everyone slept on the roof. Luckily, Aunt Evîn just kept talking. But Leyla could not concentrate; she just stared at Aunt Evîn and nodded at everything. Her cheeks turned red and started to glow. Come, let's go back down to the living room, Evîn said suddenly, pulling a pack of Marlboros out of her jeans and smoothing out her tightly fitting T-shirt.

⁓

Leyla had never seen Evîn without makeup. Even in extreme heat she at least had on eye shadow and mascara. She painted her nails, which nobody in the village did, since the nail polish flaked off during work. To protect her hands and nails Aunt Evîn would put on plastic gloves when cleaning or doing the dishes, and she was always putting lotion on her hands, which, like her Marlboros, she always had with her.

Once, when Evîn was visiting them in the village, she forgot her pack of Marlboros on the windowsill in the living room.

Leyla quickly put a book over the cigarettes before anyone noticed. She waited until the evening and was quite anxious. Impatiently she waited for a moment when nobody was watching her. Such moments were rare. Whereas in Germany Leyla spent her afternoons after school home alone or, at most, outside with Bernadette, during the summers with her grandparents she was seldom alone. Everyone slept together on the metal lofts, her grandmother at the far edge with the grandchildren next to her, a few meters away her grandfather on his own small bed, since he was too old to climb up to the loft, the other men not far away from him on the roof above the kitchen. They spent their days together in the large living room underneath the fan, and the evenings, as soon as it got cooler, together in the yard, where her grandmother laid out mats and pillows and the neighbors came by for tea. Sometimes Leyla would go to the garden, claiming she wanted to do some work, just so she could be by herself. But even then, someone usually came along with her, her grandmother to help her or

Zozan to tell her what she wasn't doing right, or Mîran, Welat, and Roda, because they were always bored and their favorite pastime was to get on her nerves. She wasn't even safe from those three while showering. Even when she locked the door behind her, Mîran, Welat, and Roda would climb up the wall and look through the window into the little house with the shower. By the time she had rinsed the lather out of her hair, gotten dressed, and run past Zozan and her grandmother through the kitchen, bent on slapping her cousins, they had long since made off.

Her cousins also liked catching frogs and lizards and torturing them with rocks and sticks until they died miserably. Because they saw that Leyla hated it and it made her furious, they enjoyed doing it all the more.

Leyla never went alone into the village, onto the mound in the middle of it, or even into the fields. It was impossible to go for a walk without someone noticing it because the land was so flat and there were no trees outside the village, so you were always in somebody's range of vision. Leyla sometimes wondered whether she preferred the long lonely afternoons in Germany or the hot summers in the village, always surrounded by the family. The more weeks that passed in the village, the more she longed to be alone again.

But when the day of departure approached, she got nervous. By that time, when Zozan made fun of her she simply shrugged it off, but when her cousins pulled her hair or hid her book, she quickly became angry. On the day of departure, she wept into her grandmother's floral dress, her *yadê*.

∼

When Aunt Evîn forgot her cigarettes, it was a long time before Leyla was alone again in the living room. She took the pack, stuck it in her pants pocket, and later shoved it between two clay bricks in the wall behind the chicken coop.

The next day she waited until midday. Finally, it was so hot outside that everyone else was asleep in the living room under the fan. Only Zozan and her grandmother were in the kitchen, already preparing dinner. Leyla fetched the pack of cigarettes from the hiding place in the wall, went to the sink behind the kitchen where the pink bar of soap was that she used to wash her face every morning, and stood in front of the mirror. But without Evîn's tight-fitting jeans and loud T-shirts, the cigarette in her mouth did not look right. The village was not the right place for Marlboros, Leyla thought. She was wearing a loose skirt that her aunt had sewn for her the year before and a T-shirt faded from the sunlight, and she stared at the chicken droppings in front of her on the floor. The village was a place for her grandfather's self-rolled cigarettes; Marlboros were town cigarettes.

Nevertheless, Leyla took the lighter she had stolen from her grandfather's tobacco can and lit the cigarette. She took a puff but did not dare to inhale, for the least little cough would betray her. She blew the smoke out from her cheeks and quickly extinguished the tip on the wall of the house.

The next few days she waited for the right moment to pack the Marlboros in her suitcase. But how would she take the cigarettes out of her suitcase in Germany without her parents noticing? In the end, she left the pack in their hiding place.

The following summer, the first thing she did after arriving was go to the wall behind the chicken coop, but the Marlboros were no longer there.

~

Uncle Memo drove to town with Leyla and Zozan. They ate at Aunt Havîn's along with Aunt Evîn's parents and brother, walking afterward, as they did every time, to the street with the stores and to the market. The shops were not lit up and didn't have shiny glass display windows like the ones Leyla knew in Germany; they were windowless garages with wares stacked on wobbly tables and tin storage racks. Even the clothes were different from what was in fashion in Germany at the moment. Everything glittered, the skirts went all the way to the ankles, the sleeves to the elbows. Whereas in Germany simple clothing was valued, here people liked everything to be dazzling and showy. *Unpractical*, her mother had said. Fake brands everywhere, sequins, logos. And plastic, everywhere plastic: the shoes, stacked up on the tables, bracelets, necklaces, toys. The merchandise, sewn in Chinese factories, came on trucks across the steppe, dust, and mountains, on the old Silk Road, as Leyla's father had told her, past countless cities and little villages until at some point they were stacked here in Tirbespî on a plastic table in one of the windowless garage shops, or dangled in front of it on hangers.

Pick something out for yourself, her uncle said, and Zozan lunged for the clothes, immediately pulling out a pink floral blouse with trumpet sleeves, whereas Leyla hesitated. In the end she decided on a yellow T-shirt with plastic rhinestones glued on it and an imprint of a swarm of butterflies, because Evîn had something similar. Leyla knew she would never wear this T-shirt in Germany anywhere but at home and in no case at school, where she would be laughed at for it. But her mother wasn't there, having remained in the village to help her grandmother bake bread, and since she wasn't there and couldn't say, You'll never wear that at home, her uncle nodded, and the vendor put the T-shirt in the plastic bag with Zozan's blouse, and Uncle Memo bartered. In the end, the vendor did not lower the price but added a set of glittering socks, and both the vendor and her uncle seemed to be content.

Before Uncle Memo headed back with them, they went to the tailor to pick up a dress that Leyla's aunt had measured her for the previous week. Green sequins were embroidered all over it, and Leyla felt that when she wore it, she looked like a fish—the many sequins were like scales.

Leyla only wore the green sequined dress later when she went to weddings. Back in Germany she laid the clothes in the top compartment of her wardrobe, and when she took them out the following summer, they were already too small.

In Germany, she stored away all the plastic jewelry she had received over the summers in shoeboxes, all the barrettes and chains. Sometimes when she was home alone, she took out the boxes, pulled the bracelets over her knuckles, and stuck the butterflies in her hair, then did her homework or read. Before her parents came home, Leyla put them back in the boxes and stuck the boxes back in the wardrobe.

~

Her grandparents were cousins. They had already been promised to one another as children. Nobody could say anymore what year they had married. They must still have been very young, maybe fourteen, fifteen, sixteen. There were no photos of the wedding.

Leyla sometimes wondered if her grandparents had felt fortunate at that time. But probably her grandparents had never even asked themselves this question.

Illnesses were misfortune, accidents and poor harvests were misfortunes. Her grandmother had told her about the expulsions when she was a child, the ferman, the massacres, the way the village she grew up in had once been surrounded and all Yazidi families forced to flee overnight. That is misfortune, her grandmother said. That Uncle Nûrî's oldest daughter, her first grandchild, had died when she was still an infant, that little Aram, the neighbor's boy, was bitten by a snake, or that the secret service had found her father's forbidden books and the list of members of the Democratic Party of Kurdistan that Nûrî had kept. All that was misfortune. That her grandfather and Nûrî had been arrested and the family had lost their fields.

That Leyla's father had even survived growing up in the village bordered on a miracle. Her grandmother never talked about it, but her father told her stories. Children had died in the village like flies. They were bitten by scorpions, had sicknesses and accidents. One child from the village, her father said, had died miserably from being attacked by a whole colony of bees that had stung him so badly he couldn't breathe anymore.

There were not only her father's two brothers, the older Nûrî and the younger Memo, and his sister Pero. There were other siblings who had not lived beyond childhood. The family was not in agreement about how many there had been exactly.

One child had died in his sleep, when he was still very little: Selim. Another child had been born dead, another one, also a boy, had died at an older age, three or four. He could already speak, her father told her. Mizgîn was his name. A smart child, very sweet. It was midsummer. He was lying in the living room taking a midday nap, Grandmother having laid a wet towel over his body because of the heat. Before Mizgîn fell asleep, he is said to have asked, When is Nûrî coming back?

Nûrî was much older than her father and at that time was already working a hundred kilometers away on a construction job, digging wells. He only came home every few weeks. Mizgîn had asked about him, then slept for a little bit, and then he died before my eyes, Leyla's father had told her. The little boy woke, stood up, then collapsed next to the living room door. The neighbor ran over to feel for his pulse. We buried him the same day. Grandfather cried the whole night and the next morning Grandmother said: Perhaps God needed him.

Her father told her how her grandmother had not cut her children's hair until they were old enough to talk. That was supposed to protect them from misfortune and illness. Yet the long hair and many prayers did not change the fact that there were no doctors in the village and not in the nearby town either.

In the family it was said that her grandmother had never cried in her life; each one of her children and grandchildren confirmed this. Sometimes her children searched for the reason for the unshed tears she had carried with her to the grave, sometimes finding it in the murder of her father when she was still little, sometimes in her brother, who years before had gone to Mosul and never returned. The exact point in time when her tears had dried up, however, nobody could say.

～

Whenever her grandmother talked on the phone with Leyla's family in Germany, she always wanted to know first if all her children and grandchildren were healthy. Once she had been assured that everyone was doing well, her grandmother would communicate how the family in the village was doing, as well as the family in Tirbespî, Aleppo, and Efrîn.

Because she herself had grown up without a father, with four siblings and a mother who worked from morning to night to feed her children, she thanked God that she was not a widow. Grandfather was a good husband for her, and he was alive, that had to be enough. He had provided for the family, had worked the fields, smuggled goods over the border. He had never hit her grandmother, at least Leyla had never heard about it. Maybe her grandmother had not been in love with him from the beginning. But maybe that had come in time, as the people in the village say.

∼

When her grandmother had been a little girl herself, every day her sisters had woven her black hair into two braids. Seyro had done the left side and Besê the right, her grandmother said. Now her hair was white but she still wore it the same way, only that she had long since woven the braids herself. Leyla loved watching her, observing how after washing her hair she carefully ran her green plastic comb through her wet hair. The comb was one of the few objects that belonged to her grandmother and truly just to her. She guarded it like a treasure and hid it from her grandchildren on the ledge over the door along with a pocketknife, a bar of soap wrapped in a piece of cloth, a metal box with needle and thread, and a few old photos tied up with a piece of yarn.

Just as rare as the sight of her grandmother's possessions was the sight of her long white braids, which she kept hidden during the day under floral headscarves and everyone else only got to see after she washed her hair.

Her grandmother's skin was furrowed like bark. She was the shortest, daintiest woman in the village. If it weren't for her headscarf and her wrinkled skin, she would have looked like a girl. When she laughed, she held her hand in front of her mouth, as if it were unseemly to laugh out loud. She was slender, her arms sinewy, her hands bony. Leyla was often amazed at how strong these slender arms were, how much weight they could carry, how inexhaustible they were. Her grandmother's body, she thought, consisted of nothing but muscle, tendons, and bones. There was not an ounce of fat on her. Probably, under different circumstances, it would have taken on a completely different form. It was the work in the fields that had made it into her tool, her beast of burden. It was like a mule whose every muscle and every fiber stood in the service of her work.

Her grandmother walked with her torso leaning forward slightly. She always looked like she was bent over and, because of that, seemed even shorter than she actually was.

She often put her hands on her hips and rubbed her back. The small of my back hurts, she would say. Her back had carried so many children and grandchildren, sacks of grain and water canisters, that at some point it had bent under the weight, and since then she was hunchbacked.

The decades of work could not only be counted on her grandmother's body, on her hunched back, her muscles and callused hands, but also in her movements. Whenever, for example, she tossed food to the chickens, she always did it with the same hand motion. With the metal bowl filled with grain in her left hand, she grabbed the kernels in her right hand and flung them in a clocklike manner that never changed. Even years later Leyla could still see her doing this as if in a movie. When her grandmother watered the garden, holding the hose as she went from bed to bed, kneeled on the soil, picked weeds, hoed the field, or swept the yard, her movements were different than Leyla's when she carried out the same tasks. While each of her grandmother's movements reminded her of the cogs of a machine, Leyla's looked awkward.

Nothing about her grandmother ever raised any doubts. She simply always knew what to do. If someone had asked Leyla who the smartest person in the world was, she would have answered: her grandmother. If Leyla had an earache, her grandmother would tie onions in wool hand-kerchiefs and lay them on her ears. She could mix flour and water into bread dough like nobody else so that it did not get stuck on the inside oven wall and fall into the blaze. If a snake strayed into the pantry or the living room, she would put a metal bowl on a tripod and put sheep's wool and herbs in it. Her grandmother would ignite the mixture, which didn't burn, but created smoke, a biting, stinking smoke. Snakes cannot stand the smell, her grandmother said.

~

Beware of the snakes, her grandmother often said. When you go into the garden put on real shoes. Watch where you step. When you take a walk, don't go through the thicket or the fields. Don't play in the ruins. Other-wise, you will end up like Aram, who was bitten by a black snake and died; this was the one story that Leyla was told over and over again about snakes, the other one being how her grandfather had once found one under his pillow after his midday nap.

In the summers they slept on the roof or the lofts not only because of the heat but because of the snakes. But Leyla didn't trust either spot. Who said that snakes could not climb or wriggle their way up the metal poles of the loft?

Leyla's fear of snakes did not abandon her when she was back in Germany. The expressionless eyes of these creatures, how silently they glided over the ground. Even in Germany Leyla did not run out into the field when the grass was high. She always wore real shoes and never picked up stones from the ground.

Sometimes she dreamed that the snakes showed up in Germany, in her bicycle basket, under her schoolbag, under her bed next to the dust bunnies, behind the thick winter sweaters in her jam-packed wardrobe. She woke up, couldn't move, and had to turn on the light and check under the bed to make sure there really wasn't a snake there from the village.

~

Leyla always stayed near her grandmother since the very first summer; she was perhaps three or four years old the first time she had traveled to her father's country. Since Leyla had first set eyes on her grandmother, she followed her.

If her grandmother watered the plants, Leyla held the hose. If her grandmother fed the chickens, Leyla filled the bowls with water. She followed her grandmother into the kitchen where she was mopping the floor. She stood next to her at the clay oven when she baked bread. She waited for her when she took a shower in the small room behind the kitchen. She sat in front of the door when her grandmother once again threw all her grandchildren out of the bedroom to hold her office hours, when she treated the ailments of the village women with herbs and other secret methods. Having her grandmother as an ally was good, Leyla knew. If she was with her grandmother, she suddenly was no longer afraid of snakes or scorpions, and even Zozan's scornful glances did not bother her anymore. Leyla simply buried her face in her grandmother's floral apron when her cousins aggravated her. She fell asleep next to her grandmother and woke up next to her.

Grandmother is an old woman, her mother said. Who knows how long she will still make it.

Every year before they climbed into the car to drive to Aleppo to spend a few days with Aunt Xezal and Uncle Sleiman and then continue on to the airport—back to Germany for ten long months—Leyla thought it was the last time she would see her grandmother.

⌒

If I were as old as Grandmother, thought Leyla, I would have long since lost my patience with being so polite. For her grandmother was truly very polite. Even to the chickens. When she fed the chickens in the morning, she talked to them. When they strayed into the house, she shooed them out, but in a friendly manner; she never threw shoes at them like Zozan and Aunt Havîn did.

Her grandmother also didn't gossip like the other women from the village did when drinking tea together. In reality, the village women did not come for tea, after all, but to talk. They loved to complain about their illnesses, pity their neighbors for their illnesses, laugh themselves to death about their cousins' foibles. All the women could gossip for hours about Leyla's father having not married a Yazidi. But still, she was a nurse, they would say. Even her grandfather gossiped, which in turn led the women to gossip about him. They would talk over and over in the living room about how he just sat on his mat the whole day out in the yard and cursed.

Her grandmother sat in their midst, held her tea glass in her hand, and never gossiped, never cursed, and kept to herself what she knew about other people. Her father said that her grandmother was a religious woman. And although her father constantly complained that religious people were uneducated, that they didn't know any better, it was a compliment when he said about his mother: She is devout.

⌒

Zozan made fun of Leyla. When Leyla came into the kitchen or the living room looking for a pair of scissors or spool of yarn to bring to her grandmother, Zozan said she followed her grandmother around like a dog. Leyla is hardworking, her uncle said and slapped Zozan. But I work hard the whole year, cried Zozan, and didn't say anything else, at most raising her eyebrows whenever Leyla once again came back from the garden with her grandmother.

One summer, when Leyla was already twelve or thirteen years old, her grandmother put two little plastic boards on the kitchen floor for herself and Leyla. Today we are making *aprax*, she said and set down a bowl full of grape leaves with a second bowl of rice, beans, and spring onions next to it. She and Leyla chopped up the spring onions and mixed them with the beans, rice, and tomato paste. Then she and her grandmother each laid a grape leaf on their little board. Like this, said her grandmother, and piled the rice mixture in the middle of the leaf and rolled it up. Leyla's first grape leaf fell apart immediately. Her grandmother gave her a new one.

They stacked the grape leaves in a pot full of lemon slices and garlic. Her grandmother put a plate over them so that they wouldn't boil up over the edge of the pot while they were cooking and put the pot on the stove.

Today we'll make *kutilk*, her grandmother said the following day as they were expecting a visit from relatives from town, and she and Leyla fried onions and ground meat and then coated the mixture with semolina.

And today we'll make *dew*, her grandmother said. Two parts yogurt, one part water, and a pinch of salt. They mixed it in a bowl, stirred it with the whisk until it was foamy, and then added dried mint.

Who else could have taught Leyla to cook, said her grandmother to her grandfather at dinner, when she has a German mother? Although it is so important: after all, Leyla will also get married one day! Her grandmother talked constantly of marriage, since in her eyes neither Leyla's father nor her mother concerned themselves enough about it. She suggested various second cousins to Leyla—What do you think of that one? Do you like him?—while they kneaded bread together, chopped onions, or watered the garden. She taught Leyla to serve tea, not to look strange men on the street in the eyes, to sit in such a way that her skirt covered her legs at all times.

One evening the neighbor came for tea. He didn't talk long but simply suggested that Leyla could marry his oldest son. She can go ahead and finish school in Germany, he said, then we'll celebrate the wedding in the village. The neighbor talked about the bride-price, saying how much he was willing to pay. It wasn't much; the neighbor was not a rich man. Others were said to have paid much more for wives for their sons. Aunt Rengîn's husband, for example, was said to have paid a whole pile of gold for Aunt Rengîn. But what price can be asked for Leyla, Zozan laughed later, after the neighbor had left. Leyla can't do anything. And to Leyla she said, They just want your German passport.

～

Repeat after me, her grandmother said in the morning. Leyla was still tired and could barely keep her eyes open. They were both sitting on the loft bed in the yard, shoulder to shoulder, gazing at the horizon, where the first small strip of light was emerging. Look, like this, her grandmother said and laid her hands one over the other in her lap. Leyla imitated her.

Amen! Amen! her grandmother said. God is the creator of the origin, with the wondrous power of Şemsedîn. Shaykh Adî is the crown from the beginning to the afterlife. God, bless us with good deeds and ward off harm from us!

Leyla could barely follow what her grandmother was saying. The words coming out of her mouth were strange to her. She had never before in her life heard what her grandmother was saying and how she was saying it. Her grandmother's words came very quickly, following uniformly one after the other like a single stream; she had been repeating these words for decades. Her grandfather claimed that since their wedding day not a single morning had passed when she did not say her prayer. Her grandmother did not herself speak of such things, neither about her praying nor her fasting. She prayed and fasted as naturally as she fed the chickens or pulled the laundry from the clothesline.

But she started waking Leyla daily before dawn. It seemed to Leyla that her grandmother was initiating her into something that was larger than she was, more meaningful than she could grasp with her mind. From day to day, Leyla moved with more certainty through the prayer text. As soon as she had learned the morning prayer by heart and she and her grandmother said it together, her grandmother called her in the evenings as well and spoke with her toward the setting sun. Oh Şêşims, watch over us and those who are with us!

~

The first day God began creating, her grandmother said, was Sunday. God created an angel, to whom he gave the name Azrail, which is Tawûsê Melek, the Peacock Angel.

He made the Peacock Angel into the greatest of all the angels.

From the angels only good things come, her grandmother said.

Leyla got confused when her grandmother talked about the angels and the saints, and she couldn't remember anything. All the names and stories whirled around in her head, slipping away from her again and again. Leyla should have written them down, put together a notebook that she could use as a reference. But when her grandmother had once again told her quite a lot and Leyla said, Grandma, I have to write it down, otherwise I will forget it, her grandmother shook her head and said: No, write it down? For what? Her grandmother carried her book on her tongue.

Better in the head, she said.

There it is safe from everything.

~

In the smaller of the two living rooms, the one where the family slept in the winter and that became the women's living room during many visits, a small picture of a giant peacock hung next to the door. The peacock was almost as big as the old building behind it with two spires. That, her grandmother had explained to her, was the shrine of Lalish. Leyla saw her grandmother kiss the picture again and again.

When she learned how to pray, she started to imitate her grandmother. Her grandmother did not even have to ask her to do it. Whenever Leyla came into the room, she kissed the picture. And not only then, sometimes when she came from the garden and wanted to go into the kitchen, she took a detour to kiss the picture. As her grandmother had told her, she, Leyla, was from the tribe of Xaltî, from Xûdan the Mend, from the caste of the *murids*, a child of the people of the Peacock Angel. That seemed to her to have great significance.

But if Zozan was nearby, Leyla avoided kissing the picture. She couldn't say exactly why, perhaps for fear of looking ridiculous in front of her. In any case, she herself had never observed Zozan kissing the picture or even paying attention to it. And she never saw Zozan pray.

But one day when Leyla was kissing the picture, Zozan happened to come into the room. Zozan laughed. You can kiss it as often as you wish, she shouted, but you still won't be a Yazidi. A Yazidi, she said, sounding like a teacher, is someone who has a Yazidi father and a Yazidi mother. You are not a Yazidi, because your father married a German.

That's not true, Leyla said softly and stood defiantly in the middle of the room. It always follows the father.

Who says so? Zozan asked, as she stacked the mats and pillows on the wall shelves.

Grandpa says so!

Yeah, right! That's only Grandpa's opinion. Nobody besides Grandpa sees it like that. Now don't be sad. Somebody has to tell you the truth.

~

All that did not seem to interest her grandmother. Of course you are Yazidi, my child, she said. Who is saying such nonsense? And she simply continued telling stories.

On his lap, Êzdan, the creator, made a white pearl and a small bird.

He laid the pearl on the bird's back and it lay there for thousands of years until Êzdan decided to create the Earth.

God blew on the pearl, so that it became warm, finally turning red and bursting into several pieces. From the largest piece the sun came into being, and from the other pieces the stars were formed, and steam. From the steam arose the clouds. It rained, and the sea came into being. God now created a ship and put the seven angels on the ship. Then the ship sailed to all corners of the globe, one after the other. Since the world consisted exclusively of ocean at that time, God wanted to create firm ground. He threw Lalish into the sea, and at this spot the ocean became firm. When parts of the sea had become firm ground, the angels ran ashore in Lalish, her grandmother said.

～

After Adam had been created, God demanded that Tawûsê Melek kneel before Adam. Tawûsê Melek refused. That was a test, her grandmother said. I will only obey you, Tawûsê Melek said, for you are my creator. Thus, Tawûsê Melek passed the test. For God's highest commandment to the angels was to kneel before no one but him. Since for this reason Tawûsê Melek had opposed even God's command, he was elevated to steward and governor of the Earth. To this day, the Muslims and the Christians accuse us of worshiping evil, because the angel who opposed God's command is considered to be evil. But we, her grandmother said, do not even pronounce the name of evil.

Every year at New Year Tawûsê Melek, the Peacock Angel, the first of the seven angels, comes to Earth and meets with the Cilmer, the elder's council of the Yazidis, consisting of forty people, her grandmother said. This day is celebrated today as Çarşema Sor, Red Wednesday. I don't know if you can remember, Leyla, you were still very little, not even in school yet. You were here with us in the spring, in April, the bride of the year. Back then you and I and Zozan decorated the house with flowers and green branches, and we died eggs, and that was Çarşema Sor. We built a fire in the yard and threw scraps of cloth in it. That protects us from sickness.

～

Next to the peacock picture, hanging on a nail, there was a bag that her grandmother had woven. It held a plastic bottle filled with water from the Kanîya Sipî, the white spring, as well as a dried olive branch, two clay balls, and a little cloth bag with some soil from Lalish.

Okay then, her grandmother said and took the objects, dropping them into her skirt. I have to cook. She stood up and left the room.

Leyla would have liked to keep holding the objects in her hand, observe them from all sides and kiss them like her grandmother always did. She had a fascination for them, although she did not really know what to do with them, or maybe precisely because of that. They were simply truly magical. The water, what made it different from other water? Another day she held it up to the light when she was not being observed, shook it, and unscrewed the cap. It had the same color as normal water and it didn't smell any different, and still!

Even the olive branch could have been from their garden and not from Lalish as her grandmother had assured her.

The clay balls are laid on the eyes of the dead, her grandmother said when Leyla asked her about them.

Leyla was also fascinated by the tiny chain that her grandmother's sister wore attached to the collar of her blouse when they visited her one summer in her village near Efrîn. Tiny blue plastic pearls were attached to the chain, a tiny hand whittled from a twig and a somewhat larger pearl that looked like an eye. While Leyla was playing in the yard with her great-aunt's grandchildren, she saw that all the children, from the infants to the girls her own age, were wearing tiny chains of pearls like that on their clothes.

What's that for? Leyla asked.

Protection, said the girls.

Protection from what? Leyla asked.

From the evil eye, the girls answered.

⁓

Everything meant something. For example, you weren't supposed to spit on the ground, because the earth is holy, her grandmother said while they were sitting in the courtyard in front of the kitchen cutting the vegetables for dinner. Leyla, please be a dear and fetch me some parsley from the garden.

You were never to name the name of evil, her grandmother continued as Leyla handed her the parsley. Because God knows no adversary, she said, but I told you that already.

You also shouldn't kill snakes, her grandmother said, as she washed the parsley in the sink, for the snake is a symbol of the seasons, time, and the path. Shaykh Mend Fekhra is said to have had immense knowledge of snakes in his time. People came to him when they were bitten by snakes.

Through prayer and with herbs known only to him, he was able to draw every kind of poison from their bodies. Shaykh Mend Fekhra passed on this knowledge to his son, who in turn passed it on to his son, and so on. To this day the Shaykh Mend caste has jurisdiction over snakes, her grandmother said, loosening her headscarf a little to dab the moisture from her forehead, then taking the parsley out of the sink to lay it on the plastic board to chop it up.

Leyla's grandmother explained to her what was good and bad while she steamed the onions in the pan until they were glassy. She added zucchini, water, tomato paste, and onion. You should not kill, she said, because God gave people life and therefore, only he has the right to take it from them again.

Leyla put a large plate of bulgur on the tray, counted out the silverware, got bread and little bowls from the pantry, and carried the tray into the living room, her little grandmother behind her with the steaming pot of *trshik*.

Knowing shame, her grandmother said, knowing shame is important, and not eating leaf lettuce. But I'll tell you about leaf lettuce later.

∼

While they were standing in the kitchen later washing the dishes, she actually did explain why you weren't allowed to eat leaf lettuce, and as was so often the case, there were several reasons. One of them was that the Arabic name for lettuce, *khas, xas* in Kurdish, meant saint, so you should not eat lettuce in honor of the saints. The other reason was that Shaykh Adî had once been in flight from a man who wanted to kill him. He found refuge in a field of lettuce and hid underneath the large leaves. The lettuce saved his life, and since then lettuce was sacred and it was forbidden to eat it.

Her grandmother put water on the stove and added three spoonfuls of tea to the pot. She placed fourteen little tea glasses on the tray, then the dish of sugar.

After drinking tea Leyla could not sleep and lay with her head on her grandmother's legs.

Her grandmother looked down at her and said that in Lalish there was a tree near the sacred spring, Kanîya Sipî. Parents went to this tree when their children could not sleep and when they got back home laid a piece of bark from the tree in the child's cradle. That helped the children to fall asleep right away, her grandmother said and closed her eyes.

∼

When Leyla told her father the next morning that she wanted to go to Lalish, he shook his head appalled. What is grandmother telling you? he said. That's not good.

Once, I was in Qamişlo, her father said, and ran into a *mîr* from our tribe on the street. Three weeks later this mîr complained to my father that I had not kissed his hand when I saw him there in town.

What's the point of that? said her father and shook his head again. The mîr should first wash his hands before I kiss them. No, Leyla, said her father. Wherever you look, religions have always impeded progress—I have experienced it myself. Religions are there to oppress people. In town, there are Muslims who won't buy any meat, cheese, or yogurt from our people at the market because they think we are unclean. Leyla, religion has given me nothing. Religion has to do with lack of education: people simply don't know any better. Her father tore off a piece of bread and dipped it in the apricot jam.

⁓

Women live in Lalish, said her grandmother, who are temple guardians. They wear white and are called Kebani. Only the purest and best women can become Kebani. They must never have violated the laws of our religion. Two priests have to confirm this. Only then can the woman go to the mîr and to Baba Shaykh to ask to be accepted into the order.

As a Kebani the woman lives out her whole life in Lalish. She never marries. She is responsible for maintaining the temple, cooking for the residents and visitors, and praying in sorrow-stricken times. The most supreme among them is the Mother Sherin, who is also called the mother of the guardians. Among many other things she makes the sacred *çira* lights that are lit every day in the temple.

How beautiful the Kebanis must have looked with their woven braids, white turbans, and long white dresses as they sat in the temple courtyard under the olive trees holding spindles in their hands to spin wool into candlewicks. When I am grown, I want to be a Kebani, said Leyla.

⁓

Most people were astonished that Leyla preferred to be with her grandmother than to go into the village with her cousin and talk about things that girls talked about at that age. It wasn't a problem, but the others made fun of her because of it. Zozan, of course, and Zozan's mother, Havîn, her sisters and sisters-in-law, even Evîn. The old women, such as the old neighbor lady Xane, however, praised her for it, Such a good girl, always with her grandmother. Everyone was in agreement about just one thing: Leyla behaved so oddly because she was from Almanya.

~

In the very back corner of the garden, just in front of the fence behind which lay the fields and behind those the mountain range and the Turkish frontier, grew her grandfather's tobacco plants. Every summer, Leyla helped to harvest and thread the plants onto strings; she and her grandmother would hang them to dry in the pantry. Then in the evening Leyla would sit with her grandfather in the yard as he tried to teach her how to roll cigarettes. He took a rolling paper, laid it in her little hands, and told her to take some tobacco out of the can and roll the paper with the tobacco in the middle back and forth between her fingers, then fold the paper and moisten it on one side. He showed her, that's the way to do it and so forth, but try as she might, she never succeeded. Only many years later, when she bought tobacco for herself the first time, did she suddenly remember those moments, the scratchy smell of the tobacco, her grandfather. She asked herself for the first time how her grandfather had still managed back then to roll his own cigarettes even though he was blind. She thought about this as she laid the tobacco, filter, and paper in front of her on the table and practiced rolling. The first attempts were pitiful, and the cigarettes fell apart just like her stuffed grape leaves had. Had her grandfather put a filter in his cigarettes back then? Certainly not, she thought, but suddenly she was no longer so certain. No matter how hard she tried to remember, she just couldn't visualize it. She would never know for sure. She had forgotten this one detail, the filter in her grandfather's cigarettes back then in the courtyard in the summers in the village. How could she have forgotten that?

~

Remembering had only started in 2011. Although, no, more like shortly after that. The year 2011 was still the year of the revolution, full of news and expectations: a golden future stands before us, freedom, democracy, human rights. In 2011 they had been excited, keeping the television on without interruption, for months. In 2011 Leyla had not yet begun to remember and even her father had rarely told stories of earlier times in the village. Instead, they went on talking at the kitchen table about the revolution, revolution this, revolution that. One more year, her father had said and laughed for joy, then the dictator will be gone and we'll travel to a free country.

Leyla's remembering began shortly thereafter. It started with the massacres, the bombing campaigns, the destruction; it accompanied the destruction, followed it. After every shock came sorrow, soon to be washed away by the next shock. There was no end to it. And the memories kept proliferating, getting out of hand, and could no longer be stopped. Like a wound, Leyla thought, with blood seeping out of it.

～

Once she visited an old schoolfriend of her father. He was a shepherd and was with his flock on the pasture not far from the village. Leyla was still little, in any case the sheep were larger than she was, maybe eighty or ninety of them. She and her father stayed quite a while, the men conversing. The shepherd lit a cigarette and held out the pack to her father. Her father declined, having quit smoking years ago. Actually, the shepherd knew that, but he was polite. The shepherd had turned on a cassette tape in the car. He turned up the volume so you could hear the music on the pasture. Cizrawî sang. I am a dove, I sit above the roof of an old house. I am in love with a black-eyed girl. The music was much too loud for the old speakers: it creaked.

The shepherd set Leyla on his donkey and her father took a picture. The shepherd took her back down and the men paid no more attention to her. Leyla roamed around among the sheep, talking to them, but didn't dare to pet them, to reach into their wool caked with dirt. Leyla stared at the sheep, and the sheep stared back. They looked clumsy the way they scoured the ground for dried bunches of grass with their mouths, ate, then trotted on, thick-bellied with wool. When at some point the flock suddenly started moving, Leyla panicked and began to run. The sheep came down the hill after her like a landslide. Hundreds of hooves pounding on the dusty ground. Leyla ran and ran until she couldn't run anymore, and yet still she kept running, not noticing that the sheep had long since lost interest in her and were far behind her. She only realized that when she tripped over a rock, banged her knee, and turned around toward where she assumed the sheep to be, thinking: Well, that's it then, now they will eat me like dry grass. Leyla couldn't help crying. Neither her father nor the shepherd could comfort her. Both of them laughed and said, What, you're afraid of a few sheep? Because she could not stop crying, the shepherd gave her his prayer chain, which Leyla always liked to play with. But the prayer chain did not interest her right then.

Her father carried her back to the car and at dinner her uncle said, I heard you are afraid of sheep, and laughed. Don't you have any sheep in Almanya?

When Leyla thought back on that day, she couldn't place it in a specific summer; in fact, she couldn't put the summers in any kind of order. Her memories were nothing more than individual scenes, in part fragmentary, all completely without order. She could almost never say whether something happened this year or that year. Had she forgotten something? What had she forgotten? She became uneasy when she thought about forgetting and when she actually did forget, when she could no longer remember names and places, whether it was this baby she had carried around the garden or that one, what the name of the citadel was that she had once visited, where she had collected the pebbles that were in some box or other at her parents' house. Every time for her it was as if by forgetting she had lost everything a second time, and this time for good.

~

If I had known then what was coming, thought Leyla, I would have taken a camera along with me. I would have taken pictures every summer, all summer long, at my grandparents' house. Every house, every stone, every plant in the garden. I would also have cataloged everything, setting up a giant database. I would have called it 37°05′27.5″N 41°36′55.4″E, the village coordinates. I would have done that, thought Leyla, so that nothing could be lost.

She could have expanded her work even further, to her relatives' houses, for example, in Tirbespî, in Aleppo. Or Aleppo in general, or Haleb. Every photo of these cities was precious now. How they never could have suspected, never would have dared to suspect what was coming when they had made snapshots of a few memories, Leyla with Uncle Sleiman and Aunt Xezal in the suq, Leyla on family outings in the old city. If everything could be lost that Leyla had been so sure of, then was anything certain, she wondered now.

She could hardly bear to look at the photos of her unsuspecting family back then in Aleppo or to contemplate the city as it was then, which was so beautiful that it hurt.

~

When the websites of the major newspapers presented the before and after pictures of Aleppo to click through, she seldom made it to the final picture.

~

She couldn't believe any of it. Everything, both before and after, seemed so unreal to her. As unreal as the last piece of Savon d'Alep, that Aleppo soap that smelled of laurel and olive oil she took back to Germany with her every year. As unreal as the metal cans of baklava with the label Sadiq that they had bought shortly before the return flight in the shiny neat transit area with its duty-free shops, not suspecting that this very trip would be their last one. As unreal as the few silly stones that Leyla at some point had collected at the river. Everything would be proof, even ten or twenty years from now, that all that had really existed: the village, the towns, the people, the summers.

~

Hesso, her father told her, didn't know how long he had been standing. He stood dead still, leaning against the cold rock. He shivered. His feet were hurting more and more until he finally dared to sit down, very slowly, intent on not making a sound. When he sensed even the smallest stirring, he paused. He kept his hand on his gun the entire time. Was that the wind or an animal? He sat that way until twilight must have long since passed. Here in the cave, it was pitch black. He stared into the darkness. Outside he heard the wolves howling. He prayed to God they wouldn't find him here, neither the wolves nor the soldiers. He couldn't sleep a single second during that first night. He barely dared to breathe. If they came, he would be trapped. The cave, he well knew, was both a curse and a blessing. It could be his salvation or his death. He didn't know how many nights he would have to stay here or even whether the others had survived. Everything had happened so fast. Three of them, he found out later, had been killed and two captured. And that, he knew, was worse than death.

At some point it got brighter, his father told Leyla on a different evening—he told the story often. At first, Hesso thought he was imagining it, for he had not closed his eyes for a single second. But it was indeed getting brighter, grayer. And then suddenly he could say with certainty that day was breaking. Although he could not see the entrance to the cave from where he was seated. Yet still he did not dare to leave his hiding place. He drank water from his bottle, relieved himself on the spot, and ate a dried fig from his pouch. Although he was hungry, he always only ate one of them. He had to be thrifty, for who knew how long he would be stuck in the cave.

There was water that appeared to come out of a mountain. A rivulet on the wall. He thanked God for it, for the water gave him time—he didn't have to leave the cave.

He took his first steps barefoot to avoid making noise.

After three days he started making a row of stones, a little one for each day. He washed his face in the morning and in the evening. He counted the nuts and figs in his pouch and watched them dwindle, polished his gun with the cloth of his coat, disassembled and reassembled it, although that was pointless. But he had nothing else in the cave to fill his days and nights with. The last bullet was for his own head. He would not die in the hands of the soldiers.

He slept on the bare earth, covering himself with his coat. But his sleep was meager, every little sound waking him. He saw the first increasing then diminishing light at the entrance of the cave. He added another stone to the row.

The days passed. There was sunshine, there was rain. He saw a green light, was it a trap? Only in the dark did he dare move a few meters from his hiding place behind the rock ledge. He always stayed in the concealment of the cave. Until hunger drove him closer and closer to the exit. Until one day he stood at the exit. One step, the next one.

He went at night by the light of the moon, barefoot again to be as quiet as possible, just a few shaky steps. The first fig tree, the first apple tree, the first herbs on the ground. As if he was the first human being. They were not lying in wait for him directly in front of the cave, that much was certain. But still he did not dare to go far, and not to the valley either. He went back. He lined up thirty stones. His beard had grown long, his hair was tangled, his fingernails had black edges. When he set down the thirty-first stone, he decided to leave the cave for good. The soldiers had to believe he was dead, at least that was a possibility, but they certainly had not forgotten him. At night, he climbed down laboriously into the valley. He stumbled and fell. The moon was almost full. It was bright.

～

When he knocked on his brother's door, his brother hardly recognized him, her father said. His brother looked at him as if he had risen from the dead. And then he just called out: Hesso! He let him in. I thought you were not coming back, he said.

His brother's wife brought tea and gave him something to eat. He washed himself, then slept. He cut his nails and trimmed his beard. He stayed for one day. When it was dark again, he set out toward the border.

This was his house, Leyla's father told her as they were coming back from having tea with a family in which a child had been born two days before. They were standing in the middle of the village in front of a caved-in clay house.

After he came out of the cave, her father said, he never again slept in a bed. Everyone said that in the cave Hesso made a deal with God. If you get me out of here alive, he supposedly said to God, I will forever remain loyal to you.

He always ate only bread, onions, garlic, and figs, because they had saved his life when he was in the cave, her father said. Leyla knew that her grandmother had laid fresh garlic in front of Hesso's door every few weeks until his death.

He could have lived differently, her father said. He received a pension from the state, like all those who had fought against Saddam's troops in Iraq. But he never kept his pension, dividing it up instead among the families in the village that didn't know how they would make it through the winters, giving it to the widows who were providing for their children, had to pay the doctor fees for a sick child or buy the medicine for an infirm father.

~

His house had been deteriorating since his death a few years ago. Once, when she was playing with Zozan and her cousins, Leyla wanted to climb inside, but Zozan grabbed her arm and pulled her away. There are snakes in there, she said.

When they were back in the yard, her uncle and grandmother had set up a large tin tub. Zozan and Leyla were supposed to bring the plastic buckets from the pantry in which they had gathered the overripe grapes several days before. Flies swarmed around the plastic buckets. Zozan and Leyla poured the grapes into the tub. Her grandmother and uncle took off their shoes and stockings and climbed in barefoot. The juice squirted out of the grapes. Leyla could not remember what had been done with the trampled grapes. She only knew that at some point there was raki stored in the pantry in plastic bottles that Uncle Memo sold on the black market. Raki was a drink that only turned white when you mixed it with water. It was almost magical.

Once Leyla's father told her that the large plastic jugs in Uncle Memo and Aunt Havîn's wedding video were filled not with water but with raki. But Leyla did not think much of drinking raki out of plastic jugs. She preferred to think of Evîn holding a tall glass of raki on ice in her left hand and a cigarette in her right one. Evîn standing in front of the house, leaning on the wall with painted fingernails and red lips, as if she weren't on a visit in the dusty village but in one of the television series that Aunt Havîn was so addicted to.

Mîran, Welat, and Roda knew very well that Leyla liked to be with the adults and only half-heartedly played with her cousins. Whenever they hunted frogs with stones at the well, Leyla was disgusted and told them to stop. But her cousins did not listen to her, and in the end the frogs lay dead on the ground. And when her cousins secretly climbed the walls of the house and jumped from roof to roof, Leyla got frightened they might fall off and preferred to sit quietly enjoying the view over the yard and garden. Her cousins were often too exhausting for her. Nevertheless, Leyla was there when they raced up and down the road behind the village on the bicycle that belonged to the neighbor's child, which they were actually not allowed to do because of the giant trucks on their way to Turkey. Mîran on the bicycle accelerating when he reached the oil pump, heading directly for the throng consisting of Leyla, her cousins, and the other boys, who scattered screaming into the fields. The boys immediately chasing after Mîran, finally wrestling him from the bike.

Leyla was there when her cousins chased the chickens into the fields with sticks. She stood next to them and ran along with them. Her cousins accepted her because, unlike Zozan, she never tattled.

Later, Leyla asked herself if she would feel less alone if she had never been to the village, if she wouldn't be able to *feel* alone if she didn't *know* that she was alone.

She asked herself this in Germany as she was walking home alone from school because she had missed the bus, down the orderly streets lined at regular intervals by green trees, past cars, front yards, and empty driveways that did not even have chickens. Once she was home, it was so quiet that she could hear the gurgling in the pipes, the noises from outside, cars and airplanes. She just sat there and was only she herself. And also at night, when she tried to fall asleep, nobody was lying there to the left and right of her. Hers was the only breathing in the room. It could make her crazy.

Later, Leyla asked herself this once again, when she had not been to the village for many years and had long since been living in Leipzig, moving from one sublet to the next. Her roommates who always closed their bedroom doors behind them. And she herself who also did it because they all did, every evening this closing of the bedroom door behind them. Everyone lay in their rooms and slept. And again, Leyla's was the only breathing in the room.

In the village, there was never no one there. There were no doorbells, for the doors were always open. The neighbors came and took off their shoes in front of the house, a regular pile of shoes and plastic slippers. The neighbors stayed for tea, left sometime much later, and then soon afterward her grandfather's friends arrived, and at some point, Leyla and her cousins fell asleep in a row on the loft with their grandmother next to them on the edge. Now and then, Leyla would sneak away, follow the gravel road out of the village, past the fields or the hill in the middle of the village, up to the graves where she could look out over the region. Late in the afternoon with the sun low in the west it wasn't quite so hot anymore. To the east and south Leyla could see the oil pumps, to the north the mountains on the border strip with Turkey, where the mines used to be buried, and right below her the flat, clay-brown roofs of the village with the satellite dishes and electric wires strung on poles from yard to yard, which had no order or system that Leyla could recognize and, like the satellite dishes, did not exist here when her father was growing up.

This here was also her village, not just that of her grandparents, father, aunts, uncles, and cousins. From here she could see the garden—when she thought of it, she called it *our garden*—with its rosebushes and the olive trees that her father had planted just a few months before he had left. From up here she could see the gate at the front of the yard, of *our yard*, and in the yard right now were *our kittens*, right by the clay oven in which Leyla baked bread with her grandmother every morning.

A few houses farther she saw the village school, surrounded by a barbed wire fence full of holes that they always climbed through when the school had closed and they wanted to play soccer in the schoolyard. All that, thought Leyla, was also hers, every year for as long as the summer lasted. As if she, although she probably did not know it yet but only comprehended it later, would again and again interrupt her life for the duration of a few weeks to continue a different life in a different place that after those few weeks had run their course she would not continue until a year later. And there was never enough time; her grandmother always cried at their departure and asked her father to simply just leave her there for the entire coming year.

And Leyla knew already that she would again forget her Kurdish over the course of the year and have to collect her words laboriously. She would also no longer remember where the sewage ditches ran in the village and where she had to jump. Sometimes, thought Leyla, it would perhaps be better never to have come here or never to come back here, not to have to miss anything and not to be missed. Or maybe that wouldn't be better, but at least simpler.

When Leyla was standing on the hill, she was happy to be alone with her thoughts. Her cousins were, as always, occupied with themselves, and Zozan was the last person she would have wanted to have with her here. At precisely these moments she was ashamed of herself, as if Zozan could guess what she felt. And then she was often envious of Zozan, even if she never would have admitted it. Unlike her, Zozan had the village for the entire year, it was always her home. Were Zozan to climb the hill she would have seen nothing that she would soon have to say goodbye to again.

When Leyla came back to the village after a year had passed, the first thing she did was to take inventory. The kittens weren't kittens anymore, and the watchdog was dead. The chicken coop had been renovated, and Mîran had completed his first year of school. Rengîn from the neighbor's house had moved to town, because she had married Evîn's brother, and the neighbor Um Aziz had given birth to a daughter.

As soon as she found time, she went back up the hill and looked at the village from above. From up there all the changes seemed smaller. There was always still the same clay-brown color of the roofs, the same slightly rippled fields, the same dry landscape.

Even the shrinkage that at that time had long been underway was almost invisible from up here.

To perceive it, you would have to walk through the yard, past the crumbling facades and weathered doors with their paint peeling off, which no one had restored for ages. The snakes captured the houses, the wind carried seeds over from the fields, and the ragged weeds grew over walls and roofs. The houses that had once been masoned from earth sank back into the ground, the rain washing the straw down from the roof, the wind loosening the clay.

When her father had lived here there had been almost two hundred families. For a long time now not even half that many lived here.

The dusk spit out the mosquitoes. Leyla turned around again and looked to the north. She imagined that she was a camera, her head a strip of film.

The mountains in the north, the oil pumps in the east and south, the road to Tirbespî in the west. She set out on her way back home.

~

Perhaps it had just simply been ridiculous, the way she had stood up there then, a rich agha overlooking his estates. And yet the village was nothing more than a cluster of poor clay huts, in which the babies, in years of bad harvest, years of drought, when there was no longer enough to eat in the village, scraped the plaster from the walls and stuffed it in their mouths for the nutrients in the chalk. In which, as it was told secretly, the eldest daughter, not yet of age, sold herself to get her family through the winter when there was no more money, since her father had gone to Germany three years before and never sent the promised euros. Because he, like everyone in the village knew but did not dare to tell the family, went to the gaming halls and soon lost the little money he had earned. The village was nothing but a cluster of clay huts to which electric lines had been strung when the Arab villages of the region had long since had electricity. Clay huts and all around them garbage, plastic, bottles carelessly thrown away, bags, candy sacks. Perhaps the huts were not after all in the Promised Land, with rich, fertile soil, as her father always said. Perhaps this village in the land of the chieftain Haco, somewhere between the Euphrates and Tigris, was insignificant in every respect.

~

The landscape had changed since her father had left the village, and it would keep changing. Not only had the electric lines been strung along the road to the village, not only had the minefields been cleared, not only had the gravel path been paved. Rather, the Turks on the other side of the border had begun to build their dam, letting the river between Tirbespî and the village turn into a muddy creek. When her father had been a child, there had often been so much water that the river overflowed, but now the dryness ate at the land. The people in the village said that when the big dam in Hasankeyf was actually finished the river would completely dry up and Hasankeyf would sink under the floodwaters. The people in the village said that already they had to dig their wells deeper than they did ten years before.

~

While the men her father's age all knew how to swim, the boys Leyla's age had never learned. But the river had not only been good for swimming but also for fishing, and for this the mines from the border strip were used. Because the children were best suited for it with their little hands, they unscrewed the detonators and replaced them with cords, Leyla's father told her. The mines were all put together in a sack, and the children carried the sack down to the river.

There was a boom that made the air quake, and the water shot up like a fountain. Then it was still again, the fish floating on top.

The people from the village got the mines from the traders when they had once again been clearing the border strips. The traders came from the village, from the neighboring villages, and from everywhere, forming a complex and confusing network of negotiators and middlemen that extended across all villages and towns of the land, across national borders, into Turkey, Iraq, and Iran. The mines from the border strip behind the village had provided for the Peshmerga in Iraq during their fight against Saddam's troops, something that people were proud of.

The traders were called smugglers by the government, for naturally they crossed the border illegally. In the village, however, they were called traders, because that's what they did: trade. Their walk across the border at night was their profession. They had already been crossing the border before there had been mines. Before there had even been a border, they had been trading. They lived from this: you had to eat something, whether it was forbidden or not, and hunger drove them over the fields. They transported tea and animals, tobacco and medicine.

Take tea, for example: on their side a kilogram of tea cost ten lira, but on the other side you could sell it for double the price. A donkey could carry seventy or eighty kilos of tea. Or sheep: on the other side there were lots of sheep, since the region was mountainous and fertile. The traders had driven whole flocks across the border. Once the Turkish military was after them, but the traders were faster and were able to get their sheep to safety. So instead, the Turkish soldiers confiscated the flock of a clueless Arab shepherd a few kilometers away. People told the story again and again in the village.

The border was long, some thousand kilometers, impossible to guard it completely. Every kilometer there was a watchtower with two soldiers. The land mines were everywhere where no natural barriers such as mountains or rivers aided the border guards. The minefields were thirty or forty meters wide. The traders knew narrow trails, strips that they had cleared and only they could find.

Leyla couldn't help but think of the paper napkin on which, many years later, her father drew little crosses with a ballpoint pen, the web of mines on the fields. The soldiers had orders to defend the border by force if necessary. They sat in their watchtowers and shot at the traders. Once the traders, thirty or forty in number, shot back with their black-market guns and rifles, defending their animals and wares, and naturally this was talked about over and over in the village. Everything always had to go quickly. Before the soldiers could fetch reinforcements, the traders must have been over the border.

Nevertheless, we buried many traders, her father said.

When his father, Leyla's grandfather, had been underway at night, Leyla's father couldn't sleep a wink. He stared into the darkness of the summer, into the gray blackness. The traders only traveled at half moon. At full moon it was too dangerous.

The barking of the dogs, the scratching of the chickens in the coop. Something was in the air, threatening to rip apart at any moment. The shots and the exploding mines could be heard in the village.

Her grandmother prayed at every detonation that her husband was not among the dead.

And the children played a game. They laid little stones on the ground, the mines, and formed two teams, the traders and the border soldiers. The traders had to get to the other side as fast as possible without being caught by the border soldiers. Whoever stepped on a stone was out, dead.

∽

Once, her father told her, people from the neighboring Turkish village on the other side of the border wanted to cross over. It was an icy January and the landscape was white. At some point it started to snow again, in the middle of the dark, almost moonless night. The people must have gotten lost, having walked around in circles, their footprints blown away by the snow. It only stopped snowing the next morning. The sun was shining again, and the air was clear. The villagers climbed up the hill. They watched as the people from the other side of the border carefully walked across the plains, carrying those who had frozen to death.

∽

A few years later, the struggles between the traders and the border soldiers became more brutal. The Turkish government sent tanks. The villagers in turn dug a trench behind Leyla's grandparents' garden. Each family in the village had one or two Kalashnikovs. When they heard shots from the border, the village men would lie in the trenches with their Kalashnikovs and wait.

∽

Her father was silent for a while at their table in the kitchen, got up, poured himself some more tea, and added a spoonful of sugar, and Leyla thought he had ended his story already, but then he started talking again.

Once the neighbor's turkeys took off over the border. Probably they were just looking for something to eat. They ran farther and farther in some direction across the fields, as turkeys do. With their scurrying turkey steps they ran through the mines, which could not harm them since they were too light. With their pointy beaks they picked at the earth and ate seeds until at some point, they were in a different country without taking any notice of it whatsoever. When the neighbor noticed, it was long since too late. He stood on the road, his back to the village, yelling toward the border. The evening sun illuminated him from the side, and he screamed for his turkeys. The landscape swallowed his voice.

~

Leyla had only been to the village school one single time, with Zozan, Mîran, and Roda on an early September day to pick up the new schoolbooks. The village school was not a school like the ones Leyla knew; it was, above all, far too small for that. There were only three classrooms, and the plaster was crumbling from the walls here too. The few shelves were old and worn, even partly damaged. The coal ovens were heated by the villagers in the winter; the children themselves brought the coal from home. There were no chairs or tables, but instead a picture of the president in every room.

You weren't safe from his face anywhere in the country. It hung as a poster larger than life on public buildings, was painted on walls, looked at you from taxi drivers' key chains in the towns and from the rearview mirrors of buses, dangled next to pictures of saints and tree-shaped air fresheners, hung resplendent in frames over sofas and televisions. It was printed in books, stood on shelves. The president had his eyes everywhere, and Leyla feared his gaze when she encountered it. The president's eyes could see what she thought and what she had been told by her family about him, she believed. On the street she quickly passed by his face because she hoped that way he would lose sight of her more quickly, but then she was afraid that he would be able to see the fear in her steps and began to walk more slowly. Leyla was not used to life under the presidential eyes. She wondered how the others managed every day to walk by him without attracting his attention. She wondered whether they had all really gotten used to his eyes or if over the decades they had so perfected walking beneath them and those of his father that their fear and rage were no longer visible.

Leyla couldn't help it; she got nervous when she saw his face. Her steps faltered again and again and she stumbled. That wasn't only because of his gaze but also because of something connected to him. Her father had told her about it when she was still little.

Namely, her father had said that he has eyes everywhere, even where you cannot see them. His eyes were the very people one did not suspect. You couldn't trust anybody in the country.

Besides the many pictures of the president there were just as many of his father, who had been president before him. While the president's hair was black and thick and sat on his head like a sponge, the hair of the presidential father was light gray with thin patches and was combed sideways across his head, as if he wanted to hide the bald scalp underneath but was unsuccessful, since his hair was too thin. Both father and son had the same thin moustache, the same thin lips, the same small eyes lying somewhat too close together, the father's brown and the son's blue.

At least the presidential father was dead. But in spite of that, Leyla did not trust his eyes and was almost ashamed of her superstitious fear. The presidential father was dead, and dead eyes cannot see, and certainly not from a poster, she told herself over and over. Yet the network of eyes that her father had spoken of covered the land so completely that it continued to exist even after his death. The presidential father, just like the president, was the past, present, and future of his country.

Once Leyla got off the airplane in Germany, she knew she had escaped the eyes of the president and those of his father. It alarmed her all the more when a few years later his picture could suddenly be seen everywhere in Germany too. In the newspapers, on television, on the internet, suddenly his name was everywhere. Every time it struck a blow to her, and every time she jerked back, then admonished herself not to make such a fuss, telling herself that, unlike the others, she was safe. Nevertheless, she turned the newspaper over when his photo was on the front page.

And sometime later she quit doing that. But she still could never get used to the sight of him.

She often imagined how it would be to kill him. Although she did not want to hate, she imagined it. Imagined how, like the blacksmith Kawa in the Newroza legend, she would break into his palace and walk along the shiny polished floor. How her steps would echo and how she would finally be standing in front of him. He sat on one of his upholstered armchairs, and she drew her gun. Her hand did not shake, and she pulled the trigger. The recoil, and then—her fantasy ended here.

⁓

Her father said they had their people in Germany too.

Leyla had never set eyes on them. And even if she had, she would certainly not have recognized them.

When her father spoke about them, he usually said *they* or *his people*. Even after so many years in Germany, the fear in her father's language was still breathing down his neck. He always spoke of *him*, never mentioning him by name.

At most he would sometimes say Hafez al-Addass, Hafez of the Lentils, and then laugh out loud. That's what I always used to call him, he said, never his real name.

Leyla tried to imagine *his people*. In her imagination they all looked like him. They wore his suits, had his slim build, his black hair, even his eyes and ears. He is the head, she thought.

⁓

Uncle Hussein was Aunt Pero's husband. He was short and slight and was always smiling good-naturedly. He cut his silver hair himself and was not nearly as vain as the young men in the village today, as Grandmother said. He wore his shirts until the fabric was frayed and patched them until there was nothing more to patch, afterward cutting them into strips. He used the strips to tie the grape vines on their poles or gave them to Aunt Pero to use as cleaning rags.

When he walked, Uncle Hussein dragged his feet across the floor; his movements were slow. He always seemed to Leyla to be someone who could not withstand strong storms.

When Leyla visited her aunt, Uncle Hussein gave her sweets. Partially melted chocolate wrapped in glittering paper, sticky pieces of candy from the village shop that Leyla did not like.

When Mîran, Welat, Roda, Siyabend, and Rohat annoyed them, he cursed and waved his walking stick around menacingly.

When greeting Leyla, he pinched her cheeks. When she was still small enough, he always twirled her around in the air, holding his hands to his lower back afterward, moaning.

It only occurred to her later that her father never went with her to her aunt's house. At that time, she took it for granted just as she did the crowing of the rooster in the morning, the pounding of the oil pumps behind the village, and the heat every day at noon.

She never speculated about her father and uncle. Her father's frozen stare whenever Aunt Pero came for a visit and someone mentioned her husband by chance. Uncle Hussein sends his greetings, Aunt Pero said, as if that was the most normal thing in the world. In Leyla's memory, however, her aunt's voice trembled slightly, betraying her. For it was of course not at all normal to send greetings when her uncle's plot of land bordered directly on that of her grandparents and they all visited each other all the time anyhow. And it was also not normal that her father never reacted to her aunt's words, overhearing them as if she had never said anything. His father kept a straight face and Leyla could not read his thoughts. He looked past her aunt to the empty wall.

Why had all that never surprised her? It should have surprised her, Leyla thought. If her father was watering the garden beds in the evening and Uncle Hussein stepped into the neighboring garden, her father would freeze up for a moment until he pulled himself together again and retreated to a corner where Uncle Hussein could not see him. When Leyla now remembered this, it naturally appeared conspicuous to her. But there had of course always been conflict. Somebody was always having a falling out with someone else. Her uncle with his neighbor, her aunt with her sister-in-law, her grandfather with everyone. And most of the time they were all getting along again before Leyla even understood what the conflict had been about.

Leyla never would have thought about not going to Aunt Pero's anymore. Even if her father and Uncle Hussein had openly quarreled. Leyla took no consideration of the adults' arguments, and nobody expected that of her. On the other hand, when her uncle was quarreling with his neighbor lady from the other side, he wanted to hear from Leyla that her cookies did not taste good, that her house was dirty, and that Leyla had not gotten any tea when she was there. And Leyla told him what he wanted to hear, even if it was not true.

~

So Leyla kept going back and forth between her aunt's and her grandparents' property. She didn't even knock but just kicked off her slippers, pushed open the door, and entered the house barefoot—there was, after all, always somebody there.

Had it bothered her father that she ate Uncle Hussein's sweets, sat next to him when he watched television, and brought him water when he asked for it? If anyone had asked her one summer if she liked Uncle Hussein, she would have smiled and been surprised by the question: of course, he was her Aunt Pero's husband!

Give my regards to your father, Uncle Hussein would say. And Leyla nodded but didn't say a word to her father about it.

Years later, she wondered how it could have been like that. She must have noticed that she never mentioned Uncle Hussein to her father. It had not been a conscious decision, for certain. But why had she herself never wondered about it?

How is your father? her Uncle Hussein would sometimes ask.

It was a harmless question, coming inconspicuously. Everyone was always asking everybody, How is your father? How is your mother? Not in Germany, of course, but in the village it would have been strange not to ask. But was Uncle Hussein's question really harmless? In retrospect, Leyla couldn't say. How was her uncle's voice when he asked the question? Did he really just want to know how her father was doing? Did he hope to get information out of Leyla? Was she overestimating him by believing he could do such a thing? Or was he just a good actor?

What's your father up to? Uncle Hussein asked.

And Leyla answered: All good. This and that. He is working.

Does he still play saz? Uncle Hussein asked. Leyla nodded.

Does he still go to demonstrations? Uncle Hussein wanted to know.

Leyla shook her head. He plays saz at home, after work, she said.

Now, years later, she was annoyed by his questions. Why did he want to know that? Was he curious? Polite? Was he trying to sound her out? Did he have a guilty conscience? Did he love his brother-in-law? Did he want to betray him?

Hussein, you dog, Leyla thought.

Neither did anyone make the effort to explain to her why Uncle Hussein and her father didn't speak to each other anymore, nor did they deliberately conceal it from her. Leyla learned the reason for it through pure coincidence.

She was just coming into the kitchen when her father said to her mother: Hussein is one of them. Her father said it as if he was absolutely certain, Leyla thought.

The following summer, Leyla avoided Aunt Pero's property. Not that she did not go over there at all, but far less often. She evaded the questions: Why don't you come to visit us more often?

Her aunt's friendliness made her uncomfortable. When Uncle Hussein gave her sweets, she declined graciously, saying she wasn't hungry. Not hungry for candy? Uncle Hussein shook his head. How can a child not be hungry for candy?

If he insisted on his gift, Leyla would spit out the candy outside in the dirt. They had never really tasted good to her anyhow.

~

Sometimes in the evenings she would see Uncle Hussein from her grandparents' garden, standing propped on his cane at the fence, chatting with the shepherd on the other side who had come home with his sheep, goats, and dog from the fields. If her uncle looked over toward her, she imitated her father, turning away quickly and sitting behind the bee house until he had disappeared.

He had to have noticed that she came far less often. As if they had both agreed to avoid each other, he too suddenly came less often to her grandparents' house for tea, which he had done sometimes in earlier summers when her father was not there.

Later, Leyla said she had never liked him anyhow. She had always known everything: his whole manner was so sly, fake.

Her father assumed that it was because of Uncle Hussein that he had problems the year her grandfather died and wanted to enter the country for the funeral. He couldn't prove it, but to whom and for what purpose should he have proven it?

The questions came even later. How can he be one of them, Leyla wondered, if he is actually one of us? Can he be one of us if he is one of them?

But was he really one of them? How had he become one of them? Was it because of money, could he be bought? He was poor: Leyla knew that. It rained in Aunt Pero and Uncle Hussein's house in the winter. He had debts and three sons who were all still in school and would have to marry sometime. And to marry, they would need money for the women, which the family did not have. Did he want to go away from the village, leave the country where they were only tolerated as stateless people and where there was no future for them? Migrant smugglers were expensive. Or had he perhaps even been promised a passport and a future for his sons? Certainly, he would have done it for money. So, someone like that could be bought! Or had they blackmailed him, threatened, pressured? And what if, ultimately, he himself was a victim? And what if the whole time Leyla was only looking for excuses for the man her aunt was married to and who had betrayed his brother-in-law?

~

Every morning at seven o'clock we gathered in the schoolyard before the lessons started, her father said. The principal had chosen one student from the highest grade to raise the flag. The sky above the schoolyard was blue. The flag waved, penetrating the blue. We stood there in our olive-green uniforms, backs straight, chests out, heads forward toward the principal, right next to the flag. The principal shouted. We sang, each class separately. Protectors of the homeland, peace be with you! Our proud spirit will not be conquered, the Arabs' dwelling place is a sanctuary! Umma Arabiya Wahida. An Arab nation. And only then would we proceed row by row to our classrooms.

~

As soon as we got out of school we switched languages, her father said, just as we changed our clothes, slipping out of our school uniforms. Arabic was not our language, not the language of our parents, not the language of our grandparents. Before we started school, we could only speak Kurdish. Arabic was the language of the big cities, Damascus, Aleppo, Homs, which we had never been to. There were a few scattered Arab shepherds in our region, but as children we had nothing to do with them. The first day of school was a shock; we were not prepared for it. From one day to the next we had to speak, write, read, and calculate in Arabic.

The teacher had a pencil, her father told her. He gave the class leader the pencil and said, if you hear someone speak one word of Kurdish then give him this pencil, and he has to pass on this pencil to the next student who speaks Kurdish. The pencil wandered from student to student, and the last one holding it got a beating.

Open your hand, barked the teacher, and then his stick whooshed down, up and down, up and down, until the student's hands were red and swollen. The teacher had a list lying next to his lectern. He counted our Kurdish words, and for every word you received ten blows.

The teacher changed his methods again and again, her father said. Once I had to put my hands on my ears and he hit them with his stick. At home, my mother put out a bucket of cold water for me. My hands were so swollen that I couldn't move them for days. The teacher was a Baathist; everybody knew that. He had been sent to our village from a distant part of the country and was ready to fight against everything that stood in the way of Arab nationalism.

The teacher went after the little ones in the first grade. They trembled and could barely get a word out when he asked them something. Once, one of them even peed his pants, and that made the teacher even more furious. At some point, I decided to kill him. I swore to myself: I will take a gun, go to school, and shoot him. I imagined doing this often, how I would stand in front of him and pull my gun out of my pants pocket, how it would be lying in my hand, and then I would pull the trigger.

But then we made a different plan. In class we sat on our tin canisters: there were no chairs. We smuggled stones into the classroom in our tin canisters. When the teacher started shouting again, we shook the canisters so that it made an immense thundering noise. It was very funny. I started laughing because the teacher just kept shouting, but we just kept shaking our canisters, and the teacher's shouts were swallowed by the thunder. And at some point, things went further than that. I can't say who threw the first stone, if I did it or someone else. The teacher ran out with us on his heels. We chased him out of the village. That was five weeks before summer vacation.

The following school year they didn't send a teacher to the village. A Yazidi from town stepped in, one of us. He lived with a family in the village, and all the families chipped in to give him some money or something to eat. He was very strict. We were in sixth grade, but he taught the material from ninth grade. In the evening he went from house to house and peered through the windows. If he saw us doing something besides studying we got into trouble the next day in school. He threatened to beat us, but he never raised his hand against us. He wanted us to be good. He knew that we had no other choice than to be good, and at some point, we knew it too.

Syria is an Arab country, but we are Kurds, her father said. In 1962 there was a decree: the Kurds were called upon to turn in their Syrian passports for them to be renewed. They never got them back.

It was in my papers from the very beginning, her father said.

He held his birth certificate in his hand and read it aloud to Leyla: nationality *ajnabi*, foreigner. Her father laughed. Almost puzzled, as if he could not believe it himself, thought Leyla, the same impression he always made when he told his story with the help of documents and photographs that he took out of his suitcase as if submitting evidence. This suitcase was, as far as Leyla knew, *the* suitcase with which he had come to Germany. Since that time this suitcase had gotten stretched out, the leather had become greasy, and the edges were battered. Only her father had the key to it; Leyla didn't know where he kept it.

It always happened the same way. He started telling a story, in the kitchen or sometimes even in the living room, the bag of sunflower seeds in front of him, and at some point in the middle of his story he interrupted himself, laughed as if he could not believe himself what he had just said, and got up and fetched the suitcase from the living room cabinet. It was more like he was showing himself rather than Leyla the right photo or document that proved what he was saying was true. As soon as he had opened the suitcase, his story would always again take a different direction. In the photo he had been looking for there was an old friend or neighbor who actually had nothing to do with the story her father had just been telling but about whom he nevertheless remembered another story, and it continued that way again and again. Leyla's father took more and more photos and documents out of the suitcase, not in a random order, but selected in relation to one another, and his story went on and on.

Most of the documents in the suitcase were long since worthless: his recognition as a political refugee in Germany, something that had been rescinded shortly after being issued, or his diploma, which in spite of his good grades did not allow him as an ajnabi to study at the university in Syria and was never recognized in Germany.

After the Hasakah census in 1962, when our family and many Kurds were stripped of their citizenship or never allowed to receive it to begin with, her father said, you could hear slogans everywhere. *Save the Arab Nation in Jazira; Fight the Kurdish menace!* That was when oil had been discovered in our region. And when Syrian troops fought alongside Saddam in Iraq against Barzani. We were accused as Kurds of supporting Barzani secretly. It was precisely at that time that they took our passports away, making us stateless.

There were two groups of stateless people, her father said, the ajnabi, foreigners, and the *maktumin*, the hidden. They accused the maktumin of being in Syria illegally; most of the time they did not even have birth certificates, he said, and put his certificate back in the suitcase.

Without citizenship we were not allowed to leave the country, her father said. For rice, bulgur, and flour we had to pay four or five times as much. We were not allowed to buy cars or land, go on trips to foreign countries, or study at the university. We couldn't even get married. Your grandparents, her father said, thus stayed unmarried before the law. There was no medical treatment for us; we were not accepted by hospitals. Once my oldest brother, your Uncle Nûrî, wanted a room in Damascus. They told him that foreigners like him were not allowed lodging in hotels and he should go to the secret service to get a permit and then come back.

Who was maktumin, who was ajnabi, and who was a citizen was often decided arbitrarily. My oldest brother had to turn in his passport; I myself never received one, but my youngest brother, your Uncle Memo, was allowed to keep his.

When I was as old as you are now, her father said, we didn't even know what to eat in the winter. During the week, we were in Tirbespî and went to school there. We took grain with us from the village, and sometimes for days we would eat only bulgur with green onions and tomato paste. We also took bread from the village, but it turned hard after two days, and to buy bread in the city you had to stand in line for hours if you did not know anybody in one of the bakeries or the secret service. Sometimes I got out of bed at four o'clock in the morning to get bread. I stood in line, and over and over people who had been behind me in the line came out of the bakery loaded down with bread.

Every Thursday after school, her father said, we went on foot to the village, which took two hours. Later, there were shared taxis for one and a half lira. But for that amount of money you could eat in town for a whole week. We walked to the village, even long after the shared taxis existed.

Every Thursday we set out again for Tirbespî. We had to cross a river jumping from stone to stone, since there were no bridges. If it flooded in the spring, we took off our shoes, socks, and pants and held each other by the hand so that nobody would be carried away by the current.

Uncle Nûrî dropped out of school after tenth grade. He would have liked to stay longer, but we didn't have enough money. From then on Nûrî only went to work, illegally in Lebanon. And Aunt Pero? Leyla asked. Aunt Pero, her father said. Did she also go to school in town? asked Leyla. No, there was not enough money for that, he said. And for what purpose? Aunt Pero would get married, after all. And somebody had to help Grandma and Grandpa in the fields.

⁓

Shilan, her father said, always came to us first when she visited the village. She came every few weeks. One of her aunts had married a man in our village and moved in with him. Shilan went to my sister Pero and asked her for advice about clothes that she was sewing. Pero, by the way, could sew better than the tailors in town; women were always coming to our house for help from Pero with their sewing. The women would drink a cup of tea, another one, smoke, and then offer Pero cigarettes that she always refused because she didn't smoke. So Shilan also came repeatedly to visit Pero and I didn't give it a second thought. The two of them were friends, I assumed.

But at some point, Pero told me Shilan was getting married. Her brother wanted to marry a woman, and in order to spare the bride-price Shilan was simply to marry the woman's brother: a wedding of exchange. The wedding was to take place in our village, where the bridegroom lived. Of course, I knew him. He was hot-tempered and had a short fuse. When he drank too much he always got into fights. Pero had often said: I already feel sorry for the woman who will someday marry this man. And now it would be Shilan.

~

On the wedding day I had come home from school in town. I changed clothes; we wore uniforms at school, her father said. I was standing in front of the mirror on the wall behind the kitchen combing my hair when suddenly Shilan's little brother came into the garden and told me to come with him. He was still a child.

Immediately, he said.

Immediately? I asked.

Yes, he said.

What's going on? I asked.

Shilan sent me, he said. She wants to talk to you.

I went into the living room, put the comb back on the ledge, and tied my shoes.

She said you should hurry, Shilan's brother said.

All that was a mystery to me. What's so urgent? I asked.

I don't know, he said. She just told me to come get you.

So, I went with the little boy through the village to the house of her bridegroom, where the wedding was to begin. The courtyard was full of people. Women were standing in the kitchen cooking rice, bulgur, and meat in big pots. The men were standing around in groups, talking and smoking. A zurna player and a drummer had arrived. The people were already dancing. I saw Shilan sitting on a chair, surrounded by other women. Pero was with her too. Shilan was wearing a red dress. She looked serious, but that did not surprise me. Brides at our weddings always looked serious. Weddings are a serious matter. I went over to Shilan to congratulate her.

Congratulations, I said.

There is nothing to congratulate, she said.

And later, when even more people were dancing all in a row with the drummer and zurna player in the middle, she said to me, softly so that only I could hear: Run away with me!

I was confused, very confused. We kept dancing. She said: I'd rather die than marry this man.

Let's meet behind the garden, I said. She looked at me: Later, when we are not being observed. And I, I wondered how that would work, for naturally there was no moment when a bride would not be observed at her wedding.

I will go to the bathroom, she said, then I'll climb over the wall. And you will wait for me on the other side.

How are you going to climb in that dress? I said. And then? I asked. What then? How are you going to walk in those shoes?

It was crazy, a crazy idea. But Shilan seemed determined.

More and more people crowded into the courtyard. We danced. I stood near my neighbors, then went to the women in the kitchen to get something to eat. On my way to the kitchen, however, I changed my mind. I turned around and left.

I never found out if she really climbed over the wall.

After her wedding, Shilan lived in our village. I avoided her. If I saw her in the distance as she was coming back from the fields or fetching water from the well, I turned around. Or I pretended not to have seen her, avoiding her gaze. At some point we encountered each other again, of course; in a village like ours you can't avoid each other for long. There were new weddings and funerals. It would have been impolite not to talk to her. People would have gossiped. So, I asked her how she was.

Well, she said. Thank you.

Later, Leyla's father said, I often thought about how for one moment I considered running away with her. Just one single short moment. I liked her. But I immediately discarded the idea of fleeing. Where would we have gone? I hadn't even finished school. I was a member of the Communist Party of Syria. I had read Marx, and the poems of Cigerxwîn. I had read the poems of Cigerxwîn so often that I knew them by heart. I didn't want to marry; I wanted to read and live.

〜

Many years later—I hardly thought about Shilan anymore—Nûrî's wife told me about her. Shilan was also now living in Germany. With her husband and three of her children, near Oldenburg. They had left only the older girl with her in-laws in the village. Shilan is not doing well, Nûrî's wife said. She keeps getting thinner; she's ill.

But Nûrî's wife could not tell me exactly what Shilan had.

At a funeral, a few years later, my cousin told me that Shilan had run away from home. She had always had these bruises. They couldn't be seen under her long dresses. When she had the bruises also on her face, she tried to cover them up with makeup. But you could still see the bruises. At first, they were blue, then they turned brighter, green and purple. At some point Shilan went to a women's shelter. Since then, the family has heard nothing more from her.

～

Before the internet came to the villages, everybody sent their greetings on videocassettes.

Because the family lived scattered across villages and towns in Kurdistan, in northern Syria, in eastern Turkey, mostly in the vicinity of Batman, or in the Sinjar mountains in northern Iraq, great-aunts and uncles everywhere and their families, all of whom Leyla had never yet met, videos were constantly being sent back and forth, and Leyla's father was always getting mail too. Once, Leyla remembered very clearly, a videocassette arrived on which an old woman in a white dress with a lilac-colored headscarf, the clothing of the Yazidis from Sinjar, sat on a plastic chair and talked. All three of them sat at home in front of the television and watched her, and as always, her father translated difficult words for her mother. The woman talked and talked, endlessly. Leyla ate cornflakes. The bowl was long since empty when the woman finally began to greet the family members in Germany. She said: I greet the family of Xalil; of Nûrî; of Sleiman, his wife, Gulistan, their daughter Shirin; and then a whole list of names that Leyla was not familiar with. Once again, it was endless, until the old woman finally said, and the one, the renegade, I greet him too. And with that, the video ended. Leyla was not sure if she had understood correctly and wanted to ask her father. But he was just staring straight ahead at the television.

～

In her father's suitcase, there was a photo of her grandparents and Uncle Memo taken by Leyla's father in a hotel room in Aleppo. It had been the first time that her father could travel to Syria again after many years, under a different name with a French passport that Leyla had no idea how he had obtained; her father didn't want to tell her. The passport was genuine, or at least her father said so, even having a photo of her father and all. Only the name printed on it was not her father's.

Leyla's father, Uncle Memo, and her grandparents had seen each other for only a few hours in Aleppo. Because her father was afraid of being recognized, he couldn't travel to the village or to Tirbespî. Because her grandparents in turn were afraid of Aleppo, they only stayed a few hours. It was after her father's marriage to her mother, shortly before Leyla's birth. Leyla thought for a long time that it was a bad photo, since her grandfather and Uncle Memo were staring into the camera looking irritated.

And her grandmother's hands lay on her floral skirt like foreign bodies, as if she didn't know what to do with them. She looked away from the camera. A happy reunion after many years looked different. After her father had told her grandparents there in the hotel room about his marriage, his grandmother asked if his wife was Yazidi, surely already suspecting why he had waited so long to tell them about it. Her father did not answer, finally shaking his head. Her grandmother, Leyla's father told her, crossed her arms, pursed her lips together, looked away, and did not say another word to him. Leyla's family sat for minutes like that, as if frozen, until her grandfather finally said: You haven't seen your son for all these years and now he has traveled so far. And you don't want to talk to him just because he chose the wrong wife!

In the family, it was said that it was Leyla who first brought reconciliation between her grandmother and her father. Leyla was so sweet, Aunt Baran said, that her grandmother could not be angry anymore.

For the rules were actually clear. Yazidis who did not marry Yazidis were cast out. And with them their children and children's children. And again, their children and their children's children, and so forth and so on.

Even if her grandmother was now overriding her own rules and teaching Leyla her stories and prayers, Leyla didn't know if she was Yazidi now or not, and this question seemed important to her.

Her grandmother often said to Leyla: When you are grown, you will marry Aram. Or they would say: When you are big, you will marry Nawaf. And everyone else also talked incessantly about marrying, even her grandfather. The motorcades that would drive along the highways from village to village, from the villages to the town, from the town to the villages, the loud music booming from loudspeakers, the women whose hair was rigid with hairspray, the made-up faces, the long dresses, the cheering throngs of people: Nothing was more important here than weddings, Leyla thought.

The shaykh's wife said to Leyla, when she and her husband were once again at her grandparents' house for a visit: You are Yazidi, because your father is Yazidi. It follows the father. Leyla didn't know if that was right: there was no book in which she could look up the rules, but the question was definitely very important. And everybody told her something different.

Who was promised to whom, how much bride money was paid, if the price was too high, who had run away with whom: simply everything in life appeared to add up to marriage, but not only in the village but even in Germany. Everywhere people were getting married, or at least all the people Leyla knew. Leyla feared the whole topic; she couldn't say why, but it seemed to her like a trap that people fell into over and over. The beautiful dresses at the weddings and the loud music might be able to hide this fact, but then came the sheets with the bloodstain that the women showed everyone after the wedding night while the bride sat next to them bashfully. Leyla was horrified the first time she heard about it.

～

Leyla was happy that her father was on her side in all these matters. He was always telling everyone that Leyla would finish school and go to college. Leyla, he said proudly, would study medicine or law. And then she would go to the International Criminal Court in the Hague. My daughter, he said, raising his index finger, will not marry young. I forbid it. She is not allowed to marry until she has completed her studies. Why marry? To do her husband's laundry and cook his food?

Your father is right, said Aunt Baran. School is certainly good for you. But if you wait too long, you will be too old and end up like Aunt Evîn: nobody will want you anymore. Leyla nodded and thought about the loudly laughing Evîn.

～

Leyla, come in, Evîn called and waved her into the kitchen. Everybody was there, sitting in a semicircle. Evîn's sisters and sisters-in-law, nieces, aunts, Zozan. She is always alone, our Leyla, Evîn said and laughed loudly, so that you could see her large front teeth.

Leyla sat down with the others on the floor, and Evîn gave her a bowl of grape leaves. Leyla took some rice from the pot and put it in the middle of a grape leaf. She folded the corners, left and right, rolled the leaf and added it to others' stuffed grape leaves.

Tell me, Leyla, which one of them do you like? Evîn asked. Douran, or his little brother Firat? Faso's son Mahir, your cousin Aram, or do you prefer Dalil?

Leyla laughed in embarrassment and shrugged her shoulders. She didn't know what to say.

Come, tell us, Leyla! Which one do you like? We'll keep it to ourselves.

Leyla felt backed into a corner.

Leyla, you know we will keep it to ourselves, Zozan said, which was a lie, Leyla knew that. Zozan laughed and pinched Leyla in her side.

Dalil is certainly a handsome one, Havîn cried.

Evîn laughed and said: Everybody thinks Dalil is handsome, right Zozan? But it's such a shame that he is a shaykh. And we are not allowed to marry anyone from the shaykh family.

Come on, Leyla, tell us! Who do you like?

Leyla took another grape leaf from the bowl and some rice.

Nobody, she said, but that sounded feeble. I don't want anyone.

Nobody, Evîn laughed. Nobody is handsome enough for you or what? Our Leyla is picky! Would you rather marry your books or what?

~

At least Leyla is smart, Rengîn had once said to Evîn. Leyla heard it only by chance because she was sitting in front of the house under the window eating figs that her grandmother had given her.

Not that she is ugly, but Zozan is definitely prettier than she is, Evîn answered. Cigarette smoke wafted out of the window.

And that hairdo, said Rengîn, that hairdo! Leyla would be such a pretty girl if she hadn't cut off her hair. So short! To the chin, how does that look? Almost like a boy.

That's the fashion in Almanya, Evîn said and laughed.

I don't understand German women, said Rengîn. How can they find that pretty, such short hair?

Leyla didn't want to listen any further, got up, and went into the garden. She ran to the rosebushes, picked a rose, removed the thorns, and put the rose behind her ear like her grandmother had done to her the previous summer when her hair was longer. But the rose slipped out and fell on the ground. Leyla sat down on a stone and picked off the petals of the rose, one by one, from the outside to the inside, until the rose was destroyed forever. Leyla got up, walked along the fence looking at the trees that her father had planted before he had gone to Germany. She plucked a tomato, big, plump, and warm. She wiped it clean on her skirt and bit into it, the pulp dripping onto her T-shirt. The tomato tasted sweet.

Leyla was about to turn back when she heard voices from the rear of the garden. Somebody was laughing near her grandfather's tobacco plants. She recognized Zozan's voice. What was Zozan doing in the garden in this heat? Leyla was lured by the voices.

In the corner between the tobacco plants and the fence, with the mountains and the border far behind them, Zozan was standing before a tree trunk—Zozan, who was two years younger than she was—and next to her in the shade was Dalil. Dalil, tall and slender, hair combed back, a head taller than Zozan, was holding a long blade of grass in his hand and touching Zozan's hand with the tip. He looked very focused.

Leyla was so surprised to see Dalil that she took a step, then another, and Zozan and Dalil looked up and stared at her so startled that Leyla did not know what to do, so she turned around without saying a word and ran back to the house.

Only when she had caught her breath back at the house did it occur to her that Dalil could not have entered the garden through the courtyard, where she had been sitting the whole time under the window. He must have climbed over the fence.

Evîn and Rengîn were still sitting in the living room smoking. Leyla filled a glass with water and emptied it in one gulp.

Where did you come from? Evîn asked.

From the garden, said Leyla.

Do you want some tea? Rengîn asked.

Leyla sat cross-legged in front of them both.

Zozan, Leyla said. I saw Zozan with Dalil in the garden.

~

Come, I'll do your eyebrows, Evîn said during one of the other summers, and Leyla laid her head on Evîn's legs while Evîn ran a thread over her face and removed the hairs. Leyla felt the warmth of Evîn's body through her jeans.

And now I'll paint your fingernails, Evîn said.

~

Pull your skirt over your knees, her grandmother said when visitors came. Don't sit there like that: people can see your legs.

~

If they were out and about in town and Leyla looked back at a group of men sitting in front of a café staring at them, Rengîn would ask, Why are you looking those men in the eyes? Evîn came out of the fabric store. Finally, said Rengîn. Let's go home.

~

Something changed. The neighbor came for tea, the same neighbor who once had talked about Leyla marrying his son. Leyla has gotten pretty, he said that summer. She is hardworking, her grandmother answered. The neighbor kept talking about his son, who was two years older than Leyla. She could finish school in Almanya, the neighbor said, and then move back here to the village. The neighbor said he would pay for her.

Leyla had to laugh about that as if it were a joke.

She could not even imagine the whole thing. The thought of living in the house next door to her grandmother on the other side of the garden fence with the sheep and the chickens amused her. She imagined herself serving tea when company came, carrying the tray into the room with her long skirt dragging on the floor. Kneeling down to pour the hot tea in the little glasses, stirring the sugar until it dissolved, standing up again. Her feet getting as chafed by the dry air and dust as the feet of all the women in the village. Going to the village store in plastic slippers with a baby in her arms and another child holding her hand.

~

I wanted to live differently. I wanted to change my life, her father said. When I was fourteen years old, I joined the Communist Party of Syria. I had to pay monthly membership dues of twenty-seven piasters a month. Under no circumstances did I wish to join the Baath Youth and I also hoped that the Communist Party could give me some protection. The Communist Party of Syria was tolerated because Syria had good relations with the Soviet Union. My brother Nûrî joined the Democratic Party of Kurdistan, which was illegal.

Still, we too were careful. We held our meetings in the fields, each arriving separately. Since it was only ten minutes by foot from the village one could think we were just going for a walk. We were allowed to meet, but we were still afraid. We got off the road and went into the grainfields. In the summer the wheat was tall; we crawled so that our heads could not be seen.

In the middle of the field, we would lie down on the ground. One of us squatted in the middle and read aloud from the newspaper of the

Communist Party of Iraq, which was illegal and was smuggled over the border to us every few months. Afterward we discussed what we had heard. Once the meeting was over, we each crawled separately out of the field and walked home on different paths.

∼

I do not believe in God, her father said and spit the husk of a sunflower seed onto his plate. Leyla nodded; she had heard it a thousand times before. Her father told everyone whether they wanted to hear it or not. Religion is something just for poor or stupid people. For people who do not know any better. Religion is the opium of the people; her father repeated the sentence over and over. He forgave the poor and the stupid but not the ones that he called fanatics.

Her father talked about a fanatic who in Mosul had shot one of her grandmother's nephews, Kawa, because he sold alcohol in his store.

He talked about a fanatic who had taught religion in Tirbespî and had forced them to recite Koran verses in Mosul although he knew perfectly well that they were Yazidis. Or more accurately: because he knew they were Yazidis.

He talked about a fanatic who had been one of his classmates and had cursed him again and again as an infidel and devil-worshiper.

Or he told the story that Leyla couldn't help thinking of often, about the fanatic who in the eighties boarded a train every week from Batman and went from compartment to compartment shouting that it smelled of Yazidis, and when he recognized a Yazidi by his moustache and clothing, he gave him a thrashing.

∼

When Leyla asked her father what he himself believed in, he answered: communism. In communism and thus in something that finally made all people equal. Communism, her father said, came a long time ago already via the big cities to our village, in the form of newspapers and books. For his entire life, the only books that Leyla's father owned besides his Kurdish newspapers and books were the Arab editions of *Capital* and *The Communist Manifesto*. Leyla's father told her about the class struggle and taught her to sing "The Internationale" in Kurdish and in German. In the evening he sat alone in the kitchen in their house near Munich and sang the workers' songs by Şivan Perwer, accompanying himself on the saz.

∼

When I came to Germany, her father said to Leyla, thirty years ago, I revealed everything. I said from the beginning that I was not Firat Ekinci as I was called in my fake ID but that I was *I*, a stateless Yazidi Kurd from Syria. I had an excerpt from the Syrian civil registry sent to me that proved that in Syria I was registered as an ajnabi, a foreigner, although I had been born in Syria. I described truthfully why I had had to leave Syria.

My application for asylum was approved. Witnesses testified to the German authorities that I was politically persecuted in Syria as a stateless Kurd. I was happy, on top of the world. But just a few days later, her father said, handing Leyla the document from his suitcase, I received another letter. A message from the Ministry of the Interior stating that an objection had been raised to my asylum claim and that the reasons would be communicated to me later. My plea for asylum was blocked.

From 1980 to 1991, her father told her, there was no decision made. He laughed and sighed. All these years I was allowed neither to work nor study at the university. Eleven years. But because our family in the village needed money, I worked illegally.

It was not until later that I learned the reasons for those eleven years of my life. Naturally they were political. The official statement was that there was democracy in Syria and that Arabs and Kurds were treated equally.

In 1987, I filed a petition as a stateless person. The foreign office, the Max Planck Institute, and the German Orient Institute in Hamburg confirmed for me that I was stateless. And after a few months I actually received official recognition as a stateless person, a great day. In the document it even said that the government was not allowed to appeal; I have all the papers here, Leyla. But then, in spite of that, I was refused a passport, just like that. I contracted a lawyer, and in the end, I won my case. I received a passport as a stateless person. Look, her father said, putting a completely different stack of papers back into the suitcase. I've kept everything, every single document.

~

We're going to Italy, my mother said. It was March, and Leyla was ten or eleven years old. Her mother had borrowed the family car of an old friend. She randomly packed toys and clothing for Leyla. She was packing differently than usual, not with the care and deliberation with which she prepared for the trips to their grandparents' village in the summer. This time, her mother didn't even bother folding the clothes.

Towels, said Leyla. You are forgetting the towels.

Her mother had wet hair and her toothbrush in her hand.

She stood at the kitchen table looking for the phone number of the school. I want to report my daughter's absence for illness. Leyla Hassan, Grade 4B.

We have a math test tomorrow, Leyla said, I will need a doctor's note.

Leyla's mother looked at her as if she did not understand, then took her toothbrush out of her mouth. And now that, she said.

In the waiting room of their family doctor her mother stared at the issue of *Der Spiegel* in front of her on the table. On the cover there was a picture of the deck of a ship full of people and a caption in red letters: *Migrant onslaught,* and beneath it in bold yellow script: *Europe seals itself off.* Her mother opened the magazine and leafed through it to an article titled *Infernal Voyage to the Promised Land: The Refugee Ship Monica.*

Leyla read: *High Stakes Game: How Refugees are Smuggled to Germany.* Then the receptionist called her name.

Her father picked them up directly from the doctor's office.

I forgot my book, Leyla said.

We don't have time for that anymore, her mother said.

I'm not going without my book, Leyla said. It's not a vacation without a book.

You always get sick in the car when you read anyhow, her father said.

They drove for about half an hour when her father said to her mother: This is making me nervous. Her mother only said, I am driving the way I always drive. They stopped at the next rest stop to switch places. Leyla's mother bought her an ice cream. Her father leaned against the car door and waited. When they started driving again, he turned up the heat and it got warm. Leyla's popsicle melted and ran over her fingers; she was eating too slowly. When she was certain that her parents weren't watching, she wiped her sticky hands on the upholstery.

Her parents remained silent. Her father put on a cassette and turned up the music. *Ay lê gulê.* He sang along.

It was the first time they had all gone on vacation together by car. But nothing about it was the way Leyla had always imagined it would be: in Italy with a book at the seaside, ice cream, pizza, and her new pink bathing suit. Right now, the weather was a gray, wet fog soup. The mountains, which with a clear view you could have seen from a distance, only rose up later like dark green monsters.

Leyla had often been envious of her classmates in September when at the start of school they were all asked about their summer vacations. The others would always talk about hikes at low tide in the North Sea, the food in Italy, water parks in Spain, or sometimes hotel complexes in Tunisia or Egypt. There were differences between them too: some of them talked about the beach and the bed and breakfasts, the Turkish cities of Antalya, Izmir, and Bodrum, others about villages and towns in which their grandparents, aunts, and uncles lived. And then some of them in turn always kept it short, speaking little, avoiding the question. Leyla spoke of the village, of her grandmother's chickens and sleeping outside under the sky. My grandma and grandpa in Kurdistan, but she only said this sentence one single time. For the Turkish children came to her during recess and said: Kurdistan does not exist. And that the Kurds were dirty and did not wash themselves. They were murderers, the dirty Kurds. After that Leyla said: my grandma and grandpa in Syria. But most of the children were not familiar with Syria; one classmate mixed it up with Siberia. When Leyla said it was very hot in Syria, her classmate said: No, it's cold in Syria.

The German children sent postcards when they were on summer vacation, shiny with colorful lettering, the name of the vacation spot in big letters, underneath it a dolphin, ancient walls, palms, or a beach. In Leyla's village, naturally there were no postcards. Nor did she see any in Tirbespî either, and also not in Qamişlo. Once she found some in Aleppo in one of the shops at the entrance to the suq. Although the land was beautiful, there were no tourists, and even these few postcards were old-fashioned and faded.

On one of them there was a carpet weaver, on another a tall citadel. Leyla bought the yellowed cards and filled them with writing, and her uncle put them in envelopes, because postcards did not make it through, he said, only letters. Three of the five mailings, however, never arrived, and the two others only many weeks later.

Leafless trees whizzed past the window and grayish green pines. It was March and not the right time for vacation with sunscreen and bathing suits. But Italy, Leyla thought, was always a proper vacation destination. Maybe it would even be warm on the other side of the mountains and the trees would have leaves. Past the autobahn the mountains now loomed large.

They crossed through the Brenner Pass and stopped for a break in a roadhouse, eating potato pancakes and applesauce. Leyla saw castles on hills: that was South Tyrol. Can we stop? Leyla asked. I want to go to a castle.

In Bolzano, they paid the toll and left the autobahn. Her mother had a giant map on her lap that she had been opening and closing ever since crossing the Italian border, studying it over and over. She wanted to get to a train station following a certain route. They drove through Bolzano, went around a traffic circle three times, turned around, and looked for the right way. At some point they stopped in front of a plaza. Bolzano Main Train Station.

There they are, her mother called and pointed excitedly at the station lobby. Leyla couldn't recognize anybody. Her father parked the car, hastily got out, and crossed the street. Her mother waved, and her father held Leyla tightly by the hand. Only now did Leyla see that the people across from her were a mother with her two boys and that it was Aunt Pero and two of her sons, Leyla's cousins Rohat and Siyabend from the village.

Her aunt looked completely different than she had all those summers in the village, where she always wore a floral dress, plastic slippers, and a headscarf from which the tips of her braids always peeked out at her hips like they did for all women her age. But now she was squeezed into a glittery green sweater that she must have been sweating in and looked cheap with its large lettering *Party Girl*; in addition, she wore stretch jeans and pumps made out of imitation snake leather. Why was her aunt dressed up that way? Leyla needed some time before she understood that it was supposed to be camouflage.

Her aunt, who was still her aunt, even wearing this strange clothing in this foreign country Italy, had tears in her eyes when she kissed first Leyla, then her brother and sister-in-law.

Italian fashion, she said and laughed. Do you like it? She bought it right after arriving, at a market at the harbor. All six of them squeezed into the car. They stopped again soon, just before the expressway. You all must be hungry, her father said and laid an arm on Rohat's shoulder. They bought sandwiches and cola for the three from the village. Leyla understood that Aunt Pero's strange clothing was supposed to portray a European. Rohat and Siyabend were also acting differently than the way Leyla remembered. They were quiet and looked so tired that they might fall asleep at any moment. But they stayed awake, staring out the window for the whole ride. They didn't listen to music, remained silent, her father sometimes laughing and trying to tell a story.

Her mother said, Leyla, don't tell anyone at school anything about this. Not even Bernadette. Listen, her mother said, this is a serious matter. Leyla did not understand; they had only picked up Aunt Pero and her cousins from the train station. We could go to jail for this, her mother said.

On their way back to Germany, they stopped just after Brixen. I'll drive now, her mother said. A blond woman at the wheel is better. They won't stop me. Everybody was quiet and stared out the window until they had passed the border.

～

The house in which they soon visited her aunt and cousins was in a village whose name Leyla could not remember. The nearest large city was Ulm; Leyla saw the name on the autobahn signs. But they didn't get to Ulm, since her father put on his blinker before that. They passed fields, patches of forest, towns whose names meant nothing to Leyla. Church towers, village squares with maypoles, geraniums on balconies, big barn doors. It's good they ended up in a village, her mother said.

The house was run down. The plaster was crumbling, the tiles in the bathroom had cracks, the windows weren't sealed tightly and had mold growing in their seams. There was a custodian who came every few days for a few hours to fix something here and there, but that didn't change anything.

In the kitchen that Aunt Pero shared with the other people in the home, she cooked rice and trshik. When Leyla and her parents came for a visit, she stood every time in her plastic slippers, headscarf, and brightly colored skirt in the middle of the kitchen. She was still the same aunt as before, short and fat, the other residents of the home standing around her at the other stove burners, the cries of the children drowning out their words. Her aunt stirred a pot with her wooden spoon as if nothing in the world could knock her down, just stood there and stirred and stirred until she finally spooned the trshik onto the plates.

She and Siyabend and Rohat lived in a room on the first floor. The furniture was from charity and smelled of other peoples' lives. Leyla was secretly disgusted by it. The pieces were flung together in such a way that Leyla felt like she was in a storage room in which the furniture was just standing around for a bit until it could be put out for the garbage.

The house used to be a village school. Because there were too few children in the village, at some point they had closed it. The house had been empty for a few years until the authorities declared it to be a home for asylum-seekers. All the German families whose lots bordered the home had put up tall new fences around their gardens.

～

Although Aunt Pero could only speak a few words of German, she somehow managed to meet the families in the village that had farms and kept cows.

Every Monday from then on, her aunt would take her sons or one of the other women from the home to the farm. She handled the business even though her German was the worst of any of them. In spite of that, she bargained the best. Her aunt always got what she wanted for the price that she wanted.

She got her way, said *Danke*, *Bitte*, inquired about the family, and came back with buckets full of milk from which, under her direction, the women in the home made cheese.

They had no work visa and would only be able to get one when their asylum status was clarified. But for her asylum status to be clarified, her aunt needed documents from Syria that she could only request in person there. In spite of this, with the help of the family who owned the farm, she arranged employment for herself as a cleaning lady. The family she cleaned for paid her wages in cash. And in turn, every time Leyla's parents visited her aunt, she would force a few bills into their hands. Her parents protested, but her aunt insisted. Over the years, her aunt paid back everything she had borrowed from Leyla's parents for the migrant smugglers and the voyage to Europe, down to the last cent. Her sons helped her with this. Siyabend and Rohat picked up garbage at the lake for one euro per hour, an integration initiative of the state. Later on, they received official recognition as refugees and with this status they were then allowed to work, so the cousins could look for different jobs. Jobs for unskilled workers, temporary staff in fast-food restaurants, menial work in handicraft enterprises, furniture packing, or assembly line work.

~

Aunt Pero received no money from the agency but instead food stamps and everything else the agency assumed she would need. Sauerkraut, dumpling dough, jars of cherries, noodles, shampoo, rice packed in individual bags with holes in them. Who cooks rice in such little bags? her aunt asked.

Her aunt wanted to cook Kurdish food and proposed a trade to her mother. When Leyla and her parents visited her, at the end of the afternoon they would load the jars of preserves and bags of rice one by one into the car and her mother would give her aunt money for the Turkish supermarket in the nearest bigger town. Her aunt made the hike twice a week, returning on the bus that went only four times a day, loaded down with bags crammed full of groceries.

The cans of food from her aunt collected in her parents' cupboard; Leyla's parents also preferred to cook Kurdish food. The groceries piled up higher and higher until the expiration dates had passed and her mother threw everything away.

In the home, Aunt Pero served tea after meals and cookies, afterward fetching a stack of papers and showing them letters from the agency, forms and applications that her aunt could not possibly read with her four years of schooling and her German. Her mother filled out the applications. Leyla watched her aunt writing her signature, individual shaky letters, P-E-R-O H-A-S-S-A-N, like the handwriting of a child.

~

Aunt Pero put fruit and bread in a plastic bag. She packed towels and a blanket. They set out for the lake behind the village not far from the home.

Leyla and Rohat took the lead. Rohat knew the way. He roams around here a lot after school, her aunt said to them from behind. He shouldn't roam around so much; instead, he should be studying.

He was always with the other boys, Leyla's mother said, back home. I remember that.

It's nice that you have the lake nearby, Leyla said, not knowing what to say.

Rohat kicked a stone from the path into the bushes.

Do you still have the slingshot, Leyla asked, that you used to shoot birds with?

Rohat shook his head. I left it there.

Rohat was allowed to attend the local school, and since then they spoke German to one another.

He and Leyla stood in the shallow water and tried to skip stones. Rohat usually managed three or four skips, while Leyla's stones simply fell in the water and sank.

You have to use flatter stones, Rohat said. Look, like this. Leyla watched him. He stood sideways, lowering his head. Like this it's really easy. He spun his arm and torso forcefully. The stone glided over the water, bouncing three times before it sank.

Everything is better here, said Rohat, but I still want to go back. Leyla didn't say anything. She picked up a flat stone from the ground and imitated the movements that Rohat had just shown her.

Is this the right way? she asked.

Rohat nodded.

~

Better stay inside, her aunt said during their next visit, when Rohat and Leyla wanted to go out in the yard with the other children.

Why? asked Leyla.

It is going to storm, her aunt said and stroked Leyla's hair, but the sky was blue and there was not a cloud in it.

Leyla and Rohat sat on the bed eating gummy bears that Leyla had brought with her.

Why don't you play Uno, her aunt said. Leyla, you brought Uno along, right? We'll go outside together later. She went into the kitchen to make a new pot of tea.

They are having problems with the new family from Iraq, her mother said in the car on the way home. The oldest son spat at Rohat and pushed him, calling him an infidel. You dirty Yazidi, he said.

Just quarrels among teenagers, her mother said, adding that her aunt now always locked the door to their room at night and left the key in the inside.

∼

One day a police officer arrived in an SUV, her father said. Without notice they stood in front of the courtyard, got out, and simply came into our house. Nûrî said: Do you have a warrant? Does the head of the village know? The police officers pushed Nûrî aside.

In the living room, my mother had that wooden board, you know, over the door, where she kept her few things. The police threw all of it on the floor, pushed everything off the shelves on the living room wall, and used their boots to sweep everything together into a pile. Maybe they were just looking for tobacco, but they found paper. Gorgeous Kurdish children's books, all illegal in Syria, that I had bought the previous summer working in Lebanon. And receipts from the Newroz festival of the Democratic Party of Kurdistan, a list of its revenue and expenditures; Nûrî was in charge of the finances at that time. And lists of donations, with names. They found all of that right away, since we hadn't even properly hidden it.

The police took Nûrî and my father away, Leyla's father said. To jail in Tirbespî. As soon as their SUVs disappeared, I ran out of the house and through the village to warn everyone whose name was on the list. And then I kept running to the next village and then to the next village after that.

Two days later we drove to Tirbespî. The officials named us a sum for which Nûrî and my father could be released. They promised that if we paid, the case would not be passed along. We said we would pay. But the amount they demanded was too high. We didn't have that much money.

So, we leased out our fields that summer. We hired ourselves out as day laborers for the cotton harvest, everyone, all the men and women of the whole family. All together we rented a room near Hasakah to sleep in. In the evenings, we watered our own fields, and in the daytime we picked cotton, gathering it in big sacks under the hot sun. I can still remember clearly the vast fields there, Leyla's father said, the white cotton, the exhaustion.

After some time, they released Nûrî and my father. As they had promised, the case was not passed on to a higher level. That had been our biggest worry.

Her father was silent.

Leyla, your grandmother told herself that something like that could not happen a second time. She went with a shovel into the garden and dug a hole. She put all the books that she could find in the hole and filled it with earth.

For her, who had never learned to read or write, there was no difference. For her, everything in print was dangerous.

When I got home from school, her father said, all the books were gone. Gone, gone, gone, he said. Nobody knew anything about it. Not my brothers and sister, not my father, and my mother just shrugged her shoulders. I screamed, her father said. Somebody must know where they are, I shouted. My mother came out of the kitchen with a tray with tea and sugar on it. I don't want any tea, I said, I want my books.

～

You should never be in need of books, her father said to her often. If Leyla wanted a book, he bought it for her. Once when they were leaving the bookstore, he said: You can read every book you want to. When I was as old as you, I couldn't read what I wanted to. Today I could do it, but I'm always too tired from work.

Leyla got books for all her birthdays. As soon as she had learned to read, she read incessantly. Once she had started, she couldn't stop. For whole afternoons she would read at home by herself after school, while her parents were at work. Leyla read during the summers with her grandparents in the village, on the school bus, under the school desk, everywhere.

You have it good, her father would say. You have everything that you need.

～

I told you, Leyla, that my parents sent me away from home to town when I was twelve. The village school only went to the seventh grade; whoever wanted to keep learning had to go to Tirbespî. We rented a room from an Aramaic family, Nûrî, my two cousins Xalil and Firat, and I. Every Thursday in the late afternoon we made our way back to the village. In the winter one time it was snowing so hard we lost our way. It grew dark. Everything was white. The border with the minefields was not far away. On the hill in the village our families made a huge fire so that we could find the way.

In the three summer months when school was out it was time to work. I worked in Lebanon on construction sites, tilled fields, repaired utility poles. In Aleppo and Damascus, I washed dishes in restaurants, waited tables in cafés, sold candy in soccer stadiums. I helped out with the harvest in the village. From the time I could walk, I had worked in the fields. I carried melons, harvested wheat, picked cotton.

Once, at Leyla's school, they had discussed child labor, and Leyla told her father about it. Her father just shrugged his shoulders. We didn't have child labor, he said. We just worked as children like everybody else.

~

Leyla believed that she was a disappointment for her father. I came to Germany so that my children could have a better life, he said. You have everything you need. We didn't have that many books in the whole village.

And she came home from school with a C again, barely good enough for the Gymnasium. If I had only had the opportunities that you have, her father said and shook his head. You are lazy, he said. Do you want to have to work later on like I did? Do you want to have to work like Rohat does at sixteen in construction?

~

We are from a region, her father said, that is now in Turkey. We were living there already at the time of the Ottoman Empire. At that time there weren't any borders yet. The country was divided into provinces. The region was called Bisêri, near the ancient city of Hasankeyf. We owned land there on the banks of the Tigris, fertile green land; owning it signified wealth. We had fields and raised cattle.

We lived there at a time when there were still hundreds of Yazidi villages, when the qewals from Lalish traveled through the land to tell stories they needed a whole year. Today there are only a few villages left there. You can count them on two hands.

When in the beginning of the twentieth century the Armenian massacres started, our situation also became difficult. If we went into town the people threw stones at us. They shouted, It stinks of Yazidis here! They chased us off.

My mother, your grandmother, her father said, was still a child. It must have been in the summertime—that's the way it is told in the family—when her father, his name was Cindî, was on his way to Sirte. There were three of them, along with Cindî two other men from the village. It was a hot day. They had been underway already for a few hours and were tired. The sun was at its highest point. It was noon, and they wanted to take a break. Each of them looked for a place in the shade.

The men approached Cindî first. They recognized him by his moustache and clothing. They demanded that he convert to Islam. He refused. I would rather sacrifice my head than convert to Islam, her grandmother's father shouted. That's what Cindî shouted before they killed him with their bayonets.

Cindî's two companions were able to flee. It was a stony landscape, mountainous. They ran and hid among the rocks.

One of them, his name was Xalef, lived with us in the village, her father said. He was already old when I was born. He came to visit us almost every evening. He was the one who told me all of that, not my mother.

⌒

Cindî left behind a woman and five children. The second youngest was Leyla's grandmother. Cindî's wife was called Rende. She was only in her early twenties and already a widow. Her family urged her to get married again after the time of mourning had passed so that she would be provided for. Her children were, after all, still little, four daughters and a puny, sickly son. The children were to be distributed among Cindî's sisters' families. But Rende refused. She did not want to give up her children. She didn't want to marry again. Cindî was a good man, she said; she didn't want anyone else but him. She stayed living in the house with her five children. There was a lot of talk. A woman without a husband in a house with five children, her father said.

Rende worked like a dog to feed her children. Her face was tanned from laboring in the fields. She worked from morning until late in the night, tilled the fields, took care of the animals. There was never enough money or food. She married off her oldest daughter, Seyro, to someone in the next village. As often as possible, Seyro would walk back to her old village to help with the harvest or the housework. Her mother-in-law complained: You spend more time with your family than with us. We too have to bring in the harvest, not just your mother.

Rende and her children had a cow, their most valuable animal. Once, the cow ate its fill on the neighbor's grainfield. Leyla's grandmother was supposed to have been watching the cow while Rende was in the field. The cow had run away from her. The furious neighbor took the sated cow and led it to the trough to give it water to drink. So much water that the cow's stomach became very heavy and it collapsed and died.

From that time on there was no more milk, her father said, no yogurt, no cheese. They didn't have money for a new cow.

~

A few years later, Rende's second daughter got married but stayed in the village. A year passed with its holidays, fast days, work days, and then another year. The qewals had come and gone again. In April it was New Year and Tawûsê Melek came as every year onto the Earth to bring fortune and blessings among the people. The people in the village carried flowers into their houses, dyed eggs, received new bracelets around their arms. The grain grew, the autumn followed the harvest, then came snow, and then the snow melted again.

~

Seventy-three ferman have been passed down in the history of the Yazidis. A Yazidi life is one that can end at any moment. One day they came, her father said, and surrounded the village. The villagers, among them Rende and her children, left everything behind. There was no time to pack. They fled in all directions.

Rende and our other relatives went to the Sinjar region, her father said. Part of the family stayed there, but my mother went to Syria with her husband after their wedding, to the region of the tribal leader Haco. And that, Leyla, is how we came to Tel Khatoun, her father said.

~

Leyla tried to find the other village where her grandmother had grown up on Google Maps, but she only knew its Kurdish name and not the Turkish one. They had started renaming the villages sometime during the Ottoman period, but it was carried out systematically in the newly founded Turkish Republic after the Dersim Massacre of 1938. Over four thousand Kurdish towns and villages were renamed, her father said. But that was not enough, her father said. They were no longer allowed to give their children Kurdish names. All who had remained in Turkey had to have Turkish names in their passports. Then, in 1945 the use of the Kurdish language in public was prohibited by law, as well as the şal û şapik, the Kurdish clothing. It is important for you to know that, her father said. You must not forget it. Leyla, you must never forget that you are Kurdish.

A few years later there was again a linguistic prohibition: this time it was the letter *x*, which exists in the Kurdish but not the Turkish alphabet, as well as Kurdish music, Kurdish literature, and Kurdish newspapers.

There were no more Kurds. One spoke of Mountain Turks. Later, since Mountain Turks sounded too derogatory, of East Turks. The Kurdish national colors, red, green, and yellow, were prohibited. In the eastern part of the country green was replaced by blue in traffic lights. All the rest, said her father staring at his suitcase with the documents in it, was accomplished by fear.

Leyla knew the stories. The checkpoints on the roads, the men from JITEM, the Turkish intelligence agency, their white Renault Toros, the corpses covered with acid thrown into the fields as a means of deterrence, the wells they threw the Kurds into.

~

They were on their way to work, to the doctor, or to a wedding, at night or during the day, and were never seen again. Her father told her about the Turkish prisons, showed her the scars on his arms. For a book, for a few cassettes with Turkish music.

When I am in Kurdistan, again and again I meet fathers who tell me that their sons were hanged because of my music, Şivan Perwer once said in an interview on Kurdish television.

~

Ask pigeons, ask friends and comrades. Ask the prison walls. They will tell you the truth, he sang. Leyla could only vaguely remember seeing Şivan playing for the first time. It must have been one of the Newroz celebrations that they went to every year in March. The celebrations mostly took place in gymnasiums or halls that were also rented for weddings. Everybody was dancing, and up front on the stage sat Şivan in şal û şapik, playing and singing. Leyla was still little; it was an important moment. Her father listened to Şivan's cassettes while driving and played the songs at home on the saz. Ask the colors of spring. Ask the blossoms of the tree. For many years I have been captive. Of violence and oppression, I have seen much.

Believe me, I long for you, sang Şivan. *Min bêriya te kiriye, Kurdistan.* Leyla
knew all of his songs by heart, she always had. Sometimes she had the feeling that the songs knew something about her life.

And they knew something about her father, how he sat in the evening
in front of the television eating his salted sunflower seeds, knew something about the satellite dish on the rooftop, something about the wrinkles
in her grandmother's face, something about Leyla, who at night sometimes
when she couldn't sleep went to the kitchen and opened the cupboard door,
behind which lay the plastic bag with the okra from the garden that her
grandmother had threaded with a needle onto yarn to hang in the pantry
to dry and that, whenever Leyla took the bag out of the kitchen cupboard,
held that very scent of the pantry that always caused a throbbing tightness
in her chest.

~

Şivan Perwer, who himself had spent thirty years in exile in Europe, had
sung the praises of the Kurdish towns and landscapes over and over. Duhok,
Zaxo, Amed, Erbil, Kermanshah, Mahabad, Slemanî, towns that Leyla had
never been to and only knew from the songs she heard on Kurdish TV,
snowcapped peaks, waterfalls, blooming valleys, green fields, rivers with
crystal-clear water.

Leyla only knew the part of Kurdistan that lay in Syria and people now
called Rojava, the West. When vacation was over and Leyla had to talk
about her summer at school, she said that it was beautiful there. And when
the teacher asked what was beautiful, Leyla didn't know what to say. The
dust, the flat land, the oil pumps behind the village, the mosquitoes. She
spoke in front of the class about how she sat in front of the house in the
evening and counted her mosquito bites. Then she stopped talking and
just smiled when it was the next student's turn.

Her father said, The spring, while we are still in Germany, is beautiful.
Now the trees are blooming in the village. Her father listed them, not stopping for a long time: The pomegranate trees are blooming, the olive trees
are blooming, the cherry trees are blooming, the fig trees are blooming.

~

Leyla had played the game often. What if? What if her father had not gone
to Germany? What if they had returned? What if she had been born in the
village? What sort of Kurdish would she speak today? Would she have
become like Zozan? Maybe they would have understood each other better.
Leyla imagined herself going to school in town, then to the university in

Aleppo, walking through the old city of Aleppo in her clattering sandals, shopping in the street shops, carrying the plastic bags with fruits and vegetables to her apartment.

~

Her father told her over and over about the history of Kurdistan. The foreign rulers, an invasion of paradise. The first division of Kurdistan in the seventeenth century, between the Ottoman Turks and the Safavids. The second division in 1916, referred to as Sykes-Picot, in the northeast the French and the southwest the British mandate. Again and again, the rebellions against the Ottomans, the British, the Turkish military.

You must never forget this story, her father said. That is your story, Leyla.

This story, in which they had no country, no place, was the reason they were in Germany. Not in the country with the singing shepherds, the women with tattooed faces, the mountain villages, the vast landscapes from Kurdish television. Not in the country where the watermelons were red and didn't taste like water, where the new year began in March at Newroz and the people jumped over the fire.

Her father had all the seasons in his head, all the names, all the political conditions. Leyla got them mixed up, forgot them, had to look them up. Later when she was at the university, instead of going to her lecture classes she sat in the Orient Studies library and read up on the topic. The uprising of the Yazidis against the Safavids from 1506 to 1510, the Battle of Dimdim from 1609 to 1610 that Feqiyê Teyran had written about a hundred years later, the rebellion led by Shaykh Mehmûd Berzincî against the British in 1919, the Koçgiri rebellion a year later, the Shaykh Said rebellion in 1925, the Ararat rebellion under the Xoybûn organization from 1927 to 1930, the Barzani revolts in the Iraq sector from 1967 to 1970, the armed struggles of the Kurdistan Workers' Party in Turkey since 1984.

There will never be an end to that, her father said, when others continue to rule over us. We need our own country, a Kurdish state, with schools where classes are taught in Kurdish. Kurdish universities, Kurdish street signs, Kurdish agencies, a Kurdish military. But the foreign rulers won't simply give up their power. There will have to be a fight for the Kurdish state, her father said. People have fought again and again, her father said.

He told Leyla about Leyla Zana, who had been elected as a representative in the Turkish parliament, had sworn her oath of office in Turkish and Kurdish and worn a green, red, and yellow ribbon in her hair. Leyla Zana spent many years in prison, her father said. He told Leyla about Leyla

Qasim, who fought against the Baath dictatorship in Iraq and was executed after just having turned twenty-two. Before her murder she is said to have shouted, Kill me, but you all should know that through my death thousands of Kurds will awaken from a deep sleep. Leyla's father told her about a third Leyla, whose picture hung above the television in the living room at Aunt Felek's in Celle, just as it did at Aunt Pero's in the village. Her father had actually wanted to marry this Leyla when he was a young man; she called herself Berxwedan, resistance, and had set out from Germany to the Kurdish mountains and been killed in battle there a year later. We named you after these three Leylas, her father said and poured himself and Leyla more tea.

~

A man from town came to our village, he said. The government had sent him. He wore a shirt, pleated pants, and leather shoes and disappeared with his briefcase into the house of the head of the village. A crowd gathered before the house, the children and our agitated fathers. The head of the village came out and called for someone who spoke Arabic. It was inconvenient with our village head because he spoke only Kurdish and could neither read nor write. If he was speaking to the authorities or had to notarize documents, he always needed someone who could translate or read aloud to him. But he was the only man in the village with Syrian citizenship, so only he could carry out this function.

When the man from town had driven away, the head of the village stepped out and said that there had been a land reform. He said we had all been dispossessed, all the Kurds in the region who owned land in the ten-kilometer strip along the Turkish border.

The village chief and our fathers all had serious expressions on their faces. It took us kids a while to understand what that meant: land reform. Our fields were being taken from us.

The government man had said that in exchange we would get fields in another place, hundreds of kilometers away, on the border with Iraq.

But what were we supposed to do there? We said we wouldn't allow that to be done to us, we would defend ourselves. Besides us, only one more village in the area decided to fight back.

With the tractors that we always borrowed for the harvest, we built a barricade on the road.

When two officers came from town again, we threw stones at them.

One day later, they returned. It was midmorning. We children stood on the village hill and saw them already in the distance, a column of olive-green military vehicles, whose wheels kicked up the dust of the road. So many vehicles, I couldn't believe what I was seeing.

When they reached the village, we had long since abandoned the hill. We ran, our parents running with us. Hundreds of soldiers climbed out of the vehicles. They carried rifles, cudgels, and billy clubs. They too were running, chasing the men. They beat them, hitting them with the billy clubs, breaking arms and legs.

From my hiding place in the chicken coop, I could see our yard. I had buried myself in the straw and could hardly stand it there. The soldiers came back out of the house with my father and Nûrî between them. They each had a soldier holding their hands behind their backs, and they were walking bent over. A soldier with a cudgel walked next to them hitting Nûrî relentlessly. Nûrî reared up, trying to defend himself. My father was completely calm. The fourth soldier walked behind them, his rifle ready to fire.

My mother, your grandmother, was standing in the doorway motionless.

The soldiers herded Nûrî and my father onto the street. My mother was still standing there as if frozen, as if she had forgotten to move.

I can't say how long I lay there and how long my mother stood in the doorway. At some point she went inside the house.

An hour had passed, or perhaps much longer, when our mothers finally called for us. We had climbed trees or hidden with the animals in the stall, in the garden, in dark corners, in the pantries behind the grain.

They took forty men to prison in Qamişlo, we found out.

Our neighbor is said to have shouted, We'll defend ourselves. We will not flee. We will fight back, so it was told. But fight back how? How to defend ourselves against soldiers with machine guns?

Our teacher was the only Arab in the village. He threw himself onto his bed, so it was told, after the soldiers had driven away again, and cried. Much later, I found out that he was a communist.

It was the first time, Leyla's father said, that Nûrî and my father were in prison. The second time was when the secret service found the books and the list of members of the Democratic Party of Kurdistan.

After a few weeks, when the Six Day War began, our men were released, on bail of course. Apparently, they wanted to avoid further rebellions.

When Nûrî and my father returned from Qamişlo, my mother butchered a chicken and made soup out of it. Normally, we only had meat on holidays.

We were allowed to keep a portion of our fields.

The land that they took from us was given to Arabs. The Arabs came from the Euphrates, from the province of Raqqa, where the government had built a dam and flooded their villages. The Arabs were given everything that we had never had: water pumps, electricity.

After that we just waited for them to return. We sat night after night together talking: One day they will come again, with trucks and guns to resettle us. We were certain they would come; all the years, we were certain.

⁓

During those summers in the village Leyla often thought about how they would come, that they would already be seen from a distance. The landscape was flat, no mountains to hide in like on the other side of the border. No friends besides the mountains, her father said sometimes, but the village didn't even have mountains. It lay there defenseless; the walls of the clay huts could at most protect from the sun and wind.

When Leyla lay on the loft in the yard and couldn't sleep, looking at the sky and listening into the night, there was only the thumping of the oil pumps and the bark of dogs. Yet the night offered no protection, for naturally they could still come at any moment. Once she was awakened in the morning by a deafening boom. There was an airplane flying over them low in the sky. She panicked, jumped up, climbed down from the loft, stood in the yard, and wanted to take cover but did not know where. The airplane kept flying. Her heart pounded in her throat.

That had only been one of those airplanes that sprayed insecticide over the fields, her uncle said, when Leyla asked about it at breakfast.

She couldn't help thinking of the airplane years later in the second, third, or fourth year of the war, when she sat in front of her laptop watching the airplanes drop their barrel bombs over Aleppo and Homs. She couldn't help think that death fell from heaven and that there had never been a reason to trust the president and his people, that they would stop at nothing, and heaven and earth belonged to them. Perhaps Leyla had at least sensed that back then.

And then there was again this peace in the village when they fed the chickens and the long uneventful afternoons when she lay dozing in the living room, drank tea, spit cherry pits at the chickens in the yard, her evenings going from bed to bed in the garden with her grandmother, soaking them with water from the hose.

~

Her father had wanted a garden in Germany. Because her father wanted a garden, they moved to a village, a new development of row houses that all looked alike. Leyla was eight or nine years old at the time.

People read the name of the village on signs along the road from Munich and immediately forgot it again, since it had no significance. It was not a particularly pretty village, not a village you would have taken an outing to. You only went there if you were visiting someone or lived there yourself.

The whole village had no significance. This was not changed by the fact that the Society for Local Heritage Preservation had village chronicles printed that you could buy at the bookstore in the nearest town, big, heavy hardcover books with color illustrations on the history of the volunteer fire department, the church renovation, and the brass band that existed for a few years twenty years ago.

The Society for Local Heritage Preservation consisted of villagers whose grandparents, great-grandparents, and great-great-grandparents had already lived in the village and who themselves had also never left it. Most were over fifty, but there were a few younger ones too. One of them was the vice president of the local chapter of the Christian Social Union, the other one the grandchild of the secretary of the society.

When they moved there, her mother bought a few volumes of the village chronicles and put them in the living room in the bookcase behind the television that was always on, next to her father's Kurdish books and magazines. Neither her father nor her mother ever leafed through the books. But Leyla did. However, she didn't know anyone that was mentioned in the chronicles.

~

In the village, a distinction was made between longtime residents and newcomers. Leyla and her parents were newcomers. That meant that their family names were not already engraved on the headstones in the village cemetery and that while they had an attic, unlike the attic of the longtime residents, theirs was empty. Their house was located at the edge of the village, between the highway and a small patch of forest. From the house you could see the road and count the cars. Leyla did that for hours as a child.

~

The house was painted white and had dark gable beams and shutters made of the same dark wood, with a tile roof over it like all the other houses in the village. Sometimes, Leyla lay staring at the ceiling trying to imagine the various construction materials. Above her, the ceiling was white, underneath it there was plaster, then pipe, tiles, cables, cement. Only after looking very closely could you see what distinguished this house from all the other ones: the large satellite dish on the roof. Her mother had painted it the muddy red color of the roofing tiles so that it did not stand out too much.

~

Her mother talked a lot to the people in the village, her father as little as possible. Still, he was never impolite. Fine, thank you, how are you. Well, very well! He smiled when greeting the neighbors; he always smiled. His smile outside the house was similar to her mother's fake Bavarian dialect, a kind of hat they put on when leaving the house, an umbrella, an object of utility for the outside world.

~

Her father's smile could make Leyla furious, his constantly exaggerated politeness. The way he said please and thank you and: only if it is no inconvenience for you. His strictness with Leyla, saying she should always be quiet so as not to disturb the neighbors. How she was not allowed to play outside after eight o'clock because the neighbor children were not allowed to do that either. That's what people do here! His strictness with Leyla when the teacher said that she had not been listening in class and had been gabbing with Bernadette and had not done her homework. He slammed his fist on the table and hissed. I didn't come to Germany for that!

Don't stand out. Be modest. Always be polite, he said again and again.

~

He was spit at in the subway in Munich, verbally abused as an asylum-seeker. She often remembered how that had happened when she was a very little girl. She also often remembered how he had once come home from work and said to her mother in the kitchen in a calm, monotone voice that a man at work had said to him: People like you should be sent to the gas chamber again. When he tried to report the man to his supervisor, all of his coworkers claimed not to have witnessed it.

Once Leyla came to the defense of a classmate and was reprimanded by her teachers for it. Her father praised her for doing it. He looked at her solemnly when saying that he had never spied on anyone and never betrayed anyone. Do you understand that? Leyla nodded in confusion and didn't know what her father was getting at. Once he and a friend of his had refused to march in a parade of the Baath Party that was obligatory for all students. They had been suspended for a whole week. Do you understand? Leyla nodded.

◠

Her father bought bees and a hive from a German beekeeper. He put it in a corner of the garden just like in Leyla's grandparents' garden, protected from the wind behind the little wooden shed. In July he harvested the honey. He dug a vegetable garden that took up almost the whole yard. That's what a yard is for, he said. He built a greenhouse and grew tomatoes, cucumbers, zucchini, eggplant, even *tirozî*.

The tirozî were small, had a bright green peel, and tasted somewhat sweet, quite different from the long, dark-green cucumbers from the German supermarkets. Her father had the seeds for them from her grandparents' garden. Her grandmother had given them to him to take back to Germany, sewing especially for them a little cloth pouch from the rags of her dresses.

Her father planted green onions, garlic, garden cress, mint, and parsley. He put grape vines around the terrace, pulling them up on wires. In the summer you could sit in the shade they made; in spring he picked the fresh young leaves to make aprax out of them. On the weekends he baked naan that was as thin as cloth.

If I had a clay oven the naan would be like it is at home.

On the lawn, he planted a mulberry tree. If the summers were long and warm, the tree brought forth a lot of dark fruit. If the summers were cold and rainy the fruit stayed light-colored and rotted at some point. From spring until well into autumn, her father went into the garden every day after work. He watered, seeded, pulled weeds, harvested, fixed the fence, painted the wooden shed, transplanted the beds.

◠

There is still enough room for chickens, he said at dinner after having worked the entire Sunday in the garden. Or for goats for cheese and milk. I could convert the wooden shed into a stall.

Her father, Leyla thought, was rebuilding her grandparents' garden in his garden. Her grandparents' garden was the standard for all other gardens.

Her grandparents' garden was four times as large as theirs. There was no need for a greenhouse, the sun shining all year round. Even if Leyla would have tried, she could not have listed everything that grew there. Everything that she ate during the summers at her grandparents' house came from the garden. The tomatoes, cucumbers, onions, garlic, and the tobacco that her grandfather smoked. When they returned to Germany, her grandmother packed suitcases for them full of jars of tomato paste, apricot jam, dried okra, pickled peppers, olives, salted sunflower seeds. A half a year later they were still eating from the fruits of the garden.

It is so cold here. The fig tree hardly bears fruit, her father said. There is almost no sun; my tomatoes are not ripening.

The soil in the garden back home is more fertile, he said. Imagine all that I could have planted if I had stayed there. Olives, pistachios, oranges, lemons, watermelons.

The German tomatoes, her father said, taste like water.

As if their German garden was just a cheap copy of paradise, Leyla thought, their tomatoes only a substitute for the real tomatoes, their bread just a substitute for the real bread. And their life, Leyla thought, just a substitute life for the real life they could have lived.

∼

At some point, her father started making a list: a hundred curses and a hundred blessings. The first time he told Leyla about it on the phone, she had already moved away to college. Every few days a new saying would come into his head. Leyla counted up her own sayings and only came up with five. One hundred ninety-five, she thought, I am missing 195 sayings in order to say what I actually could say.

∼

Your grandpa is not doing well, her mother said. They called a short while ago. She poured herself a glass of water and dissolved a packet of aspirin powder in it. Like most people, Leyla's mother had headaches when she was stressed. The packet of aspirin on the kitchen table was often the only visible indication that something was wrong.

Leyla put her schoolbag in the corner, sat down at the table, and laid her head on the cool tabletop.

Do you want to eat something? her mother asked. I can stick a pizza in the oven for you. I have to make arrangements now, she said.

Leyla shook her head.

∼

Papa has driven to Uncle Nûrî's in Celle, her mother said the following day. To organize the funeral.

Funeral? Leyla asked.

Aunt Felek called a short while ago. She said that Grandpa died yesterday. She heard it from the neighbor Um Aziz, but Uncle Memo doesn't have the heart to tell her himself.

Leyla went to her room and flopped onto the bed. First, she lay on her stomach, then turned over and stared at the white ceiling. The ceiling got blurry while she stared at it, but Leyla did not cry.

⌒

A few weeks later Leyla rode into town with her mother. This time they only bought what they absolutely needed, her mother almost running through the stores. She looked exhausted when they were standing in front of the ice cream shop. Would you like an ice cream? she asked, as if she were discharging a duty. Leyla shrugged her shoulders. Then no, her mother said, and they rode back home.

Everything will be okay, her mother said the evening before Leyla and her father's departure. Leyla was already lying in bed; her mother had come in again and was nervous. Here is the cell phone; I will put it in your bag. I saved a few numbers in it. I am sure everything will be fine, her mother said. Like I said, it's just in case of emergency. They won't do anything when you are with him. But if they take him away, Leyla, start crying and screaming. Make a scene, do you hear? Just cry for Papa. And then call this number immediately. Only in case of emergency, she said, just as I told you. She stroked Leyla's hair and turned off the light.

⌒

Everything went as usual. They surrendered their suitcases, had their carry-on luggage inspected, checked in. Leyla's father bought them each a cola. The flight attendants walked past them toward the airline. At some point they were also called to the gate. Leyla almost forgot about the cell phone that was in her bag.

Her father spoke little, but he never talked much when they were on their way to Syria. I'm tired, he said. Leyla looked for her book and began to read. The stewardesses from Syrian Airlines served the little cakes wrapped in plastic foil they were given every time. Leyla's father gave her his cake. When the stewardess announced they would be landing, Leyla got nervous. She thought about the cell phone in her bag. What's wrong? her father asked.

Nothing, said Leyla.

They landed in Aleppo. Leyla stood briefly on the gangway. The warm air hit her in the face. It was late in the afternoon. The trees on the other side of the runway were bathed in orange light.

They picked up their suitcases and took their places in the line for passport inspection.

As always, a man in uniform was sitting in the booth, with two stars on his epaulettes. He had combed hair that was so thin you could see his scalp. Why do they all look alike here? Leyla thought.

Her father pushed their passports and visa over to the man, who leafed through them, looking back and forth from his computer screen to the documents. He asked a few questions in Arabic. Her father answered in Arabic. Leyla tugged at his jacket. What is he saying? she asked. Not now, Leyla, her father said.

The man in the booth had a face that Leyla could not read. But so did her father. The man turned to his left and spoke with the man in the neighboring booth.

What are they talking about? Leyla asked. Her father paid no attention to her.

What's going on? Leyla asked. Her father shook his head.

Three men in uniform came through the tidy air-conditioned hall toward them. They said something, then nodded and signaled to her father to follow them; that much Leyla understood. Her father went with them without even turning around again to look at her.

Leyla didn't move. The man in the booth waved her aside so he could continue with the people in line behind her.

Leyla thought about the cell phone and what her mother had told her yesterday evening. She was supposed to cry, scream, call out for her father. But what should she do first, call the number or cry? Nobody understood her language and, of course, shouting something in Kurdish was the wrong thing to do.

Neither the man in the booth nor the travelers paid attention to her. They didn't even look at her. It seemed to her as if they were deliberately looking away.

~

Leyla sat down on the ground. The line was gradually getting shorter. Leyla thought about taking the cell phone out now. But what if the man in the booth took it away from her? What then? How much time had passed since they had taken her father away? Five minutes, ten minutes, more?

The man in the booth called across the hall for a luggage carrier. He didn't smile or look directly at Leyla a single time. He said something to the luggage carrier that Leyla did not understand and gave her a signal to follow the carrier.

While walking, Leyla asked the luggage carrier about her father. First in German, then in Kurdish. The carrier looked at her uncomprehendingly.

Leyla followed him past the passport inspection and through the exit. Behind the barrier stood Uncle Memo. When he saw that Leyla was alone, his gaze froze for a brief moment, his eyebrows bunched up, but then he forced his mouth to smile. Uncle Memo thrust a coin into the luggage carrier's hand, then took out his cell phone and dialed a number.

She is alone, he said. Yes, and yes. I don't know either. I'll call right back. He called a second number. I can't talk now. I'm at the airport.

Let's go, he said, more to himself than to her. Leyla nodded.

Outside the terminal, Uncle Memo waved for a taxi. And Papa? Leyla wanted to ask. But she could tell from her Uncle Memo's bunched up eyebrows that now was not the right time for tears or questions.

They stopped in front of Uncle Sleiman and Aunt Xezal's house. Leyla had actually been looking forward to this visit.

She liked visiting both of them. Their apartment in Aleppo had a balcony where at night you could see the lights of the big city down the hill. In the last few years, she had loved to stand there and count the taxis on the street below.

Finally, Leyla! Aunt Xezal kissed her. Nesrin has been driving us crazy for days. Is Leyla coming today? Is Leyla coming today?

You are hungry, said Aunt Xezal. There was chicken with french fries and salad, but Leyla didn't want anything to eat. Nesrin brought tea from the kitchen and sat down next to her. And Aunt Xezal said, Come Nesrin, we'll see to it that our Leyla doesn't starve. After the meal, Nesrin showed Leyla her sticker album and asked, Which ones do you want? Pick some out! I don't want any, Leyla said. Nesrin flung her little arms around Leyla's torso. But I want to give you some, she said.

⁓

Leyla went to bed early, pretending to sleep as Nesrin lay down next to her. She lay wide awake long after Nesrin had started to snore. She thought about the brief phone call with her mother in the airport terminal and the three men in uniform, trying not to think about her fear for her father. All of a sudden, she felt lonely. She swallowed so that she didn't start crying. Outside it had cooled off a little. The window was open and the noise from the street, the constant honking and revving of the engines, invaded the room.

Leyla heard Aunt Xezal walking down the hall, then her powerful voice. Her sons were coming home, the door clicked shut several times, somebody came and left again. Sometime much later there were once again voices in the hall. Her father was back. Leyla got up and went into the living room.

Your father is back. Everything is okay, Leyla, said Aunt Xezal. Go back to sleep.

In the living room, Uncle Sleiman, Uncle Memo, and her father were sitting on the sofa. Uncle Sleiman lit a cigarette. Aunt Xezal brought another tray of food. Leyla sat down with the men in spite of what she had said. The floor was cool, and she pointed her toes upward.

Aunt Xezal set down a glass of tea for her too.

What happened? asked Leyla.

Nothing happened, said Uncle Sleiman.

Her father just nodded. Leyla, go back to sleep, Uncle Sleiman said.

～

The next morning, Uncle Memo, her father, and she rode together in the car to the village. Everything was the way it always was. After about two hours they stopped in front of the restaurant where they always stopped, sat on the floor, and ate kebabs. Then they continued on. They listened to music. Her father and uncle were conversing in the front seat, and in the back Leyla could not understand what they were talking about. She looked out of the window. Dried up fields, flocks of sheep, towns, villages, houses made out of concrete, houses made out of clay, at some point the Euphrates, that giant, never-ending river, fishermen on the bridge advertising their catch. It was hot in the car, and Leyla was sweating. In a shop next to the road, her uncle bought a bag of corn chips that Leyla loved and always looked forward to because you couldn't get them in Germany. Leyla ate the whole bag, every single chip. She felt sick, her tongue was numb and furry.

In the afternoon, they arrived.

Leyla's grandmother kissed her. Aunt Havîn came hurrying out of the kitchen with a tray and served tea. The place in the yard where her grandfather had always sat smoking his cigarettes was empty.

The living room was full of men smoking and drinking tea. In the other living room, the women smoked and drank tea just as the men did but broke out into loud weeping again and again. Leyla went to the kitchen, but Aunt Havîn shooed her out again. We have so many guests, I can't have you here. During the course of the evening more and more people came, now also sitting out front in the yard. The women kissed Leyla and started to sob. Leyla ran into the garden, where it was so quiet. Only a few chickens had strayed here. They strutted around between the beds paying no attention to Leyla.

Leyla sat down on a rock. It was as if at any moment her grandfather might come out of the house, propped up on his cane, and slowly pass by the beds, feeling the way with his cane until he reached his tobacco plants. But he didn't come.

What would they do now with the tobacco plants? Uncle Memo now smoked Marlboros that he bought in town and always kept with him in his shirt pocket.

At some point her grandmother came, brought her a plate of bulgur and chicken, salad and bread. Leyla ate a few bites, then brought the food back into the kitchen. Aunt Havîn gave her a board, a knife, and a bowl full of tomatoes to slice. At some point her grandmother came into the kitchen and said, It's late, Leyla, go to sleep.

The next morning, they ascended the hill and kissed the rock under which her grandfather already lay buried.

They ate lunch. Guests came. Leyla found her father in front of the mirror behind the kitchen. He was combing his hair. I have to go to town, he said. I will be back again this evening.

Leyla wondered where he was going and why he wasn't taking her along, although she loved town, with its streets full of people, the shops, cafés, and bistros. And her father loved it there too. They always went to the music stores, buying new strings for his saz and, one time, a drum. Every time, he asked for extensive advice and conversed for a long time with the salesclerks. Sometimes they just drank tea and picked out music cassettes, afterward buying spices at Azra's shop. On their way back to the car, their hands full of plastic bags, her father was always in a good mood and whistled through his teeth.

∼

But this time was different. This outing to town was different. The car is here, said Uncle Memo. Her father nodded.

When he returned many hours later, the living room was still full of guests. He sat down with them and drank tea. He looked exhausted.

The others were talking about politics, then about farming. Her father nodded, laughed at times, but mostly remained silent. As soon as the guests went home, he went to bed.

Two days later, he drove to town again. I will be back in the evening, he said more to himself than to Leyla. Leyla nodded.

Two days later, he again said the same thing. I'll be back in the evening. Like a promise or an assurance, thought Leyla.

When he was in town, she was busy, helping in the kitchen, serving tea, cooking along with the others.

Since Aunt Pero and her sons had gone to Germany, they lacked her directions. Aunt Havîn was on edge, sometimes snapping at Zozan, sometimes Leyla: You both can see how much is going on! In turn, Zozan snapped at Leyla: You forgot the sugar! You forgot the spoon! Some days Evîn and Rengîn came from town, and only then did things calm down a bit. Her grandmother sat with the mourners the whole time.

Leyla carried the tray of tea glasses from the kitchen into the living room, poured the tea, put the empty glasses back on the tray, carried them back into the kitchen, and washed them.

The guests talked all day long, about everyone and everything all mixed up together, and at some point, Leyla happened to hear that her father was not on a visit to town but had been *summoned*. And that it had to do with Uncle Hussein's statements. Uncle Hussein really was one of them.

When Uncle Hussein came over, her father was in town. Leyla didn't know if that was a coincidence or if her uncle had waited until her father was gone. Indeed, he actually dared to come over! Leyla was almost astounded when from the kitchen window she saw him walking slowly across the yard with his cane; he had become an old man. Leyla did not go outside to greet him. Only later, when Zozan had sent her into the living room with a tea tray did she serve him some tea. He nodded, caught up in a discussion with the neighbors at the moment. And Leyla went back into the kitchen. Uncle Hussein had not gone with Aunt Pero and her sons to Germany. Leyla did not know why. But when a short time later she saw him going back across the yard to his mostly empty house with the broken roof, she almost felt a little sorry for him.

∼

Only when they were back in Germany did Leyla's father tell her that he had been summoned to an interrogation in the secret police headquarters. Beforehand, he had gone to Mirza, a nephew of Uncle Hussein but definitely not one of them. Mirza had a Syrian passport, a Syrian law degree, and an office. He had become a lawyer. Leyla only knew him in passing. Once, when she was still little, they had gone to visit him. Leyla had been allowed to sit at his much too large desk and eat dry cookies from a box; in the end, the whole desk was full of crumbs. Her father apologized, but Mirza only laughed.

Years later, perhaps in 2013, Mirza was arrested. His family fled. They sent documents from Germany to human rights organizations, wrote open letters to the Syrian regime deploring the poor health conditions of those who had been arrested, and begged for Mirza's release. But there were a lot of people like Mirza.

∼

Where does your name come from? Leyla's German teacher asked her. That's an Arabic name, right? Leyla shook her head and looked at the tabletop. She didn't tell her teacher about the three Leylas that she was named for.

Our Leyla can certainly tell us something about Islam, her social studies teacher said.

Do you fast on Ramadan? asked the mother of a school friend as she was driving Leyla home from a birthday party. Isn't it hard growing up between the cultures? Your father must be strict. Does your mother wear a headscarf?

If Leyla answered, No, we aren't Muslims, we are not Arabs, we don't pray at home or fast on Ramadan, but yes, my grandmother and my aunts wear headscarves, the result was even more questions. When Leyla said, We are Yazidis, then the others no longer had any idea what she was talking about.

Everything about Leyla always irritated everyone. The baker in the village, the dentist, the pharmacist, the teachers at school.

Leyla stood in front of the mirror contemplating the watery blue of her eyes and her dark, almost black hair. Leyla Hassan: the name betrayed her.

My father is from Kurdistan, said Leyla, and the people would answer: Kurdistan does not exist. My father is from Syria, Leyla would then say, and thinking of her father, she was ashamed.

∼

Are you more German or Kurdish? her school friend's mother asked her. German, Leyla said, and her friend's mother nodded in satisfaction.

Do you feel more German or Kurdish? Aunt Felek asked her. Kurdish, Leyla said, and Aunt Felek clapped her hands with joy.

～

You must never forget that you are a Kurd, her father said. I will also never forget that I am a Kurd. I was in prison because I was a Kurd.

Leyla Qasim, her father said, died, because she was a Kurd. Before they executed her in Baghdad, she said: I am happy to sacrifice my soul for a free Kurdistan.

You must never forget what was done to us because we are Kurds, Leyla, her father said to her.

～

Are you Turkish? Emre from her class asked, and Leyla shook her head.

Leyla's father showed her his scars from the Turkish prison.

They beat me with an electric cable. They extinguished cigarettes on my arm. He pulled back the sleeves of his sweater. Here, here, and here, he said pointing to the light spots that Leyla knew so well, where his skin was rippled, as if it had melted.

It got spread around in school that Leyla's father was Kurdish. At recess, Pina came to her and said: There are no Kurds. Kurds are criminals, said Emre. They are born in prison. Kurds don't wash, said Esra, whose desk was behind hers. Kurds stink. But you are different, since you wash. Leyla didn't say anything. At recess she played with Bernadette, Julia, and Theresa. When Emre wanted to borrow a ruler from her or Esra wanted to have some of her chocolate, she gave Emre the ruler and Esra the chocolate. But she didn't join them when they stood outside the classroom waiting for the teacher. Had she already started avoiding them before they knew her father was Kurdish, or was it only afterward?

Bernadette never talked about these things. Once, Leyla had tried to tell her about them, but Bernadette just looked at her helplessly and changed the topic. Julia didn't say anything about it either, nor Theresa. Did they even notice any of it?

～

Her father stayed out of things. Sometimes Leyla wondered if he even noticed that she was getting older. Or if he noticed anything at all that was going on around him, if he wanted to notice it. Yet lately, whenever Leyla left the house, he started asking: Where are you going and when are you coming back? If she answered, to Bernadette's, he looked at her as if he was not sure if she was telling the truth. That was new: not his asking, but his suspicion that she might be lying. But the times when he had changed the channel when two people were kissing on television were over.

Her father's biggest worry seemed to be that she might be neglecting her schoolwork. What are you doing all that time in the bathroom? he asked and grumpily turned off the television. Hours and hours! What a waste of time!

~

Leyla mixed masks of healing clay the way Bernadette had showed her. It disinfects your skin, Bernadette had said, it's good for acne. Leyla filed her nails, painted them a loud red, and put on layers of makeup. Powder, mascara, and eye shadow that she and Bernadette had stolen from the drugstore.

Leyla looked at herself in the mirror. At the small and narrow German nose for which Zozan envied her. Be glad that you don't look entirely Kurdish, Anna had said to Leyla. I'm envious, said Bernadette, Leyla always tans so quickly. Thomas, who sat next to her in art class, said: It's so disgusting that you Turkish girls always have such hairy arms.

When he said that, Leyla rode directly home from school. Luckily, nobody was there. She locked the bathroom door behind her, sat on the toilet seat, and took the mirror that her mother always used to pluck her eyebrows. On one side of the mirror, you saw yourself in your actual size, and on the other side magnified three times. Until then, Leyla had always avoided the magnifying side, but now she wanted the certainty of knowing what she had long since suspected: everywhere on her face there were hairs growing. On her chin there were even two longer black hairs like spider legs. And some above her lip too. She felt sick when she thought of the expression *lady beard*. Her cheekbones and temples. Her bushy eyebrows that almost grew together in the middle on the bridge of her nose. Tears started to run down her face, and she couldn't bear it. She took her mother's tweezers out of the drawer and set to work. In the end, her face was red and swollen. She would have to get used to it.

Leyla took off her skirt, T-shirt, bra, and panties. Curly black pubic hair. She sat down and leaned her head against the wall. The tiles were cold.

The longer she concerned herself with her body, the more places she found where the dark curly hair was growing. Growing rampant, she thought. On her back, on the underside of her upper thigh, under her belly button. She even had hair on and between her breasts. She found some on her toes, on her hands, not to mention her armpits and legs.

Leyla got dressed again and left the house. At the drugstore she bought depilatory cream, razors, shaving cream, and cold wax strips.

Once she was back home, she called Bernadette.

Bernadette said, I know, it's bad. I have a lot of hair too.

But your hair is blond, said Leyla. You can't see it.

What do you want to start with? asked Bernadette.

I don't know, Leyla said and spread out the packets she had bought on the bathroom floor.

Leyla got a rash from the depilatory cream and stubble from shaving. The cold wax strips only worked once, when the hairs were still long enough for it. She went to the Kurdish supermarket in the next town where her parents did their shopping for the week and bought sugar paste, brushing it over her arms and legs. She removed her facial hair with a thread the way she had seen Aunt Havîn do it. The hair was a problem, but you could solve it. This reassured Leyla. The brief pain when you pulled off the wax strip was like an exercise. You have to practice it, Leyla said. The reddened, burning skin. Leyla loved running her hands over her smooth arms and legs.

~

Later, when she looked at photos from the time period, she saw a made-up face with her two thin eyebrows, plucked down to two lines, the dark eye shadow and lashes clumped with black mascara. Her lips were pressed together so that they looked smaller. She looked like she was wearing a mask. Her father had made fun of her: Take a look inside a book instead of in the mirror! Her mother knocked on the bathroom door: I have to go, Leyla, hurry up! Leyla bit herself on the lip and opened the door, running without a word past her mother to her room and locking the door behind her. Do we have enough money to buy new doors all the time? her father shouted. Leyla bit her lip again. Just don't cry or the makeup will be ruined.

~

She seemed constantly to be bursting into tears, like an uncontrollable torrent. At school, when the teacher talked to her in a certain tone, at home when her father asked her why she had been on the phone with Bernadette for three hours although they saw each other every day at school. Bernadette was the only one who did not make her cry. Bernadette just stroked her head when Leyla laid it on Bernadette's knees, her tears dripping onto

Bernadette's jeans. Bernadette was always on Leyla's side, whenever there was a side to take. Even when Bernadette did not know what it was about and she actually had a different opinion, when she thought Leyla was exaggerating, she was still on Leyla's side.

Leyla often cried for no reason. On the school bus, on her bicycle. In the kitchen, when she got hungry at night and made a sandwich. Later, Leyla did not understand who she had been when she cried every day. But at some point, the crying too lay far behind her. Eventually, it stopped and seemed strange even to her, this constant crying.

～

Her father spoke a German that had no umlauts and in which the word order was mixed up: subject object verb, with all the articles mixed up or simply omitted. She only noticed that now that she wasn't living at home anymore. Her father spoke a German that people called broken German.

In this German he didn't speak much at one time, unless he started telling a story. And she only noticed this now that she was no longer at home. True, he was overly polite to the neighbors but was mostly monosyllabic: thanks, yes, no. I don't know. If he wanted Leyla to come home at eight o'clock he would say: You are home at eight. He never gave a reason for anything. If you asked him how he was doing he said: good. Or, I have a lot of work. He spoke that way with his coworkers, with Leyla, with her mother.

～

But in Kurdish, he would tell stories for hours on end, went back and forth conversing when friends and relatives came to visit or called; he joked, poked fun, antagonized, laughed until he cried, and cursed with relish. Even his posture changed the very second he switched languages: suddenly he would gesture with his hands. He also talked louder in Kurdish, like somebody talks who is somebody, Leyla thought. Silo Hassan, the son of Xalef and Hawa, father of Leyla, brother of Nûrî, Memo, and Pero. From old video recordings she knew that he had only spoken Kurdish with her when she was a toddler. At some point he had switched to German and stuck to it whenever he talked to her.

～

Leyla stood in front of the mirror in the bathroom. She had painted her fingernails red and put on lipstick of the same shade. She held a cigarette in her right hand but didn't light it. Her parents couldn't know that she smoked. Leyla only used cigarettes to practice. Cigarettes were valuable: she could only get them from the students in the upper grades and you had to pay them. Leyla was in charge of bargaining with them; she was good at that. Bernadette stole makeup and clothes for bartering, and from the drugstore, peppermint chewing gum and the perfume that she and Leyla sprayed themselves with in order to hide the cigarette smell from their parents. Nobody could steal as well as Bernadette. She looked harmless, just like the country girl that she actually was. She spoke the thickest dialect of anyone in school, had a soft face, blond curls, and a light, silvery gaze, all advantages when stealing.

She and Leyla always worked as a team, walking through the shops pretending they didn't know each other. Leyla distracted the salesclerks, asking about a T-shirt in her size and having the women search for something while Bernadette stuffed the items into her schoolbag. Later, they always had to patch the holes they made when they cut out the security tags from the clothes.

Shopping had become uninteresting for Leyla. The only place she never stole from was Veneto, the ice cream shop where she used to always go with her mother. Why shop when you could always just steal everything?

She and Bernadette wore stolen lipstick, stolen underwear, stolen makeup, stolen mascara, stolen nail polish, stolen key chains, stolen earrings, stolen gold-colored necklaces made out of plastic; Bernadette had grabbed two of them at once, calling them friendship necklaces.

I haven't seen that sweater before, her mother said at dinner. It's new, said Leyla. Another new sweater already? Didn't you just buy yourself one last week?

Nothing but shopping in her head, her father said. Nothing but makeup, fashion, clothes.

And when she got her math test back, he said: Already another C.

～

Her father insisted on signing all of Leyla's tests. No matter how exhausted he was from work, how tired he was sitting in front of his Kurdistan TV or KurdSat, reviewing the tests was reserved for him. To do so, he took his reading glasses out of their case, which he never used otherwise, since he had not read anything in ages. I am too tired from working for that, he always said. He had not taken his old Kurdish books off the shelf for years; they stayed in the bookcase next to the village chronicles behind the television. Sometimes he would walk over to them and pick them up like demonstration pieces in a museum, using them to illustrate something he happened to be talking about. And indeed, he could still find his way around in them amazingly well. If he was looking for a particular picture, a specific Kurdish demonstration in Cologne in 1985, he grabbed exactly the right magazine, turned three pages, and said: See, Leyla, take a look at that!

Already another C, he said and put his reading glasses on. He stood up with effort to get a pen. When I was in school, he said, I always received full points. He sat back down. On TV a shepherd was herding his flock of sheep through the mountains; a voice-over narrative was saying something about Kurdish cheese production.

I don't understand it, her father said. You have everything you need. If I'd had the opportunities you have! I didn't even have a desk. I walked around outside in the fields to study, her father said. Leyla stared at the screen; she had heard it all so often. The program was over; now they were showing an excerpt from some Şivan Perwer concert somewhere in Europe.

I took my book in hand and walked across the fields, her father repeated. That's the way I had to study. He shook his head angrily and signed the paper, a German essay that he surely did not even understand half of. The tears shot into Leyla's eyes. She bit her lip; under no circumstances did she want to cry in front of her father. He'd soon give her the essay back and return to the TV; the tears couldn't be held back any longer than that. Her father thrust the paper into her hand and stared past her; Leyla scurried to her room. She threw the paper in a corner, but throwing paper was pointless: it floated slowly to the floor with a tranquility that made Leyla furious. She would have liked to throw a plate or a glass. She wanted to see shards, wreckage. Leyla didn't know which she found worse, her father's disappointment with her—she was his disappointment, he had only come to Germany so that his children would have a better life—or his anger when he simply just ranted about everything. Leyla couldn't hold back her tears any longer, and she pressed her face into the pillow.

∼

Once—Leyla couldn't remember anymore why her father had been scolding her or why she had felt unfairly treated—she mimicked his accent. Stunned by such disrespect, her father's face instantly turned to stone. You don't talk that way to your parents, he finally said in German. First learn how to speak proper German, Leyla said. Her father slapped her in the face.

Afterward, Leyla sat in the bathroom with the door locked. An hour later you could still see a red handprint on her face.

Her mother knocked on the bathroom door, saying: Open up! Leyla did not react. She sat on the toilet seat staring at the tiles. Sometime much later she opened the door a crack and looked into the hall. No one was there. She crept to her room, quickly stuffed a few random things in her bag: clothes, makeup, her Walkman, and ran out of the house.

Leyla, it's not okay that your father hits you, Bernadette said. You can report him for that. But what actually happened?

They were sitting on Bernadette's bed while Bernadette painted her fingernails.

I hate him, Leyla said. Whenever I get a C he says, Why didn't you get a B? Whenever I get a B he says, Why didn't you get an A? He wants to monitor everything. Where are you going? What are you doing? Whose house are you going to? When are you coming back? That's too late. Why is your skirt so short? Do you want to go out of the house looking like that? I know, it's about boy-y-y-s—and Leyla stretched out the word, rolling her eyes.

Bernadette laughed. If there really were boy-y-y-y-s, she said. But there is only Boris, said Leyla. Bernadette laughed.

Boris is much worse than my father's worst nightmares, Leyla said. They went to Boris's house to smoke pot. For some reason or other, Boris let them smoke with him, and unlike the other students in the upper grades, he didn't want anything in return. They sat around with him on his sofa, listened to music, and talked, while Boris played some computer game or other, listened to them, and sometimes handed them the joint. Bernadette always laughed loudly and seemed wound up. She blamed the weed, but Leyla knew that something else was the reason for it.

Once they had left Boris's apartment, Bernadette usually said how much fun it had been, how funny Boris was. Shortly thereafter her mood would turn sour and she quit talking. Leyla was surprised, since Boris was anything but funny. He always just sat stoned at his computer, playing his games, and even when they talked, he didn't say much and it was Bernadette who made everybody laugh.

~

Leyla and Bernadette took vodka from her house and went to the elementary school, climbing over the fence to sit behind the gym.

Porno vodka, said Bernadette and took Ahoj fizzy powder out of her bag.

She ripped open the packet of fizzy powder, poured the contents into her mouth, and washed it down with vodka.

Now you, said Bernadette. Which flavor?

Raspberry, said Leyla.

The fizzy powder tasted sour, and the vodka burned. It foamed up in Leyla's mouth, and she swallowed.

Bernadette took out the second package of fizzy powder.

Do we also have water? Leyla asked.

Only cola, said Bernadette.

The stone slabs beneath them were still warm from the sun, but the evening was full of mosquitoes. The mosquitoes landed on their naked arms and legs. Leyla swatted at them with her hand.

Smoke, then they'll go away, said Bernadette, lighting a cigarette and handing Leyla the lighter.

They sat shoulder to shoulder, puffing away. The smoke actually did drive off the mosquitoes. It was Bernadette's idea. She said: You have to practice. When you have a boyfriend, you'll know how it works. Leyla just nodded.

Bernadette and Leyla squatted behind the bushes and peed in the grass. When they stood up, she staggered and grabbed for Bernadette's shoulder.

Here behind the gym is the perfect spot, Leyla said. Bernadette nodded. There is nobody here. It's not strange. No, said Bernadette, what should be strange about it?

Leyla drank cola, while Bernadette lit up another cigarette. Vodka? Leyla asked. Bernadette shook her head. And then Bernadette kissed Leyla on the mouth. Or Leyla Bernadette.

Bernadette's mouth tasted like smoke, vodka, cola, and the lip gloss that she had stolen for them both. Leyla grabbed Bernadette's hair like she had seen in the movies. While she was grabbing Bernadette's hair, she thought about how it was always the boy who reached for the girl's hair and about how often she had touched Bernadette's curls when they did each other's hair or sat next to each other in the classroom and Leyla looked out of the window, bored, playing around with Bernadette's curls.

At some point, Bernadette freed herself from Leyla and reached for the bottle of cola to take a gulp. Do you want some? she asked. Leyla shook her head. Vodka? Leyla nodded.

～

They staggered back to Bernadette's house. The streets were empty. They held hands. When Leyla rode her bike home the next morning and unlocked the door, she had a headache and was ashamed.

～

At home, her father was once again, or still, in front of the television watching the news. On TV students were planting trees in the Kurdish mountains. Since Saddam was gone and the autonomy of the region was written into the Iraqi constitution, things were looking up. Leyla had never seen her father so happy as on the day the Americans pulled Saddam out of his hole in the ground. Out of that cellar hole of a farm near Tikrit, and Saddam was an old man who, Leyla thought, looked like a homeless person from the train station, with his long unkempt, almost matted hair. Her grandmother had been more excited on the telephone than Leyla had ever seen her before. They pulled him out of his hole like a rat, she said, like a dirty rat. I am so happy, she said. Her father went into the kitchen and opened the bottle of raki that her grandmother had distilled and given to him to take back after his last visit. Today, the three of us are celebrating, he said.

After work, for the entire week after Saddam had been apprehended, her father sat in the living room watching the trial, which was broadcast in its entirety on Kurdish television, Saddam being transported daily in a helicopter from his prison cell to the courtroom in the green zone, and then back again. Saddam saying he did not recognize the court. The president of Iraq saying that Saddam deserved not to be executed just once but twenty times a day. The reading of the charges, war crimes, crimes against humanity. His death by hanging in December 2006. Her father did not shut off the television now either. Finally, he said. Her mother said, Finally! Leyla nodded.

～

Leyla lay on her bed. She had a headache. She told herself that it had been nothing. Bernadette was just her best friend. On the way back they hadn't talked about anything at all; there wasn't anything to talk about. Leyla had told her parents the previous evening she was going to sleep over at Bernadette's. Bernadette's parents didn't ask questions when she came home late; Bernadette could even have said they were going to Boris's. Whereas Leyla would never have dared to even mention Boris's name in front of her father.

～

In social studies class they talked about dictatorships, and Leyla raised her hand to give Syria as an example. The teacher was kind but always wanted to be precise. While it was true that Syria had authoritarian features, it was not a dictatorship according to the definition, she said. People disappear, Leyla said, and the president's picture is hanging everywhere. The teacher

thanked Leyla and declared the discussion to be over, but Leyla kept talking anyhow. That's enough now, the teacher said, and then Leyla started
screaming and said the teacher had no clue about anything. The teacher
smiled uncertainly, took a few steps to the left and the right, then pounded
her fist down with all her might on the table, demanding what the meaning
of this was. Leyla should stop. Leyla shouted that the teacher was Assad's
stupid whore.

You completely flipped out, said Bernadette later. What happened?

When the letter arrived at their house, Leyla's mother became agitated.
That was unnecessary, she said. The teacher, Leyla repeated, said that Syria
is not a dictatorship. I don't care, said her mother, looking furious. You
don't call your teacher a stupid whore. Her father signed the letter without
hesitation. That woman has no idea, he said. Her mother left the room,
exactly as she always did, but she was furious.

～

One Saturday morning when it was still dark, Leyla's mother woke her up.
Her father was already sitting in the kitchen drinking tea. We are driving
to Cologne.

Why? Leyla asked only after they were already sitting in the car.

As it happened, her father had been sitting in front of the television
again every evening, the way he had done the year before when George W.
Bush had given Saddam Hussein an ultimatum to leave his country within
forty-eight hours or Iraq would be attacked, then bombed Baghdad ninety
minutes later. Leyla could remember the green nighttime recordings, satellite photographs of Baghdad, missile bombardment, tanks and dead people,
the monotonous voices of the newscasters. Saddam had been caught three
months before that; now it was spring and it was about the unrest in Syria.

～

I don't feel like it, said Leyla. Neither her father nor her mother even
reacted. Leyla stared out the car window.

They drove past green patches of forest and fields. It was a gray day,
having just stopped raining when they arrived. The demonstration started
at the main train station. It was Leyla's first time in Cologne.

Look, her mother said, the Cologne Cathedral.

Leyla thought it had an ugly color, like the autobahn.

Many people had come. The whole square was full. The people shouted
bijî Kurdistan and held up photos of people who had been killed in the
unrest. The photographs looked as if they had printed them themselves at

home and then glued them on cardboard boxes. In many of the pictures, the dead lay in pools of blood, all blurry and pixelated. The blood looked a little like a red mosaic.

They all walked together. Leyla, her mother and father always next to each other. Her father constantly encountered people he knew. The acquaintances nodded at Leyla and her mother, then conversed with her father without paying any further attention to them. All of them looked worried. Leyla felt like an appendage. Her mother did not seem to have a problem with it. The longer they walked, the angrier Leyla became, but at what? The demonstration was endless. At some point they were standing on a square. In the middle, a stage was set up, with huge speakers. The square filled up. Everyone was standing around waiting.

Her father kept finding more acquaintances to talk to. The acquaintances nodded to Leyla, said something like, My, how you've grown! The last time I saw you, you were still a small child. Then they continued talking to her father.

Leyla took a few steps, then pushed her way alone to the edge of the crowd. A speech was given, then another one. After that a singer came on stage, and everybody pushed toward the front. It was Şivan, Şivan Perwer.

Şivan started singing. *Min bêriya te kiriye.* Leyla knew every song. Ask the colors of spring. Ask the blossoms of the tree. For many years I have been captive. Of violence and oppression, I have seen much. Believe me, I long for you. A fat woman stood next to Leyla crying into the corner of her headscarf. The woman cried so loud and forcefully that her body shook from the sobs. Leyla looked away. She stepped even farther back, imagining she had only come by chance to be among these people, that she was a passerby who had just come out of one of the clothing stores on the square and now observed the gathering with interest. It all had nothing to do with her.

Şivan sang with a powerful voice into the crowd. *Kîne em.* Who are we? Suddenly, Leyla's eyes filled with tears. She bit her lip, trying to keep her facial expression under control and not burst into tears. Şivan's voice boomed through the loudspeakers. Leyla turned away, pushing through the crowd to a booth even farther back and bought herself a cola.

~

Years later, Leyla read the headlines about the time of the demonstrations, *The Riots in Qamişlo in 2004.* She read about them when the country had long since been plagued by new riots and these had long since no longer been called riots but war and civil war. Leyla sat on her bed with her laptop on her knees, in the city where she went to college, reading and reading and trying to understand what she had not been able to understand for a long time. Riots were superimposed on riots; the civil war had buried the war; ruins lay on top of ruins. Leyla read *Qamişlo 2004* and could only remember the dead bodies in pools of blood in the pictures held up by the demonstrators and that the dead had something to do with a soccer stadium.

At that time, the riots began on March 12, she read, during a soccer game. The fans of the visiting team were able to get into the stadium without the normal security measures and sit directly next to the fans of the home team. Before the game, they started to throw stones and bottles at them. One team was considered to be pro-government, the other Kurdish. Already during the game there were reports over the radio about violence between the fans; more and more people came to the soccer stadium. Shortly thereafter, the Syrian security forces fired their first shots. The fans of the pro-government team shouted out anti-Kurdish slogans, insulting Kurdish politicians. The police did not drive them out of the stadium, instead evicting the other team. Although the people amassed outside the stadium had no guns, the Syrian security forces shot into the crowd with live ammunition. Nine people died.

The next day, the dead were to be buried. The Kurdish parties agreed to hold a funeral procession with the participation of several thousand people. The procession proceeded peacefully at first. When some of the participants, however, started calling out slogans in support of the American President Bush and threw stones at an Assad statue, the security forces first shot into the air and then, at the end of the demonstration, at armed civilians in the crowd.

～

The summer after the riots in Qamişlo was the first summer that Leyla did not travel to the village. Too dangerous, her mother said and shook her head decisively. It's out of the question. The riots can break out again at any moment. Her father said: We don't know how things will develop. The situation is unpredictable.

Grandma, Zozan, Aunt Havîn, Rengîn: Leyla listed all the names for her parents. Evîn, Douran, Uncle Memo, Aunt Xezal, Nesrin. As if it weren't dangerous for all of them too!

Why should they have to live with a danger they wanted to protect Leyla from? That makes no sense, said Leyla back then. Why did she deserve that? How was that just?

I want to go to the village, she said. I don't care if it's dangerous. Nonsense, her mother said and stood up, as she always did when, for her, the discussion was over.

You're crazy, her father said. He fiddled with the remote control in his hand. Leyla went to her room and just stood there staring at her bookcase with all the brightly colored book covers. That wasn't fair, she said to herself. What was supposed to be fair about that?

~

I passed my high school exams with 96 out of 100 points, her father said. I decided to become a pharmacist and applied to pharmaceutical school in Damascus. But they told me that as an ajnabi without Syrian citizenship I would not be allowed to study. There was no waiver for stateless people. They didn't even look at my application. Still, I tried to enroll, first in English literature, then Islamic theology, although I really did not want to study Islamic theology. But each time they rejected my application.

I left Damascus and took the bus back home to help with the harvest. I put my bell-bottoms in the wardrobe. I had bought them in Damascus when I could still imagine going to the university, sitting in the lecture halls and, afterward, in cafés.

I was at home for a few weeks. It was 1980. I got up at the crack of dawn to help my father in the field and my mother with the cooking. In the evening I walked across the fields, strolling aimlessly through the landscape. I walked along the gravel path to the river, took off my shoes, walked barefoot through the riverbed and along the large rocks, then back to the fields. Only just before the next village did I turn around every time, not feeling like running into any acquaintances who would ask me how I was. I stayed awake until late into the night, sat under the gas lamp smoking, staring at the poems of Cigerxwîn without reading, not knowing where I was going. I had handed down my schoolbooks to Memo, since I didn't need them anymore. Who knew, maybe he would be luckier than I was? Everything that I had learned seemed meaningless to me. I was almost ashamed of my plans to study English literature. I wanted to become someone, simply just someone, a pharmacist, a teacher, a doctor. I had studied for that and now regretted it. I didn't want to go to town anymore, didn't want to see the Arab students who had not been stripped of their citizenship, who unlike us were allowed to study even with bad grades. I also didn't want to go to Damascus anymore to work during summer vacation, selling coffee and juice to these very students on their way to university.

So, I stayed in the village. I worked hard, not wanting to be a burden to my parents. I helped out with the harvest, fed the chickens, watered the plants, hauled watermelons, harvested garlic. I took a spade and went with it into the garden. What are you going to do? my father asked. Dig a well, I said. I wanted to do something meaningful. So that mother and Pero did not have to keep hauling water, I said. That won't work, my father said. Still, I went to the garden. I dug for half a day, sweating. At some point I stood up to my waist in the earth, and finally to my chest. And then I hit rock: firm, thick rock. See, my father said, didn't I tell you so?

I had been back home in the village for a while already when the men in the pleated pants and shirts came driving up. They wore patent-leather shoes and bulky watches that a few hours later they would polish with their spit, cleaning off the dust from the village before they got back into their cars. We need someone who can speak Arabic well, they are reported to have said, and as a result, I was called over. I translated, and as soon as I was finished translating, I got up to leave. One of them asked me what the rush was. Another wanted to know where I was headed. To the field, I said. The men laughed. In such a hurry to the field! The grain won't run away from you, they said. They asked what I was doing here in the village. Just working in the fields, I answered. Huh, they said. Such an educated young man like you who speaks such a pure standard Arabic. What does he want in the fields? They asked why I wasn't in town at university like the other men my age. I became furious. Naturally, they knew all too well why I didn't go to the university but, instead, to the fields.

I bit my lip and said: Because my application was rejected.

Huh, they said, but your grades must not have been bad.

As an ajnabi, I am prohibited from attending a university, I said, trying to speak in a calm voice. Oh, what a waste, the men cried and shook their heads, laughing. Such a smart young man as you!

Whenever the men came to the village from then on, they asked about me every time. If one of the sons from a different family was brought to them, they sent him back and said to call me from the field. They had time; they could wait. I had to drop my work and go to them. They patted me on the shoulder and laughed. There he is, our translator.

They invited me to their office in town; they really did call it an office. Now don't look so alarmed! We just want to drink a tea with you and chat a bit. They didn't give me the address, for everybody knew, of course, where this office was. And I knew that I could not refuse their invitation without making trouble for myself. Nobody would have dared not to go when they were asked.

I took the bus to the city. I wore my pants with the best pleats and my light-blue shirt, which I had bought in Damascus and had worn there for the last time. I was clean shaven and had tried to tame my curls. It was a warm day. I kept wiping my sweaty hands on the upholstery in the bus.

I told the gatekeeper I had been summoned. I showed him my papers and gave him my name. The gatekeeper smiled at me. He nodded. You are expected, he said. Stay here for a moment; they will come get you.

One of the men I knew from the village came out the door, walked across the yard toward me, and greeted me like an old friend whom he had not seen for a long time.

So, did you have a good trip? He patted me on the shoulder.

I followed him up the stairs to the third floor, then down the hall to the second door on the right. He led me into a room where two men were sitting at a desk under the president's picture. He pointed toward a chair and then left.

⌒

Nice that you've found your way here. Tea, cookies?

I declined.

Now, come, drink some tea, we haven't poisoned it, said the man, and he laughed out loud as if he had made a joke. The other remained silent and just looked at me.

We can give you work, the first one said. What you are doing there in the village is nothing for a man with your abilities and your grades. You don't want to have to toil your whole life long in the fields.

He spoke of cooperation. I could, of course, decline their offer, he said, but I surely wouldn't. I knew that it was a threat; he didn't need to say anything else. He would just want to know what this or that man in the village was doing. *Provide information*, he added.

You would be of great help to us, he said. The other man next to him just smiled. Don't stand in your own way.

I said: No thank you, no. I won't do that. I am not cut out for that work; it's not for me. I can't do that, I said.

⌒

A short time after that, they came to the village again. This time they wanted to have a different translator. But they passed on a message to me that I was expected again the following Thursday in their office.

The evening of their visit to the village, I sat under the gas lamp. I hadn't even opened the book of Cigerxwîn's poetry. I smoked and watched the insects flying over and over into the light.

The next morning, I made a decision.

I am leaving, I said to my father. He didn't seem to believe me. Tomorrow, I will be gone, I said.

$\sim$

I went to our neighbor Um Aziz. I've come to say goodbye, I said. The daughter brought tea.

Where was I going? Um Aziz asked.

Damascus, I said.

The next day, when I got up my mother brought me tea and scrambled eggs, bread, yogurt, and tomatoes from our garden. She sat next to me until I finished eating.

Where is Father? I asked.

He went to the mill, she said. That surprised me, since he had been to the mill the week before already and we had enough flour.

It was only many years later—you had long since been born, Leyla—that she told me he had returned shortly after my departure, asking for me.

Where is he? he asked.

He has left already, answered my mother.

Then my father went to Hesso, who owned a car, and said, Drive me to Qamişlo. Right now! I want to say goodbye to my son. I can handle it.

He was in Qamişlo for two days trying to find me. He went from café to café asking after me. But he didn't find me. Qamişlo is a big city.

While I was packing my things, I didn't think about the word refuge. I only became familiar with it in Germany. *Political refugee, asylum.*

I just said to myself, I'm leaving. I cannot stay, so I'll go.

I am leaving, different than the way my mother had left when the Muslims surrounded her village and she was still a child. Those were Kurds, Sunnis. My mother did not walk. My mother ran.

And I am not leaving the way my father left as a young man when the Turks wanted to draft him into the military. My father went to the Sinjar region, hiding for months in the mountains.

Nûrî had already left before me. He had already been in Germany for two years and sent the family money from time to time.

$\sim$

Leaving, I thought at that time, her father said to Leyla, looking at her across the kitchen table, is first of all a series of steps, nothing more. Merely steps.

I had no passport when I left, only my papers indicating my name, year of birth, place of birth, and my identity as ajnabi, foreigner. With those I would not get far. But I knew a Kurd from Nusaybin, the next city beyond Qamişlo, on the other side of the border. He was a Yazidi like us. His name was Sharo. He had visited us a few months before; even then I had already told him that I would soon need help.

I might be considering leaving, I said at that time. He replied that he could arrange everything for me. I should inform him when I was ready.

I took the bus to Qamişlo. I went to Mustafa, a friend of Sharo who had a Syrian passport and traded in Nusaybin. He suggested that we should cross the border together at the official crossing time. We tried it.

First, we had to pass through the Syrian checkpoint. Since I had no ID, they didn't want to let me pass. I told the customs officer that I just wanted to help Mustafa carry his wares across the border and I would come right back. The customs officer let me through.

I arrived at the Turkish side. Two border guards were standing there simply waving people through. There was a steady flow of people on the move toward Turkey. I blended into the crowd, with Mustafa behind me carrying my bag. In this way, we slowly moved forward until we came to the next Turkish checkpoint. Everyone was requested in a loud voice to show their passports. Mustafa hissed at me to just walk past the police officer. I shuffled ahead with the crowd, staring forward. It succeeded. Thus, we came to the third checkpoint.

IDs, said the Turkish police officer there. You couldn't get past him so easily. The officer next to him searched everyone's bags. I tried again just to walk by, but a third officer stood in front of me demanding my passport.

I didn't know what to say.

He had an argument with his father, Mustafa said, and ran across the fields and the border to Syria. He didn't have his passport with him, Mustafa said. I just picked him up to bring him home again.

Naturally, the police officer did not believe him.

How much should we pay you? Mustafa asked.

Two thousand lira, said the officer.

Two thousand lira is much too much, said Mustafa.

I didn't care; I just wanted to be on the other side. But Mustafa shook his head, determined. We turned around and blended in again with the crowd on the border strip.

We waited for the changing of the guard and got back in line.

How much should we pay? Mustafa asked again.

Twenty-five hundred lira, the officer said. This time I paid.

In Nusaybin, at first, I just sat down in the shadow of the dusty border station and looked back. Syria lay behind me. The invisible border that I had gazed at so often, the border my father and the other villagers had always crossed so often at night, in whose minefields so many people had died, the border that was first drawn up at the end of World War I, determined in the treaties of Sèvres and Lausanne, and was completely artificial—now I too had crossed it.

I was supposed to go to the village of Qûlika, some twenty kilometers from Nusaybin. Sharo, who was going to help me get to Germany, lived there. Mustafa asked about the bus connection to Qûlika, and when he found the right minibus for me he explained my situation to the driver. It was the summer of 1980, shortly before the Turkish generals' coup. The Turkish military was already preparing for it; there were checkpoints on every corner. But I didn't have any identification documents.

At that time, the bus drivers had assistants who loaded the luggage and took the tickets. The assistant on my bus was friendly. He said he had just been called up for military service, where he had had to turn in his ID. As a substitute, he received a letter that confirmed his identity. He gave me this letter. He said I should show the letter at the checkpoints, for he himself was no longer asked for his ID since he rode this bus several times a day and the soldiers had long since gotten to know him.

I said goodbye to Mustafa and sat down in the bus as a man who, according to his papers, was called Cemil Aslan and was born in 1962 in Nusaybin, a Kurd with a Turkish name and Turkish citizenship who in a few days would start his military service in Diyarbakir. The bus started to move. And we weren't underway long when we came to the first checkpoint. Everybody showed their IDs, and I produced my piece of paper. Luckily, the soldiers did not ask me anything, otherwise it would have immediately been discovered that I wasn't Cemil Aslan as indicated on the paper. For, at that time, I spoke not a single word of Turkish, Leyla. We continued, following the border for a while before finally turning away from it. The landscape was hilly and bleached out from the long summer months.

Like that, I was able to make it to Qûlika. I asked around about Sharo until I found his house. He came running from the field when he heard I was there. Completely out of breath, he slapped me on the shoulder and kissed my cheeks. Finally, he shouted and told the same joke he had the first time we met, that I was so short he simply had to help me, and in fact he must have been two heads taller than I was. His sister brought tea, and his mother cooked for us.

~

The next day, Sharo and I made the trip back to Nusaybin. This time I had no letter to produce, but I knew where the checkpoint was. Shortly before it, Sharo and I got off the bus. Along the road there was a large garden store. We walked through all the facilities, past the greenhouses, entering town that way without having to go through the checkpoint.

In Nusaybin, Sharo brought me to Majed, a Garachi with a thick moustache who was supposed to help me out. I went with Majed to the photographer. We had two passport photos made of me and then went to the local residents' registration office.

I was able to figure out that once we arrived at that office, Majed had said in Turkish: I am here to register my son. The agent paid no attention to him but instead looked at me and asked if I was from Qamişlo or Aleppo. He asked from the start in Arabic, but I did not answer, pretending that I didn't understand him. Majed said: I swear by the head of your father, he is my son. The agent didn't believe him. And why should he have believed him: my skin was much lighter than Majed's, and besides, Majed was shorter than I was. He was fat, while I was tall and thin. The agent demanded my ID. He doesn't have it, said Majed.

Why doesn't he have an ID? the agent said, still in Arabic; he could see right through us. The military is everywhere; how could he even have gotten here without an ID? Then he wanted to know where I had hidden. Majed said I was a shepherd and had not needed an ID in the mountains. The agent didn't seem to believe that either. Only when we laid money on the table did he nod and register me as the ninth child of Majed. Firat, said Majed, like the river; his name is Firat Ekinci. I nodded. We left.

Majed took me to his family. His parents were already well over ninety. I kissed their hands. They asked where I was from. From a village in Hasakah, I said. Which family? they asked. Originally from this side of the border, I said, from Bisêri near Batman. When I mentioned the names of my grandparents and great-grandparents they smiled, having known them from way back.

I stayed with them for two days, during which they butchered a chicken for me and bought sweets at the confectioner's. For two days, I ate, drank tea, sat with Majed's parents, and played soccer with his youngest son. Then Majed went with me to Mardin, where I was to get a Turkish passport with the certificate from the local residents' registry office. At the agency they told me I would get my passport, but first the police wanted to check my identity. They gave me a letter and said I should come back in nine days.

I took the bus to Qûlika to Sharo and his family, and the nine days passed. Then I set out again for Mardin, again in a minibus, this time to the police. Sharo accompanied me. It was July 9, 1980, two months before the military coup. The police station was completely packed, we had no idea why. There was a flurry of activity, men in uniform and civilian clothes everywhere, men from here and men from elsewhere. Sharo and I didn't know what to do. We went to a café near the police station and met one of Sharo's friends there and had coffee with him. We didn't stay long, paying quickly and returning to the bus station.

⁓

Later I asked myself what would have happened if the police department had not been packed that day and they had simply handed me the passport. Or, if having no luck at the police station we had gone straight to the bus station without first meeting Sharo's friend at the café who gave him Gulistan and Şivan Perwer cassettes. Or if the friend had forgotten the cassettes at home that day, the cassettes with the music that was illegal in Turkey. What would have happened? I wonder that often, Leyla.

We were sitting in the minibus looking out the window when suddenly it was too late to do anything. Outside of Mardin, a new checkpoint blocked our way. Military vehicles, sandbags stacked up, soldiers with shouldered rifles. We all had to get off the bus. We stood in a row in front of the minibus, our hands held up to the roof of the bus while the soldiers searched us.

We were supposed to show our IDs. But I didn't have a damned ID. Instead, I showed them the certificate I had received from the registry office and the letter that they had given me at the police station in Mardin. A soldier asked me something that I didn't understand. Sharo translated for me. The soldier yelled at Sharo to shut up and asked me his question again. I looked at him. He was as tall as I was, but his face still looked so young. How old was he, sixteen, seventeen? Doesn't he speak Turkish? the soldier asked, and I vaguely understood. Sharo shook his head: no.

Come with me, the soldier said.

Sharo and I were loaded onto a military vehicle. They tied our hands behind our backs and pulled sacks over our heads. I couldn't see anything. My breath was hot under the coarse material, and sweat was running down my forehead. Sharo, I said. The vehicle started moving.

At some point we arrived somewhere. A soldier shouted something that I didn't understand. Sharo translated: Get out! Somebody ripped the sacks off our heads. We were standing in an interior courtyard. The harsh light was blinding. In the courtyard, Sharo translated and nodded his head toward a door. There were soldiers in front of us and behind us.

Hardly had we entered the room when we were separated. Two soldiers grabbed Sharo by the arm and shoved him to the next door. Don't tell them anything, he called to me in Kurdish, upon which a soldier started pummeling him.

No, I called, I won't tell them anything. But Sharo was gone already. I had no time even to look around. An officer came into the room and directed a soldier to put a chair in the middle of the room for me. He ordered me to sit in it. They blindfolded me again. My arms were tied behind my back near my neck and my legs shackled to the chair. I heard the officer say something that I didn't understand. A door opened and clicked shut again. It was quiet. Suddenly, it was quiet.

Was I alone in the room? I didn't know. Minutes passed, and since I didn't hear anyone breathing, nobody moving or clearing their throat, I assumed that I was alone. I heard the sound of a car outside, a gate being opened, and voices: somebody was shouting something. Then this same silence again. I tried to move but couldn't. My arms were fastened high on my upper back, the rope tied around my neck. That gave me only two possibilities: either I could sit in a halfway natural position with a straight back and relaxed muscles, barely able to breathe, since the rope cut into my throat, or I could sit bent over and tensed up with a horribly twisted back, but then I could breathe normally.

I decided on the second option. With my eyes blindfolded I couldn't tell whether the light was changing, whether it was already evening or still late in the afternoon. I noticed how thirsty I was. The last thing I had had to drink was the coffee in Mardin. How long ago had that been? Four or five hours? My thirst was greater than my hunger. Sharo's sisters would certainly have cooked for us and were waiting with lunch or dinner. By dinner at the latest they had to know that we wouldn't be coming back.

Soft music tore me away from my thoughts. I heard a saz and thought I was going crazy. Then I understand that the music was coming from a recording. Still, I thought my ears were deceiving me. Where was this music coming from? I knew that melody! It was the melody to a song that my mother always sang while baking bread, an old song that shepherds sang in our village when they were watching their sheep. My sister sang it while sewing. It was the melody to a Kurdish song. I asked myself what this song was doing there in the jail.

Then I heard Şivan's voice and knew immediately: They had found Sharo's cassettes.

Malan bar kir lê çûne waran lê, I heard Şivan sing. The family has packed its things and returned. The mice and snakes have eaten our flesh. I am an orphan, my hands are tied. The family has packed its things and returned.

⌒

I cannot say how I survived the night, Leyla. I didn't sleep, not for a second. To still my thirst I tried to chew, gathering saliva in my mouth and swallowing. But that didn't help. My twisted back hurt, and my twisted neck hurt. The pain in my back and in my neck shot into my head, into my hands, into my legs. I sat there that way. Time passed as it always passed, but every second hurt tremendously. Then I heard someone open the door. Someone came into the room, walking toward me. He stood in front of me. I saw his boots. He touched my throbbing head, ripped the blindfold from my eyes, and I squinted. He said something that must have meant stand up and then left. I got up, but I could hardly stand.

I looked around. There were mirrors and sinks in the room. A group of soldiers entered noisily. They walked past me as if I wasn't there and started shaving at the sinks. I just stood there and waited. A soldier came and instructed me to sit back down on the chair and shaved my head roughly. I suddenly couldn't help but think of Cemil Aslan, who had unquestioningly given me the letter on the bus from Nusaybin to Qûlika that verified his identity and who in a few days would have to start his military service in Diyarbakir. Or had he started already? In which prison were we? In Mardin or in another city? Although I knew how silly such thoughts were, I thought about this Cemil Aslan, imagining that perhaps he could help me a second time. After I was shaved, the soldier left me to drink some water at the sink. I drank and drank, greedy, as if I wanted to drink the tap dry. After all, I didn't know when I would get water the next time. Enough, said the soldier and led me out of the room down a long corridor. At the end of it there was a staircase leading into a basement. I was supposed to shovel coal. They locked the door behind me, and I was alone.

I was still wearing the clothes in which I had set out from Mardin to the police station: a shirt, bell-bottom pants, and the leather shoes that I had bought back in Damascus when I still thought I would attend the university dressed like that. A beautiful shirt, a beautiful pair of pants, beautiful shoes, but no shepherd ever wore such clothing. And I was supposed to be Firat Ekinci, the ninth son of Majed and Canan Ekinci, a shepherd in the mountains. How was anybody to believe I was a shepherd when I was wearing these clothes? While I shoveled the coal, I scuffed my shoes again and again on the rough concrete wall until the leather was completely scratched up. I smeared my pants with coal dust and tore my shirt. I tossed the top button into the pile of coal. Maybe I had a chance of someone believing me looking like that.

∼

When they brought me back to the room with the chair and the sinks, a bed had been placed there. They let me sleep on the bed and I was allowed to drink water too. I couldn't explain it. I was so astounded that I asked myself the whole time what the trap was.

In jail, they always made everything into a trap; that was the first thing I learned. In the morning, after the night sitting on the chair, when my throat was burning because I was so thirsty, and when I had still been given no water while the soldiers were shaving and my head was being shaved, they had started spraying a jeep with water from a hose out in the courtyard. I could see it through the window. And the soldier shaving my head could see me looking at the puddles of water under the jeep, my greedy gaze. In spite of that, he made me wait. No, not in spite, precisely because of that he made me wait, continuing to shave my head with relish. He waited for me to beg for even just a sip of water from the faucet that was only a meter away. And the moment that I begged for a sip of water he would refuse me this sip. Precisely because I begged for it so much. In prison, you and all your own needs were a trap.

When the soldier finally allowed me to drink, the way you let a thirsty dog drink, and when I was drinking as if I could never stop again, that was the next trap. That he saw me drink like that, that he saw I was about to cry about this little bit of water, so happy I was to finally drink: that was the trap. That he saw how I saw myself, submissively kneeling there in front of the faucet while he loomed over me with his gun at his belt: that was a trap. And, being sensible as he was, he had to tear me away from the sink so that I didn't drink too much, since I couldn't stop drinking: that too was a trap.

Sharo explained everything to me later. He said, The first night when they let you spend all those hours on the chair, an officer was on duty who was a fascist, a member of the Nationalist Movement Party, the MHP. I know this officer already from the last time I was here, said Sharo. He hates Kurds. The second night, when they let you sleep on a bed, a different officer was on duty. He is still an officer, but he doesn't especially hate Kurds. You had to spend the third night on the chair again because the officer from the MHP was back.

After three days, we saw each other again, Sharo and I. Sharo was already sitting in the back of a military van, once again blindfolded and hands tied behind his back. Sharo, I shouted. He nodded but they didn't let me sit next to him. And I was blindfolded too. The van started moving, and I felt the road underneath the tires. At some point a new gate, at some point voices. Get out! When they removed my blindfold, I was in a room with thirty-three other prisoners; I counted them later. But Sharo was not among them.

This second prison was in a military zone that was isolated and cordoned off. Nobody but the military had access. The prisoners were not allowed to receive family members from outside, nor attorneys or journalists.

There were, however, journalists and attorneys inside the prison; there was even an attorney in my cell. When we were given soup, one plate for four people, and when we were given bread, six loaves of pita for thirty-three people, the attorney saw to it that everything was distributed fairly. He cut the loaves of pita into thirty-three pieces of the same size, giving each prisoner his portion. When there was an argument in our cell, he would also be called over to mediate.

Leyla, her father said, the military prison was like a university. Prison was my university.

I was led to an interrogation. Once again, they spoke Turkish with me. And once again, I did not understand them. This time I had prepared a sentence that a fellow prisoner had taught me beforehand. *Ben türkçe bilmiyorum*, I don't speak Turkish. I repeated it over and over: *Ben türkçe bilmiyorum*. The soldiers kept talking to me in Turkish. I said in Kurdish: *Ez tirkî nizanim*, and they hit me. I said: No matter how much you hit me, I don't speak Turkish. They hit me in the face.

I was told to sit on a chair. I waited. They came back with a translator. I could hear that the translator was a Kurd; he spoke the same dialect as Sharo. While he translated, his hands were shaking, his body trembling. He could look neither me nor the soldiers in the eyes. His eyes fluttered, and I asked myself what they had done to him to make him so panic-stricken with fear.

I could hardly concentrate on the officer's questions, staring again and again at the man sitting to my left translating.

Which political groups did I have contact with, the officer wanted to know.

None at all, I said. I spent my days with my sheep and goats in the mountains.

I considered whether the translator might be an ally. Or would he betray me and tell the officer that I didn't speak the dialect of the people from Dibek.

Sharo was one of them. He told me later that they had tortured him so much that at some point he told them he had hidden weapons, in Qûlika under a pile of straw at his uncle's house. They grabbed him and, since he could no longer walk, carried him into a military vehicle. On the road, there was a military van in front of them, a military van behind them, a whole throng of soldiers was underway, Sharo told me. Shortly before their destination he saw his brother from the window of the military vehicle; he was, like on any other normal day, sitting on his tractor in the field. They drove past him. In the village, at Sharo's uncle's house, the soldiers got out and searched through the straw, looking everywhere but not finding any weapons. Then they just drove back to the torture facility with Sharo.

I learned during my time there who I could trust. For example, the man who came back from an interrogation with his arm covered with burn marks. The man said to me: Don't talk to anybody here. I know that you're from Syria. I can tell from your dialect. When you talk, the others can hear it too. I also learned during my time in prison who I could not trust: the man who came back from every interrogation without a hair out of place.

I learned not to beg for water, because then they definitely wouldn't give it to me. I learned not to beg them to stop doing something, because they never did what they were asked.

I learned to tell people apart. The politicals, for example, who belonged to an organization, the PKK or the Kawa. The politicals knew why they were there and were prepared for prison, similar to those who weren't there for the first time. Or those who were there because of their beliefs and had done their work out of conviction, as journalists perhaps, or lawyers. But there were also those who were not prepared, the ones that had simply been picked up off the street: villagers, shepherds on the way to a wedding, to the fields, or to run errands in town. There were so many who were not prepared for what happened to us. I remember an old man who whimpered every evening: Who will they come for tomorrow? Until I couldn't stand it anymore and said loud enough for everyone in the room to hear: They will come for one of us tomorrow. One of us will be interrogated. How many days have you been here already? You well know that they always come for one of us.

During the interrogation they wanted names from me. Soon a different Kurd translated. This one didn't tremble; this one seemed to be translating not for the first time. Because he spoke so calmly, I concluded that he worked for the Turkish secret police. I was asked if I had political contacts to Kurds. Which organization did I belong to? Did I know this guy or that guy? The questions repeated themselves. If I had political contacts to Kurds was the question that came again and again. No, I said I was a simple shepherd and only knew about goats and sheep. We know you are innocent, they said. I would be released immediately if I gave them names. Why was I together with that Yazidi? they asked. How did I know Sharo? I said I only knew him from sight. My brothers played music at weddings in Qûlika. Qûlika is a small village; everybody knows everybody. I said I had met Sharo the day of our arrest merely by chance at the bus station and we had just wanted to ride home together.

They laid three music cassettes in front of me on the table. They were the Gulistan and Şivan Perwer cassettes. Was I familiar with these cassettes? I shook my head. No, I said. I am a simple shepherd; I don't have a cassette player.

They lashed the soles of my feet with electric cables. The hit me with their rifle on my shoulders and back. They locked me in a filthy bathroom for a day. There was almost no ventilation and it was over a hundred degrees. They led me into the yard, where a guard was washing his feet in a bucket. They gave me that water to drink.

They took me back to the cell, again and again.

I slept on a dirty mattress on the floor, laying my head on my shoes for a pillow.

For three days we got nothing to eat and almost no water. Then a soup that was so spicy we could barely get it down. And afterward no more water.

The man with the burn marks on his arms was taken for interrogation three days in a row, and on the fourth day they came for him again. Whenever he heard steps in the corridor he cringed. Eventually, he cringed even when no steps could be heard in the corridor.

Every evening there were a few men who told each other jokes as if they were crazy. They told the jokes until late into the night. They laughed, but the next morning when the interrogations began, they were silent.

A new prisoner was brought into our cell who wanted to know my name. Firat Ekinci, I said, son of Majed and Canan. He responded that he knew my family. Everybody knew them in the region. But he had never seen me before. Everybody in my family was dark, but I was so light-skinned, he said. He wanted to know which instrument I played in my family. *Kemençe*, I said. He nodded but did not seem to believe me. I kept quiet.

I was led to yet another interrogation. When they hit me, I didn't scream.

Leyla, her father said, I swear to you that I have always remained strong. They beat me, but I was able to bear it. Never did I beg for water, never begged for them to stop. Her father laughed and cracked sunflower seeds.

One day, we suddenly heard that five hundred new prisoners were coming. Where are they supposed to go? we wondered. There is barely room for us in this cell. We were afraid.

But on the very same day they once again took me to a military vehicle. Once again, the sack over my head, once again my hands tied behind my back. They took me to the military court of Diyarbakir.

There, an officer asked me several questions, in Turkish, of course. When I said *ben türkçe bilmiyorum*, he came at me and hit me. A translator was brought in. Once again, the same questions as always: whether I belonged to a political organization. Which organization was it? Could I name names? And again, the same answers: I am a simple shepherd, I don't care about politics. I go to the mountains with my sheep and goats. The translator said that the officer declared that my claims were supported by the fact that I had never attracted attention before. There was not a single note in the file under my name. The file was completely empty. When the judgment was proclaimed, I looked at the translator questioningly, unable to comprehend what he translated so routinely. Then everything went very quickly. Soldiers brought me to the gate and spoke to the guard. The guard opened the gate, and I simply walked through it.

~

The next morning, I took the bus to the police station in Mardin to pick up my passport. I could hardly stand, my back was in terrible pain, and I had to lean against the wall. But finally, it was my turn. For the first time in my life, I had an ID and was a citizen. Firat Ekinci, born in 1961 in Nusaybin, Turkish citizen. From the police station I went to the bus station and rode to Nusaybin, to Majed and Canan's house. I kissed their hands. I didn't know how to thank them for helping me even though they didn't even know me. But Majed was furious with me. I told you not to hang around with Sharo, he said.

I replied that none of it was Sharo's fault. On the contrary, I was the one who had gotten Sharo into trouble. But Majed didn't want to hear it.

Canan gave me some food and then more food. She butchered a chicken, cooked bulgur, bought sweets for me. You have gotten very thin, my son, she said.

When I heard a few days later that Sharo had also been released, I took the bus to Qûlika, although Mejed was against it. Do you want to get in trouble again? he asked.

I stayed with Sharo for a whole day.

He was still very weak. We sat in the yard of his house under the grape vines. He said that he wanted me to go with him to Istanbul, as we had recently planned, drink coffee on the Bosporus. Of course, that was completely out of the question; the military coup was in the air. You're too weak, I said to Sharo. How do you plan to get to Istanbul? How will you manage that? He gave me a photo that we had taken together by the passport photographer in Nusaybin before our arrest. Do you see the difference? Sharo asked and laughed. Our hair is gone and we've gotten thin, although it was only a few weeks. The hair will grow back, I said. And we'll gain weight too, Sharo.

I took the last bus back. I never saw Sharo again in my whole life.

Majed insisted on bringing me to Istanbul. We took the bus, twenty hours. In Istanbul I got on a plane. I landed in Hamburg, Leyla.

I 2 I

ate in the evening on February 15, 2011—Leyla had to look up the date—
a group of boys sprayed a slogan on the wall of their schoolyard in
Daraa in the southwestern part of their country.

That's the way it all started, or rather started again, Leyla imagined.
When one of the boys pressed down on the knob of his spray can and the
red paint gushed out, hitting the ocher-colored schoolyard wall, it was as
if everything that happened from that point on came directly out of that
can. No revolution started with just a can of spray paint. Without forty
years of oppression, this revolution would not have happened. But every
revolution needed its own story.

~

The school custodian in Daraa was the first to read the graffiti in the morning: It's your turn, Doctor! Down with Assad!

The custodian informed the principal, Leyla read. The principal informed
the police. The police arrested the students. The students were tortured.
The students were in prison for a month.

Their parents didn't know if their children were still alive and demanded
their release. Atef Najeeb, the chief of security forces in Daraa and a cousin
of the president, answered them as follows: Forget that you ever had children. Go home. Make new children. And if you can't manage that, then
bring your women to us and we'll make new children for you.

But the children's parents did not go home; instead, they took to the
streets.

More and more people joined them. And in other cities people protested too. In Damascus, but also in Kurdish Qamişlo, they demanded the
release of political prisoners and called for reforms.

Two years later, journalists found one of the boys from February 15,
2011. They believed him to be the one who had pressed the knob on the
can of spray paint back on that night in February. They asked him if he
regretted his deed. Wrong question, thought Leyla, regret: What kind of a
word is that? As if it were a child's prank to be regretted. But what did the
journalists know of this boy? He had sat in classrooms with pictures of the
president and the presidential father hanging on the wall; he had been

required to enroll in subjects that were called National and Military Education. He had been required to march in parades in honor of the president; he had been required to shout slogans countless times. Maybe he had a third cousin or an aunt or a great-uncle who had been arrested and returned from prison permanently broken. Maybe he had only heard stories about the Shabiha, the ghosts that only came at night, breaking into houses, arresting, killing, and raping. The large military prisons were cordoned off; there were thirty of them spread across the whole country. People were incarcerated there without an arrest warrant, disappeared for a long time, were never seen again or released for ransom, broken forever afterward. Fear that eventually turned to anger, thought Leyla. Perhaps it was like too much pressure in a sealed jar pushing outward, shooting out, and there was no way back.

~

Her father never left the sofa, the television turned on in front of him. The images from the news cast a pale light on the living room walls and on his face. At none of Leyla's friends' houses was the television on as often and for as long as at their house: KurdSat, Kurdistan TV, Roj TV, Rudaw, Al Jazeera, Al Arabiya. Her father sat in front of the TV eating sunflower seeds and the fruit from the living room table. Sometimes he watched the German newscast, when her mother wanted to see it, but afterward he switched back to one of his Arabic or Kurdish networks.

It was as if something was exploding behind the screen. As if the surface were shattering, the noise and the images spilling into the room and washing over Leyla's family on the sofa. From 2011 on, the television was never turned off anymore.

Her father leaned forward, propping his arms on his knees. He looked agitated. Leyla, look at that! On TV a huge crowd could be seen, a public square in the evening—it was dark already—with buildings all around. The crowd—you couldn't make out individual people since the picture was too grainy—wiggled, danced, cheered, jumped up and down. Get lost, Bashar, somebody sang. The crowd repeated it: Get lost, Bashar! The singer's voice was amplified by a megaphone, resounding over the whole square. The people clapped in rhythm. Get lost, Bashar!

Look at that, her father said. Just look at that, Leyla!

Bashar, you are a liar. Freedom is at the gate. It's time to get lost. Get lost, Bashar!

Her father stood up. He stretched his fists into the air and cheered in front of the TV. He walked back and forth between the sofa and the cabinet. Get lost, Bashar, he sang and laughed.

Uncle Memo sent an email with an attachment: a photo of Zozan and Mîran. They had both wrapped themselves in Kurdistan flags, standing arm in arm with many other people around them. Both of them laughed happily for the camera. Qamişlo, her father said; they all drove together to Qamişlo, to the demonstration.

They are taking to the streets in every city, shouting: The people want the overthrow of the regime. Arabs, Kurds, Armenians, Arameans, Druze, her father said. Christians, Alawites, Sunnis, Shiites, Yazidis. They are all shouting: The people want the overthrow of the regime.

It is only a question of time, her father said. One or two months until we'll be traveling to a free Syria.

Her father talked over and over about what this free Syria would look like, at dinner in the kitchen or in front of the TV. There will be a democratically elected parliament and, of course, freedom of the press. Kurds will no longer be second-class citizens but actual citizens. One, he said, they are shouting: One, one, the Syrian people are one. Can you imagine it, Leyla? They are all shouting—Kurds, Arabs, Christians, Alawites, Sunnis—Syria is one!

⁓

To such a Syria, her father said, I will return.

Let's wait and see first how everything develops, her mother said. But her father didn't even really listen to her. He flipped back and forth from Al Jazeera to Al Arabiya, from Al Arabiya to Rudaw, from KurdSat to BBC Arabic and back to Al Jazeera. He sat at the kitchen table in front of his laptop with several different news sites opened, watching the videos of the demonstrations on YouTube at the same time.

Next to his laptop, as always, was his bowl of sunflower seeds. He spit the seeds onto paper napkins that her mother threw in the trash when she straightened up. He stayed sitting in front of the laptop long after Leyla and her mother had gone to bed, and the next morning he was watching the news again while drinking his coffee before he went to work. He never seemed to get tired.

Lately, he didn't even ask where Leyla was going when she left the house on Friday evening. Leyla sat with Bernadette on the sofa at Boris's, and at

Boris's everything continued the same as it had before. He squatted in front of his computer and fought as he had for years against hostile armies. Bernadette had turned on music to drown out the shots coming from the computer speakers. Bernadette handed Leyla the joint and Leyla took a puff. Leyla ran her finger over the burn holes in Boris's sofa. Bernadette rolled a second joint, and Boris got a bag of chips and sat down next to them.

Leyla staggered home completely stoned. In the living room, a light was still burning. Leyla took off her shoes, went barefoot to the kitchen, and drank some water from the faucet. She heard her father turning off the TV in the living room. He came into the kitchen. You're still awake, Leyla said with effort. Her tongue was heavy. Maybe talking was not a good idea, she thought.

But her father still didn't ask her where she had been.

They found his body in the river, he said.

Whose body? Leyla asked.

Ibrahim Qashoush, her father said.

Who?

He sang at the demonstrations in Hama; you saw it on TV. They slit his throat and ripped out his vocal cords, her father said. Then he immediately went back to the living room.

~

In May, Leyla took the exams for her Abitur. For three days she sat at one of the tables in the large gym and wrote. It went neither well nor poorly.

They received their report cards on a Friday afternoon. A podium had been erected in the large gymnasium. The principal gave a speech and called upon each student from the graduating class to come forward individually to the stage, past the clapping crowd, to shake the hand of the class leader and finally receive her report card from the principal.

Later, the whole class sat behind the gym. Bernadette took a bottle of champagne out of her bag and Leyla a pack of cigarettes from her jacket pocket. Someone had a speaker and turned on music. The champagne cork banged against the gym wall. Who cares, said Bernadette, they can't kick us out of school anymore.

Bernadette and Leyla had sat together in class from the first to the twelfth grade. Because Bernadette had picked Latin in seventh grade, Leyla also picked Latin, and because Leyla had chosen French in tenth grade, Bernadette also chose French. They copied from each other and shared sandwiches during recess. They had done everything that best friends did together in movies and in the novels they had borrowed together from the public library. They gave each other friendship bracelets, wrote their initials on the pages of their notebooks and the bathroom stalls of the school, went together to all the parties and left again together. Bernadette drew black eyeliner on Leyla because she had a steady hand and because Leyla's eyeliner always looked scribbly, as if a child had attempted it.

Who will put my eyeliner on for me? Leyla asked. Who am I supposed to watch my TV shows with now? asked Bernadette.

Eventually, Leyla went home. She was drunk. Her father was already home from work, sitting in front of the TV, of course. She stumbled toward him to give him her report card. Her father nodded, not even really looking at it. He stared at the television. What's your average? he asked. B minus, she said. Her father nodded again. Okay, he said.

Leyla went to her room to change clothes. The main thing is that you passed, her mother would say, straightening out her practical clothing for the hospital, and that was it for her graduation.

Leyla put on her new bikini and a short dress over it. She rode through the early evening to the lake where her class was celebrating. Loud music came out of speakers, everybody was drinking everything: beer, vodka, champagne. Leyla sat down on the picnic blanket that Bernadette had spread out. Bernadette handed Leyla a beer and lit a cigarette. Leyla pondered the purpose of the party. To really get drunk, Bernadette had always said. When we finally have our diploma, then we'll get really wasted, Bernadette said, although too much alcohol always just made her tired and she ended up falling asleep somewhere, on one of the sofas in the youth center or in the host's bed.

Bernadette took one of Leyla's cigarettes and said, Now we have this whole summer! You're not going to Syria this summer?

Leyla shook her head. My parents say it is too dangerous.

Then we'll finally have a summer together, Bernadette said. To the summer, Leyla! She raised her beer bottle and drank. Leyla laid her head on Bernadette's legs. We can finally go to Annalena's birthday party together. Annalena's birthday parties are the best, said Bernadette. And you missed all of them! Leyla closed her eyes. Hey! Don't fall asleep, said Bernadette. Boris is still coming. Imagine, he actually wants to leave his apartment!

Later, they went in the water with Boris. Let's go a little bit farther out, said Bernadette. I don't feel like being examined by the boys. Leyla swam ahead, looking back at some point. Bernadette was lying on the air mattress with her arms hanging in the water, floating. Boris swam next to her, sometimes holding onto the mattress, still always careful not to touch her. Leyla suddenly felt no more need of returning to them. The water was cool, and Leyla plunged her head under, taking broad strokes. She swam farther and farther out, leaving the two of them far behind. Only the lake lay before her, the trees all around stretching their roots into the dark water. When she put her head underwater, the music fell silent, the shouts and whooping of the others ceased. So, this year they were not going to Syria. Already last summer Leyla had hoped they could return to Germany earlier, wishing that just one time she could go to Annalena's party. Now she was ashamed of her wish. When she had just turned four years old, they had put her on an airplane for the first time. Her father had said to her that if anyone asked where they were going, she should say to their grandparents' house. You must not tell anyone that we are going to Kurdistan. Leyla had stumbled out of a car into her grandparents' courtyard. The old woman who hurried toward her with the floral dress, who kissed her and cried—that was her grandmother. The old man who came slowly out of the house leaning on his cane was her grandfather. And now she simply wouldn't be visiting them. Leyla felt like a piece of driftwood that had been thrown into a deep, sluggish river. She swam to the other side of the lake. She sat alone and exhausted on the shore and watched the drops of water run down her arms and legs.

～

Where were you? Bernadette asked. We were worried about you. Next to them on her towel, Boris lit up a joint. Here, do you want it? Leyla nodded, spread out her own towel, and took a beer for herself.

Eventually, people started to dance and kiss. When the girls were drunk, they kissed other girls, but they had to be drunk to do that. Normally, Leyla was careful to kiss some boys every once in a while so that she was not too conspicuous, but that didn't matter to her now. At some point, Leyla didn't feel like dancing and smooching anymore, so she just drank.

On the way home, Leyla braked, climbed off her bicycle, laying it carefully on the ground, and puked into a field. Only then did she become so dizzy that she could barely stand, but puking still felt good.

Bernadette got off her bike too and held Leyla's hair out of her face. Are you okay? she asked. Leyla nodded and sat down on the shoulder of the road with her head between her knees. Eyes open, eyes closed, the dizziness did not go away.

Do you want some water? asked Boris. Thank you, Leyla said and took a drink.

She would have liked more than anything to stay there forever, lying down on the gravel between the field and the asphalt like a wounded doe that had been hit by a car and was now lying on the shoulder of the road waiting for death, or like a person who had been shot. Leyla was too tired to feel ashamed of her self-pity. Dawn was already breaking behind the fields. All around Leyla and the two others it was quiet. She knew that Boris and Bernadette were standing in front of her and that her bike was lying next to them. She knew both of them were looking at each other hoping the other one would know what to do now. And then they looked down at her. She knew that Boris and Bernadette were waiting for her to move again. But Leyla did not want to move: why, after all, what for?

Come on, Leyla, said Bernadette, you can't fall asleep here. We'll push, said Boris.

~

The summer was a German summer, sometimes about twenty degrees Celsius with some sun, then rainy or cloudy again like in the autumn, although it wasn't autumn yet. At some point it finally got hot after all, a muggy, oppressive heat that gave Leyla headaches. Her father sat every free second in front of the TV; they were still reporting on all channels. From time to time, her mother would sit next to him on the sofa as if she couldn't let him sit by himself. She seemed to expect Leyla to sit with them too. At least she kept saying so: Leyla, come sit with us. But eventually her mother would always get up too and say, I can't watch that anymore.

On TV, things changed over the course of the summer. Bashar al-Assad announced reforms, but at the same time shots were fired into crowds at demonstrations. Someone filmed something with a cell phone camera. The picture shook, somebody ran, people screamed, people were buried, funeral processions became demonstration marches. The songs of mourning turned into protest songs, and then there were shots again.

Homs was sealed off, cut off from its food supply. In Daraa, the residents discovered a grave with thirteen bodies. Syrian security forces advanced on Hama with tanks. One hundred thirty-six people died.

The newscaster said that since the start of the revolution twelve thousand people had been arrested.

Her father Skyped with her Uncle Memo while staring at the television. The picture on the laptop froze. Uncle Memo's face kept freezing up. When the image resumed, the pixels were jumbled. The connection was broken. Her father turned up the volume on the TV.

～

Leyla and Bernadette rode their bikes to the lake. They laid their towels in the sun. Leyla was wearing her new green bikini with the white polka dots and her sunglasses with red frames. Bernadette had the same ones.

Leyla's arms and legs were tanned from the sun. Sometimes, when her parents weren't home during the day because they were working, Leyla took off her bra and lay on the lawn in their garden so that her breasts would tan too.

Leyla leafed through a magazine that Bernadette had brought along. She didn't read magazines like that in front of her father anymore, since he had asked her once what she was reading and when she held up the magazine he had said: Always just fashion and makeup, nothing else in your head. Why don't you look at your schoolbooks so that your grades will be better? Now that he did nothing but sit in front of the television, he didn't say things like that anymore, but since they had been counting the dead on television Leyla felt ashamed of the magazines.

Leyla dropped the magazine beside her, got up, and ran to the lakeshore. There were sharp pebbles in the water at this spot, and she teetered a little. She was quite woozy from lying in the sun so long. She walked into the warm water, swam a few strokes, then let herself drift. There were ducks next to her, also motionless, as if in a daze. Leyla dove under the surface, opened her eyes, and stared into the cloudy water. She only came up again when she was almost out of breath. Panting, she kicked her feet until she found ground. Then she went back on land.

In the meantime, Bernadette had gone to the kiosk and bought french fries. Do you want some? she asked. Leyla shook her head and lit a cigarette. She smoked and stared into the air. The nail polish had flaked off her fingers. Leyla thought about Evîn, about how Evîn had always smoked the way she was smoking now, her fingers spread, the Marlboro between her index and middle finger. Where was Evîn now? Where were Zozan, Aunt Havîn, Uncle Memo? Presumably, they were sitting at midday in their living rooms or lying there on mats sleeping. Her grandmother was preparing the midday meal, cutting peppers. It's peaceful in the village, her Uncle Memo had said. You don't sense anything in the village. But nevertheless, in the evening nobody is outside. People sit in front of their televisions. It has never been so quiet here before. Leyla thought about the village, straining herself to imagine it as exactly as possible. Everything okay? asked Bernadette. Leyla nodded.

It was late in the afternoon when Bernadette woke her up. She had a nasty taste in her mouth and grabbed for her water bottle to take a drink. The water was warm and tasted stale. She pulled her dress over her head and slowly packed up her things. They set out for home. Because they were tired, they pushed their bicycles. The way back from the lake to the village went through a few meters of some woods that were too small to call a real forest. Under the trees, the air was humid, and it smelled of earth. They walked across the autobahn bridge and then between the fields back to the row house development at the edge of the village. Bernadette had once asked Leyla how she stood the heat in her grandparents' village, since it was at least ten degrees warmer than here. Sometimes it was even forty-five degrees Celsius, Leyla had said. But it was a different kind of heat.

They went into the village to the ice cream shop.

Since kindergarten they had sat here on the plastic chairs in front of the shop, first with their mothers, then alone when they were old enough.

That's coming to an end now too; it was the very last summer they would both be living here, said Bernadette, and Leyla just nodded. Bernadette had been accepted to a university just barely two hours away and Leyla was going to study in Leipzig, far enough away that she couldn't come home every weekend. Why Leipzig? asked Bernadette. Who goes to Leipzig? You've never been there before. What if you don't like it there? I don't understand why you applied there. We could have moved to the same city; that was always our plan, she said. We could have lived together.

Leyla didn't know the answer. She had decided on a city no better or worse than any other. The most one could say was it was far enough away from northern Germany, where her Aunt Felek and Uncle Nûrî lived and her father's many cousins, and just as far away from her mother's family in the Black Forest. Her grade point average had been just good enough for Leipzig, and besides, neither she nor anyone in her family had ever been there: Leipzig was a blank slate.

Bernadette said she was excited. In the fall she would begin studying elementary education. Already when they were in grade school, Bernadette had written *teacher* under Dream Job in her workbook, and Leyla in turn had written *flight attendant* because she loved airports so much. And now Bernadette would actually become a teacher, whereas Leyla just read through the lists of possible majors only once and decided on Germanistik. Why not law? her father had asked, and Leyla shrugged her shoulders. Why not medicine? My GPA isn't good enough, Leyla had answered. Who benefits from Germanistik? Who in the whole world? When Leyla said that she could also become a teacher that way, her father finally nodded and said, Okay, that's good. The children are the country's future.

Bernadette said: I am afraid I won't find a room. I will miss you. I will miss Boris.

Leyla said: I am sure you will find a room. You and Boris can visit each other! And as for us, we'll talk on the phone every day.

Aren't you excited? asked Bernadette. Leyla shrugged her shoulders.

⁓

She sat on the bed painting her fingernails. She was watching her favorite series on her laptop and had headphones on. When she took off her headphones, she heard the TV in the living room. Outside, it had long since gotten dark. Leyla was sweating, although she only had a T-shirt on. She first watched one episode, then a second, then a third. Then she took off her headphones again and listened. The TV was actually turned off, so her father must have been sleeping. In the foyer, it was dark. Leyla went into the bathroom and brushed her teeth. Then she sat down at her laptop again. Rohat had shared a video on Facebook, a demonstration in Damascus. Leyla only watched half of it before she clicked on the next video. This one she let play. It showed the naked body of a boy. He was lying on something that looked like a plastic tarp. A male voice spoke calmly but firmly in Arabic. The camera zoomed in on the head of the boy. His skin had an unnatural color, dark red, and in some places gray and brown. The camera zoomed to his torso, to something that looked like a wound but that Leyla could not recognize exactly because the picture was blurry.

The video had English captions. Leyla read: His name is Hamza Ali al-Khatib. He is from Jeeza, in the province of Daraa. He was thirteen years old. On the Day of Rage he participated in a rally for the ending of the siege of Daraa.

He was arrested, Leyla read, and brought back to his parents. Now the camera zoomed in on his arm. A hand in a plastic glove reached for his lifeless arm, lifting it a little. A bullet pierced his right arm, Leyla read. And hit his chest here.

The image shook. The camera zoomed in on his abdomen. Leyla read: This bullet hit his abdomen. And his left arm was also penetrated by a bullet that also hit his chest. The gloved hand again reached into the picture, pointing to the other arm and then the chest.

Leyla read: A fourth bullet was shot directly into his chest. Look at the blood splatterings on his face. His neck was broken.

Once again, the hand. Briefly you saw the boy's face, his closed eyes. Then the torso again, the chest.

Look at the wounds in his right leg. Leyla saw a wound.

But all these tortures were not enough for them, Leyla read. They also cut off his penis. They cut off his penis!

Take a look also at the reforms that Bashar announced so deviously. Where is the Human Rights Committee? Where is the International Court of Justice? Where are those who are calling for freedom? And with that, the video ended.

Leyla closed her laptop and put it next to her bed. Although it was warm in her room, she pulled the blanket up to her chin. She closed her eyes but couldn't sleep. The images were still there.

Leyla thought about her grandmother, Aunt Havîn, Uncle Memo, Zozan, Mîran, Welat, and Roda, who right now must be lying on the loft or sleeping under the olive tree next to the chicken coop. Did they even still sleep in the courtyard? She thought about the thin mosquito net, patched in many spots, that hung over them, so thin that you could see the starry sky through its mesh. Leyla had lain under it so often, right next to her grandmother, and breathed in her grandmother's scent and the scent of the pillows and the mattress that her grandmother had sewn and stuffed with wool. The branches of the tree moving over Leyla. The fear that overcame her when she stared at the night sky for too long. What if the laws of gravity reversed themselves and she fell into the infinite universe? The barking of the dogs in the village, the thumping of the oil pumps like her own heartbeat.

Maybe they didn't sleep outside anymore. Maybe it had become too dangerous, thought Leyla. As if it were less dangerous in the house than outside under the net. Although the house had thick walls and barred windows, as well as a metal door and a wooden one, neither one was locked, even at night. Maybe they locked them now, Leyla thought. But what good would that do? When it came down to it, a locked door was worth just as little as a mosquito net, thought Leyla. Welat was thirteen, like the boy in the video. What if she were suddenly to see Welat in such a video—she couldn't finish her thought—or even her grandmother? What if they were sleeping and then suddenly . . . She stared into the darkness of her room, thinking that the darkness here was just as endless as the darkness above the mosquito net. She closed her eyes again. The images were still there, on the inside of her eyelids.

~

Leyla rode to town with Bernadette and bought herself a backpack. She tried on clothes with Bernadette in the changing room. She didn't like any of them. What about this one? Bernadette asked. Leyla shook her head, finally buying a T-shirt that she actually thought was ugly and didn't even try on.

Are we grown up now that we don't steal anymore? asked Bernadette, who laughed and poked Leyla in her side. It's a shame: we would have become such good gangsters, she said. Leyla nodded and wished she could turn back time to when she used to stand watch while Bernadette hastily stuffed T-shirts, makeup, and flashy earrings in her schoolbag. And when later they sat together on Bernadette's bed sewing up the holes from the magnetized pieces they had cut out.

They drove together to the lake, Leyla with her new backpack and the T-shirt that she was already annoyed about. On the way, Bernadette bought beer, two bottles for each of them that rattled in her bag and that they opened right away at the lakeshore. Leyla didn't really feel like drinking beer, but they were, after all, at the lake. They sat shoulder to shoulder on the boardwalk, Bernadette with her head on Leyla's shoulder. She said again how sad she thought it was that they wouldn't be living in the same city anymore.

They had not yet finished their second beer when clouds began to gather. Leyla poured the last gulp into the lake as the first raindrops were already falling. When they reached their bicycles, a wind was whipping through the trees. The boughs were bending, and there was thunder and lightning. The raindrops got heavier. When Leyla and Bernadette reached the row house settlement and stood under the bus stop shelter, their clothes were sticking to their skin.

~

They smoked, shivering from their wetness, at the bus stop, and Bernadette didn't ask any questions. Nor had she asked any back on the boardwalk, nor on the way to the lake, and also not before that on their way to town. Yesterday in front of the ice cream shop she had not asked Leyla anything, and also not last week when they were sitting on Boris's sofa smoking a joint. Leyla looked askance at Bernadette. She was staring at the street and smoking. The rainwater poured from the roof of the bus stop shelter in a single sheet. Bernadette lit the next cigarette and said: Luckily these stayed dry.

Didn't Bernadette watch the news, or why didn't she ask her anything? Did she not realize what was going on or did it not matter to her? Surely it mattered to her, Leyla thought. But did she understand at all what was happening? Everybody was talking about it. But what could Bernadette have asked her? It's very simple, thought Leyla: Bernadette could have asked how Leyla's grandmother was doing, how her cousins were, her aunt, her uncle. Or she could have asked something completely different, for it wasn't really about her grandmother, her cousins, her aunts, her uncle. It was about so many people that Leyla did not even know. It was about more, thought Leyla.

How are you handling *that*? Bernadette could have asked without saying what all *that* meant. The rain had let up a little, at least Leyla imagined it had, and she was almost happy that Bernadette didn't ask her anything.

∼

Bernadette had found a room in a shared apartment. It wasn't big, but it was at the edge of Nuremberg's historic center. Leyla helped Bernadette to disassemble the furniture in her old room, load it on the van, and re-assemble it in the new room in Nuremberg. It was warm and they were sweating. Bernadette's bangs were sticking to her forehead. Leyla kept pouring water over her own head.

Bernadette was jumpy, although her parents, her sister, Boris, and Leyla were helping her. She was nervous, although she had planned the move for weeks and talked over her plans with Leyla again and again. She wanted to paint the walls in her room, but she didn't know which color. She had saved and wanted to buy a new bed, but the one she wanted was too expensive and the beds she could afford were too ugly. Should she take her bulky old wardrobe along or instead buy a clothes rail? You aren't even listening to me, Bernadette had said to Leyla at some point, interrupting herself midsentence. It's just a move, Leyla had answered. Then they argued in a way they had never argued before. Leyla said she didn't know a single person who was as selfish as Bernadette. Bernadette said she didn't know a single person who had such little interest in her fellow human beings as Leyla. Leyla stood up, got on her bike, and rode home.

But now they were sitting in Bernadette's new room eating pizza from cardboard boxes. Leyla was happy that they were too exhausted to talk. When she left, they hugged for a long time. Then Leyla got in the van with Boris and they drove back. Pop music played on the radio. Leyla looked out the window and didn't think about Bernadette. She felt relieved.

Leyla moved three weeks later. She packed her new backpack full of clothes, stuffed the rest in a gym bag, bought a train ticket, and sat down in the train with her backpack and gym bag. For the time being she had a sublet. Maybe that was a good thing, her mother had said to Leyla; she could always still look for something else. And Leyla nodded.

~

The apartment was on the west side of Leipzig. Leyla accidentally rode one stop too far and had to walk back. She was tired when she arrived. The gym bag was heavy and cut into her shoulder.

But her room had everything she needed: a bed, a table, and a clothes rail. She unpacked her backpack, hung up her clothes on the rail, put her laptop on the desk, set her shampoo, makeup, and hairbrush on the ledge in the bathroom. The room had two large windows that faced south. Leyla opened one of them. There was an ashtray on the windowsill. A streetcar went down the street below. Leyla sat on the windowsill and lit a cigarette. Later, she lay down on the bed and stared at the ceiling. It was white, with molding at the edges from which cobwebs were hanging. Beneath the cobwebs there were leafy vines and grapes made out of plaster.

Sophie, whose room Leyla was living in and who was studying abroad for a semester, had left her bicycle there. The seat was too high; Sophie must have been taller than Leyla. But the bolt was stuck and Leyla didn't bother looking for pliers. While she was riding through Leipzig on this bike that was too high for her, she imagined herself becoming Sophie. Through Sophie's eyes she saw the concrete apartment blocks, the Gründerzeit houses, the socialist showcase apartments, the overgrown vacant lots, the city park with its little lake, the completely normal houses, the statues just before autumn, rays of sun falling on the facades. It was still warm; the summer was not quite over yet. Leyla imagined herself as Sophie cycling a bit farther, to the river, getting off her bike on the pedestrian bridge to smoke a cigarette. Afterward, she would return as Sophie, Leyla thought, and maybe she would just stay Sophie.

~

Leyla read on her cell phone that the Shabiha had come back in force, the ghosts. If one had believed in the nineties that they had disappeared, now they were again driving through the streets in their shiny black cars without license plates. Big, muscle-bound men in sneakers with shaved heads and long beards. They shouted: Assad, or we will burn down the country. They came into the villages and towns, shot people down, looted, raped, tortured their captives until they said: There is no God but Assad.

～

Leyla read that the secret service was now in the hospitals. A doctor from Homs said: You are admitted with a bullet in your leg and discharged with a bullet in your head.

Leyla read that the jails were filling up and that they were stuffing the bodies from the jails in garbage bags, one garbage bag over the torso and one over the legs, driving the bodies in their garbage bags in a garbage truck to the mass graves. She read that many of the dead had their organs removed and these organs were sold in Lebanon or Egypt.

In Aleppo, in Deir-ez-Zor, and in Idlib, Leyla read, they were turning parks into cemeteries, because there were not enough places for the dead anymore.

Leyla couldn't help but think about how her grandmother had long ago gone into her garden and dug a pit for the forbidden books of her father. How she had simply put all the books in the pit without distinction. She imagined her grandmother filling the hole with earth over the books. As if the earth were greedy, Leyla thought. And she immediately thought that of course the earth was not greedy, the earth didn't care how many books and how many dead were buried in it.

Leyla did not complete the sentences in her mind that she was thinking at that time. But you need complete sentences, Leyla told herself again and again; without complete sentences you can't tell anyone about it. But who could she tell about this when her thoughts were incomplete? She couldn't even tell herself about it.

～

Leyla went to her first lectures. Fundamentals of German Linguistics; System of the German Language. Leyla sat in the lectures and didn't listen.

She took notes disinterestedly on what the professors were saying, arranged her notes in binders, and downloaded lecture notes. She sat in the library and studied. She liked the lectures better than the seminars in which the instructors asked questions and expected you to give your opinion. Leyla read silently, working through the theories and not remembering them just a few hours later.

Soon, Leyla only went to seminars with so many students that it would not be noticed if she didn't say anything. In the margins of her notepad, Leyla drew parallel lines in regular intervals, connecting the lines from top to bottom with each other to create a braid pattern. She drew the lines on all the pages of her notepad, until every page was lined on the left and the right by the same braid pattern. Ultimately, she threw the pad away and bought a new one with blank white pages.

⌒

Leyla signed up for an Arabic course. She imagined cramming verb conjugation tables, learning vocabulary, doing grammar exercises. In the end, she would be able to speak the language. Her classmates who had taken Arabic the previous semester said that Arabic was a lot of work; it took up all your time, and they themselves had dreamed at night only of verb conjugation tables. Leyla thought how great it would be if the verb tables entered her dreams and could push out the village, her grandmother, the dead.

After one of the first Arabic class sessions, Leyla went to the cafeteria with two classmates. One of them had a new roommate from Syria and for that reason was interested in the language. The other one wanted to work later for an NGO, and Arabic would be helpful for that.

On the telephone her father said: Why are you learning the language of our oppressors? You can't even speak proper Kurdish, and now you want to learn Arabic?

⌒

Leyla stopped attending the class. The exams were approaching. Leyla sat in the lecture hall and listened. Fundamentals of German Linguistics. System of the German Language. Language Variations. Linguistic Communication.

⌒

Leyla read that activists had gained access to Bashar and Asma Assad's email. They had worked through three thousand emails: the messages between Assad and his wife, short notes, insignificant stuff, sound files of country songs; the messages between Assad and his advisors, between Asma and her assistants. Shoes that Asma wanted to buy, her online shopping, her jewelry. Ladies' gloves with inlaid crystals, candelabras from Parisian goldsmiths, handmade furniture from London, curtains, vases, paintings. The two of them shopped through a middleman in London due to the trade restrictions. Leyla watched a video of Assad's state visit in London in 2002, both of them beaming, Bashar nevertheless with pursed lips, Asma holding her oldest son in her arms, who was only a toddler at the time. The photos from London, Leyla read, were illegal in Syria because they showed the president as a family man and not as a stern statesman.

⌒

The path from the streetcar stop to the seminar building consisted of large stone slabs. On the way from the seminar building to the library, Leyla had to walk across the slabs again. She couldn't help but think every time of the gaps between them. Death lurks in the gaps, Leyla thought.

⌒

Somebody could come from the road in a pickup truck, past the sign with the name of the village in flaking letters, up to the fork, then along the gravel lane past the garden and into the courtyard where her grandmother, Uncle Memo, Aunt Havîn, Zozan, Mîran, Welat, and Roda were seated eating breakfast. The very same moment that Leyla was walking across the stone slabs from her lecture to the library, the dark gaps beneath her. She never stumbled a single time. She might also be sitting in the cafeteria or putting her groceries on the belt in the supermarket or be at a party with a beer in her hand, or be standing with Anna like she did last weekend when Anna pressed her up against the wall, toppling over the beer bottles next to them on the floor, but that didn't matter to her: Anna pressed her against the wall and kissed her.

Leyla might be coming home from a party, lying down on her bed while her grandmother, Aunt Havîn, Uncle Memo, Zozan, Mîran, Welat, and Roda were also lying in their beds and while someone else was now coming into the courtyard. Would the dogs bark? Would the barking wake them up? When Leyla woke up the next morning they might be long dead. Lying there on the floor exactly like all the others in the photos and videos she had seen so often.

⌒

Her father would say to Leyla three days later on the telephone: I am worried. I haven't been able to reach them in three days. And eventually, sometime later they would find out. You always found out somehow.

If someone came to kill them, Leyla couldn't do anything. She would keep going to her lectures and to the supermarket. It wouldn't make a difference if she went to a lecture or went to the supermarket.

Whenever Leyla walked across the stone slabs she always kept trying not to step on the gaps. As soon as she stepped on the gaps she would die, she told herself, knowing at the same time that the gaps had nothing to do with anything.

~

During her first summer vacation, Leyla went to her parents' house. It was the second summer in a row that she did not travel to the village, the second summer that she would not see her grandmother, aunt, uncle, and cousins.

Leyla walked to the lake with Bernadette, and they lay in the sun on their towels, sat on plastic chairs in front of the ice cream shop, went to Boris's to smoke weed, watched him playing computer games, and listened to music. Bernadette talked nonstop about her studies, about Nuremberg and her new friends, whose names Leyla immediately forgot. Leyla nodded. Are you even listening to me? Bernadette asked. Leyla rode home to her parents' house with her headphones in her ears, but she wasn't listening to music. The headphones in her ears muffled the exterior noise, the whooshing of the driving wind while she rode her bike.

~

Her father was home sitting in front of the television. War raged on TV. The Free Syrian Army was now recruiting minors. Among the green, white, and black flags of the Syrian Revolution more and more black flags were popping up with the Islamic confession of faith; foreign fighters had come to the country by the thousands. The Islamic Front fought alongside the Free Syrian Army against the regime, and alongside them the al-Nusra Front. The al-Nusra Front had been founded by members from al-Qaeda in Iraq and the Islamic State of Iraq. Her father told her a schoolfriend of Uncle Memo named Ahmed had joined them. You know him, Leyla, her father said. He sometimes came to the village to visit and then used to sit for hours with Uncle Memo in the courtyard drinking tea and smoking. He could also be seen on Uncle Memo's wedding video dancing in a line with the others, the drummer in the middle of them. Once he invited us over, her father said; you were still little. You played with his nephew and nieces in the garden. Ahmed didn't come to the village anymore, but he at least called Uncle Memo on the phone and said: As long as I am in charge of Hasakah Province, we will leave you all alone.

On TV, Leyla saw men in black face coverings standing behind sandbags. The men fired shots, and dust and black moved across the screen. A man dressed all in black with a long beard ran through the street holding up a black flag. A group of veiled men posed in some landscape, holding their weapons into the air, crying Allahu Akbar and firing.

~

Leyla was glad to be back in Leipzig. Before she left, her father had asked her: Why don't you stay longer? But Leyla had to move to a new apartment in her new city. Sophie was coming back from her semester abroad. Leyla packed her clothes into her backpack again, stuffing the rest into her gym bag, and took the streetcar straight through the city. Leyla liked her new room in the new neighborhood. Here too there was a park close to her new shared apartment, but without a pond and instead, only beaten-down grass, bleached out from the summer. There were a few skateboard ramps, a youth center, and a wall on which you were supposed to spray graffiti legally. Families picnicked and grilled. Women who spoke the language of their fathers and grandmothers sat on the benches behind the skateboard ramps. On the sidewalk, there were bowls of salted sunflower seeds, there were hookah lounges, Arab, Turkish, and Kurdish supermarkets, many different restaurants.

In one of the supermarkets where the cashiers normally spoke Kurdish but always German with Leyla, she bought a double teapot, half a kilo of black tea, little round glasses, and saucers. The cashier packed it all in blue plastic bags and Leyla carried it home. She was the only one in her new shared apartment who drank black tea. The teapot was the smallest one you could buy in the store and yet it was still huge. Leyla made tea in it as if for a large family with a lot of visitors. Leyla drank it with a lot of sugar, alone at night sitting on the windowsill, smoking and looking down at the street devoid of people.

The villagers had now dug a trench, her father said on the telephone. Every night they lay there with their Kalashnikovs and kept watch, a different family every night. To defend the village in case someone comes, her father said.

Defend the village with what? asked Leyla. A few shepherds, a few farmers with Kalashnikovs? That's ridiculous, she said. Could they even shoot? Once a year in Newroz, they fired into the air, she remembered, but war was a different story. Nobody in the village had served in the military; oh yes, there was one man, Miro. Nobody had a Syrian passport besides Miro. But Miro served in Deir-ez-Zor in the mess hall. And, as the story went, was always beaten up by the others when they didn't like how the food tasted.

~

Leyla imagined the villagers in the trench, old Abu Aziz next to her uncle, shoulder to shoulder in the dark cracking salted sunflower seeds in their mouth, trying not to fall asleep. Leyla imagined the men there in the trench, the starry sky above them, the village behind them, that collection of clay huts of no interest to world history where Abu Aziz's family and the family of her uncle were sleeping, while they held their guns into the darkness before them, that nearly endless darkness.

Everybody in the village, her father said on the phone, has bought a suitcase now. That didn't used to be the case. What would they buy one for? her father said.

Nobody had vacation, nor a passport. Aleppo was five hours away by car, and the coast, the port of Latakia, beyond reach. But now the few suitcases that had already been in the village were being taken out of the wall cabinets, out of the corners behind the sacks of grain in the pantry. They were being dusted and wiped off and soon were standing next to the newly purchased suitcases at the door, already fully packed with the most important things.

After all, it's a Yazidi village, her father said. Leyla knew: because it was a Yazidi village, the people there knew there would be no time to pack when they had to flee. They knew their suitcases could not be heavy if they had to run. And they knew that sometimes you had to just start running without a suitcase.

~

Leyla went with her new roommates to the park. They bought beer and sat on the grass. It was a Saturday afternoon in October and still warm. A friend of one of the roommates came over and sat with them. Leyla told him her name. The roommate's friend wanted to know where her name came from. Are you Arab? Leyla shook her head. No, Kurdish. The roommate's friend said he thought that was fantastic. He talked for a long time about the Kurdish struggle for liberation, about the women in the PKK. Leyla nodded. He asked where her family was from. From Syria, she said. The roommate's friend said it was really bad there now. Leyla nodded and drank some beer.

Then she stood up abruptly and went to the bathroom in the café at the edge of the park. On the way back, she passed a large family sitting on the lawn grilling: grandparents, parents, and children, perhaps also uncles, aunts, cousins, or simply just friends of the family. She heard them speaking Kurdish. All of a sudden, she didn't want to go back to her room-mates and their friends. She would have liked more than anything to sit down with the family, but it wasn't her family. Leyla couldn't help but think about the picnic outings with Uncle Memo, Aunt Bahar, Zozan, Mîran, Welat, and Roda on the Tigris. They had sat on the banks of the Tigris and grilled. They had taken walks along the riverbank. Had climbed back into the pickup truck and gone back to the village as the sun slowly set. Leyla had held her face into the wind and squinted her eyes.

～

Leyla read in the newspapers that Assad's army had withdrawn that fall from the Kurdish territories.

One year later the government relinquished control of these areas.

The Kurdish territories received an official name: Rojava, the West. Rojava was divided into three regions called cantons: Efrîn, Kobanê, and Cizre. The Kurdish Democratic Union Party took over the administration of these cantons, along with the Syriac Union Party. Kurdish units now had military control, the People's Defense Units (YPG) and the Women's Defense Units (JPG), men and women Leyla's age in uniform. An admin-istration was formed, Assad's photo removed from classroom walls and replaced by pictures of Abdullah Öcalan, the man with the round face and moustache who looked a little like Leyla's Uncle Memo. Kurdish was taught in the schools and the towns and villages got their old names back. Leyla had to learn the old new names. Al-Qahtaniyah was again called Tirbespî, Ras al-Ayn again Serê Kaniyê, Ain al-Arab again Kobanê.

～

Leyla went to a party with one of her roommates. The parties here in Leipzig were different than the ones she used to go to with Bernadette. With Bernadette she had put on high-heeled shoes and a short skirt, put on makeup. Here people wore jeans, sneakers, and T-shirts, and partied in former auto mechanic shops, in basements or empty stores. Bernadette would have rolled her eyes and said, They think they are cool, and then gone to get beer.

There was a long line on the street. We are friends of Sascha, her room-mate said to the bouncer. The bouncer nodded, went inside, and came back with a woman who introduced herself as Sascha. And you?

Leyla just nodded.

That's Leyla, her roommate answered.

I have to bartend, said Sascha. Leyla nodded again.

Leyla and her roommate danced and sweated. The music was so loud that Leyla imagined she was swimming in it. At some point they sat down on a sofa in the next room where the bar was. Leyla's roommate went to get beer for the two of them. Leyla took a drink. She was thirsty. From the sofa, Leyla could see the woman called Sascha. She watched very closely as Sascha stood at the bar, threw money into the till, took bottles out of the refrigerator, leaned briefly against the wall when nobody came, took a sip of her gin and tonic or rolled a cigarette, laid the rolled cigarettes next to the till because somebody had come, cut off a lemon wedge, poured gin into a measuring cup, poured tonic in the glass, lit her cigarette, smoked, and looked over from time to time at her roommate and definitely also at Leyla. Whenever Sascha looked over at them, Leyla felt like she had been caught in the act and tried to focus again on what her roommate had just been telling her over the noise.

～

Sascha was beautiful, Leyla thought. So beautiful that Leyla couldn't think of any other word, just beautiful. She was tall, slender, and wore a T-shirt that was much too large for her with a faded pastel imprint; it looked like a T-shirt that Leyla would only have worn to sleep in. Along with that, she had on a loose pair of jeans that she had tucked the T-shirt into and around her waist was a wide leather belt, and still she look elegant. It was the way she leaned against the wall, how she smoked, how she got beer out of the refrigerator, Leyla thought. She had a narrow face and short hair, with the sides of her head shaved. Leyla could have stared at her forever.

I'm going back to the dance floor, her roommate shouted over the music and stood up. Are you coming along? Leyla shook her head.

She stayed seated on the sofa, smoking and drinking. Sascha looked over at her again and then Leyla did get up and walk over to the dance floor.

Later, Leyla went back to the bar and bought another beer, but Sascha wasn't there anymore. Once, she saw her in the crowd, but then she lost sight of her again. Leyla drank a lot, one after the other. Her roommate ordered schnapps.

Eventually Leyla was standing face to face with Sascha.

Well? shouted Sascha over the music.

Well? shouted Leyla. Is your shift over?

Obviously, shouted Sascha.

Leyla nodded and wanted more than anything to turn around and leave. She didn't know what to say. They stood there in the crowd looking at each other. Leyla thought, what on earth should she talk about? She didn't even want to talk! She wanted to touch Sascha while she was standing there in the hall in front of the bathrooms. She wanted to grab hold of her shoulder, kiss her, press her up against the wall.

⌒

Leyla only saw hours later when they were leaving that Sascha's hair was the color of mud. Outside it was bright. The bakeries on the corner had long since opened. They bought two chocolate croissants. They climbed the stairs up to Sascha's apartment. Sascha's room was full of plants. On the windowsills, on the desk, even some on the floor next to her mattress. Are those all yours? Leyla asked. Sascha nodded and said: Who else would they belong to? She named them all one after the other, slowly, as if each one was significant: succulent, marantaceae, spider ivy, monstera, Mediterranean dwarf palm.

Besides the plants there was nothing but books in Sascha's room. They were spread out everywhere, stacked on the floor: art catalogs, novels, volumes of theory.

⌒

The mattress was on the floor next to the window. Outside the window stood a large tree. The branches of the tree filled the entire window. Leyla lay down next to Sascha on the mattress and looked up at the branches.

Sascha buried her face in Leyla's hair, kissed her neck, pulled off her T-shirt and jeans.

⌒

Sleeping with Sascha was different than with Anna or with the other women she slept with since she had moved to Leipzig. She couldn't say what was different; it was like she was suddenly able to surrender the border that she always guarded between her body and the other bodies. At some point she no longer knew where her body began and Sascha's ended. Their hands, fingers, lips, and tongues reached out for every little piece of each other's body that they could touch. Capitulation, thought Leyla, as they eventually lay exhausted and entwined with one another, and she soon fell asleep breathing in the hollow of Sascha's neck.

⌒

Leyla stayed with Sascha for two days. There was no reason to go home. Saturday passed, then Sunday. Leyla's cell phone was turned off, and she didn't even think about it. She lay next to Sascha and watched concert highlights of Sascha's favorite band, and when they got hungry, they went to Mr. Wok around the corner, carried the food in plastic containers and plastic bags up to Sascha's apartment. They sat on the sofa in the kitchen and ate. Sascha talked and laughed a lot while they ate, and Leyla also talked and laughed a lot. They didn't finish the food, putting the half-empty containers in the refrigerator for later.

When Leyla was back home and had plugged in her cell phone, she had three missed calls from her parents.

~

Leyla dialed Bernadette's number. She said: Sascha has short hair, shaved on both sides of her head, and tattoos on her arms and legs that she did herself. She said: Sascha has a room full of plants. I've never seen anyone before who has so many plants. But that's nice, said Bernadette. Yeah, said Leyla. Then I don't know what your problem is, said Bernadette.

Leyla called her parents' number. Her mother answered. You called, Leyla said. What's going on?

Reber, Uncle Sleiman and Aunt Xezal's son, was traveling on the bus from Deir-ez-Zor to Hasakah to visit his cousin. They were stopped near Deir-ez-Zor. Three men on the bus were shot. One of them was Reber, her mother said. It's horrible, said her mother. Yeah, said Leyla. Her mother said: Your father is going to Bielefeld tomorrow, to Reber's uncle's house.

When they had hung up, Leyla buried her face in her pillow, biting the material until she could feel the down stuffing and taste the wool, pressing her face farther and farther inside. Finally, she stood up and went into the shared kitchen, poured herself a glass of water, drank the water, put the glass in the sink, and walked back to her room. She felt sick. A rush of guilt shot through her head, radiated into her neck, her shoulders, her torso, her arms, hands, tips of her fingers, into her legs, which buckled from the guilt. Leyla had to sit down.

It was her fault, she said to herself. She had danced, imbibed, and slept with Sascha while Reber sat on the bus. That's the way it was, even though Leyla knew it wasn't true: her mother had said it happened four days ago already. When she had been dancing, Reber was long since dead. In that case, Reber was dead and still she had danced.

~

In November, Reber's younger brother Welat was drafted. In December the news came that he had fallen in battle. Can you remember him? her father asked. A little, said Leyla. They had only seen each other at Uncle Sleiman and Aunt Xezal's house in Aleppo, when Leyla was staying overnight there at the beginning and end of her summers. She remembered how her father had been arrested at the airport and she had sat with Nesrin over her sticker album. How another time she had stood with her on the balcony and counted the taxis on the street below, and how yet another time she had walked next to her on a stroll to the suq. Perhaps she only remembered Nesrin because Reber and Welat had been too cool to give a girl the time of day. In the photos from Aleppo, it was always just she and Nesrin, both of them in braids. Aunt Xezal had woven them for them. Leyla thought about Nesrin. Her whole family had gone from Aleppo to relatives in Tirbespî when the fighting got more serious. Leyla thought about the switch from the big city to the town far from her classmates, then the death of both of her brothers. Nesrin was now alone in Tirbespî with her grieving parents. She still had three brothers left, but they were all married and gone already, and two of them were now fleeing to Germany.

As part of the refugee group? Leyla asked on the phone. No, not in the refugee group. With migrant smugglers.

Her mother sent Leyla a different photo. Leyla couldn't remember the picture. In this photo it was also summer. Leyla sat in her grandparents' courtyard under the grapes, a boy on her right and one on her left. Neither her face nor the faces of the two boys were clearly recognizable, since they were shaded by the grape vines. All three of them held a piece of watermelon in their hands, and in the bowl in front of their bare feet there was a sliced melon. I wonder how old you were in that picture, her mother said, maybe four or five. And Reber and Welat were only one or two years older than you.

～

Leyla went with Sascha to the Baltic Sea. Sascha's great-aunt had a cottage there that she rented out to tourists. It was empty in the winter. Sascha spent her childhood summers there. She had said, It's pretty there, pulling Leyla toward her.

In the train they ate nuts and the sandwiches that Leyla had made for them. Sascha read and Leyla fell asleep, her head on Sascha's shoulder.

The house was cold when they arrived, freezing. They gathered together all the blankets in the house and lay underneath them, hugging, but they were still freezing.

The next morning Sascha suggested they take a bath to warm up. They ran hot water into the tub, boiled even hotter water in the tea kettle, then lay together in the bath, drinking coffee and smoking. Sascha read again and Leyla just smoked until eventually they got hungry and they left the house, walking down the street to the supermarket that in winter was only opened half days.

Sascha didn't ask Leyla any questions. Sascha hardly spoke. Everything okay? Leyla asked. Yeah, everything's fine, what should be wrong? said Sascha, raising her eyebrows. While Leyla cooked, she just sat on the kitchen bench and watched.

Every day, all day long, an icy wind blew, and when they walked along the beach it was as if they were beating back a resistance. The wind furrowed through the layers of their clothing, through their jackets, sweaters, and T-shirts, even under their skin. Seagulls sat on wooden posts and buried their beaks in their feathers; the sea was gray and had the same color as the sky. Leyla collected seashells in her jacket pocket, and when she had gathered so many shells that her jacket pockets were filled with them, she threw them all back into the sea.

The sea was new to her: the gulls, shells, rows of posts that were called *buhnen*, the wind. For Sascha, it was different: We always went swimming here. Back there on the beach we would eat ice cream. Leyla nodded to everything. Only when you are at home in a landscape can you name it. Making it sound like an important piece of information, Sascha said: When you follow that path back there then you come to the Bay of Greifswald.

At night, Leyla dreamed about the village. About the days when the wind stirred up the dust so much that there was no horizon and the sky turned as gray as the fields, the houses, the village. The dust of the village was as hot as it was cold here at the sea. A longing that hurt had coated her skin when she awakened, but maybe she dreamed that too. She thought about the mountains behind her grandparents' house while she was sitting next to Sascha on the beach looking at the sea. She thought about the bleached-out fields, about her grandmother's floral skirt, the loaves of bread in the oven vibrating with heat, the long summer afternoons spent dozing. About the hot wind. The cities where she visited her relatives, sitting in living rooms eating together. About the interior courtyards, the chickens in the streets. Heleb, Raqqa, Deir-ez-Zor. Hasakah, Qamişlo, Kobanê, Efrîn. The car ride from Tirbespî to Damascus through the desert when they had stopped in Palmyra once early in the morning, all by themselves outside of the houses, since the museum had not yet opened. They had walked across the broad market street along the Temple of Bel. They had taken pictures, gotten back into the car, and simply left, forever.

⌐⌐

Sascha said: I told my mother about you. Sascha had grown up with just her mother. Her mother had still been young when she had given birth to Sascha, as old as Sascha and Leyla are now. Sascha's mother went on vacation with her, visited her in Leipzig, called her up just to chat. If Sascha was on the phone with her, it was like she was talking to a good friend. She said: My mother would like you.

⌐⌐

Leyla in turn could not imagine telling her parents about Sascha. Her parents wanted above all to know she was doing well. Her father asked her on the telephone: How are you? and expected Leyla to answer simply: *fine*. He continued to sit every evening in front of the television, flipping back and forth from Al Jazeera to Rudaw, KurdSat, BBC Arabic, Kurdistan24 while her mother continued her search for ways to get the family out of Syria, writing emails and making phone calls.

Does your family know about you? Sascha had asked. Leyla didn't know how she should answer that.

An absurd notion: Sascha at their house with Leyla's parents and Leyla herself in front of the television with the war on. Sascha at Aunt Pero's in Hanover, Aunt Pero loading her plate with kutilk, salad, bulgur, and bread, like she did for everybody who came for a visit. German women, Aunt Pero would have said later, just as the other aunts always asked again and again: Do they really think that's pretty, such short hair? She would only have spoken of Sascha as *the girl with the short hair*. At least, her aunt would have thought that her niece was studying and thus didn't have any men yet, just girlfriends. She would have brought Sascha a plate of freshly baked kûlîçe in the living room, where just like at her father's house the television was on, and on television: the war. The remote control on the living room table was still packed in plastic wrap; they only had the television since they no longer lived in the home for asylum-seekers.

On the beach and in the house and when Leyla and Sascha lay together under the blankets, Leyla couldn't help constantly imagining Sascha at her family's house since Sascha had asked if her parents knew about them. Impossible, Leyla thought and kissed Sascha. When they were finally sitting in the train back to Leipzig, she suddenly attempted to talk about herself. But all that came to mind were stories about a person whom Sascha didn't know, about a completely different Leyla. Still, she tried. Leyla said that she was named after three women: Leyla Qasim, Leyla Zana, and the Leyla her father had wanted to marry but who went to fight in the mountains and was now hanging as a photograph in Uncle Nûrî and Aunt Felek's living room above the television. Leyla soon could no longer stop talking, just stroking Sascha's hand. She said that there was a type of photograph that was only circulated after the person had fallen in battle and that the fallen soldier was called şehîd. What did Sascha know about that? Leyla thought. Some things just can't be told, she thought.

~

The beginnings of summer, for example, the way Leyla rushed into her grandmother's arms. The way her grandmother kissed her hair, her eyes, her hands. Or how they were once invited to a wedding and her grandmother dressed her in a tulle dress in which Leyla looked like a princess, combed her hair and wove it into a braid, and put Leyla's little black patent-leather shoes on her. Her grandmother held her hand as they walked together through the village, jumping over sewage ditches. Not so fast, not so fast, her grandmother said, until they reached the wedding. The men were standing with the groom on the roof of the house smoking. A musician was playing the zurna in the courtyard and somebody was drumming. The crowd clapped and the women let out their piercing cries, repeating their loud trills over and over until, finally, the bride arrived.

Bride and groom stood at the threshold of the house. They held a clay jug together in their hands that they flung onto the ground. The clay jug shattered, releasing coins and sweets that the children lunged for. Go on, her grandmother said, run!

The bride wore a red ribbon around her hips.

Leyla saw the bride before her, her hair stiff with hairspray, pinned up and falling in waves over her shoulders, gold jewelry on her hands. The dancing crowd.

~

Whenever Leyla came out of the seminar building, Sascha was already waiting on a bench smoking. Sascha even waited for Leyla in front of the library. When Leyla came from a seminar or the library, Sascha had already rolled her a cigarette. Then they went together to the park and sat on the benches next to the meadow that was empty in the winter. Leyla in turn picked up Sascha at the café where she waited tables. It was a café that she and Sascha would never have gone to in different circumstances. Sascha had to wear a blouse, serve whip cream with the cake, and bring the coffee in little pots. But the tips are good, said Sascha every time Leyla picked her up there. Sascha also worked in a bar. There were no tips there, but she could stand around in a T-shirt, jeans, and sneakers smoking when she didn't happen to be hauling beer crates from the storage room to the counter, pouring vodka into shot glasses, or emptying ashtrays. The bar did not have a liquor license and Sascha had no employment contract. She and the others paid themselves in cash and closed as soon as they no longer felt like working. While Sascha was working, Leyla sat at the bar. If Sascha was not working, they still hung out together there. Sascha attended the university but only irregularly, sometimes not for three weeks in a row and then from morning until evening again, even going to the library afterward. Now I'm really going to finish writing my term paper, Sascha said, borrowing so many books from the library that Leyla had to help her carry them, but a week later she no longer mentioned the subject. And she almost never read the books. She forgot to return them or didn't bring them back in hopes of eventually reading them after all; Leyla didn't know. Eventually the late notices arrived from the university library, and Sascha packed up the books again and Leyla helped her carry them back. They stood at the machine where you paid library fines, Sascha shoving bills of money into the slot saying: Those were my tips from three weeks. Doesn't matter; next week I'll earn new tips.

Sascha never cooked. If she was hungry, she went to Mr. Wok, to Asia Express, to Haci Baba or Tito Pizza. Or she ate bread spread with soft cheese or meat, or instant soup from a bag she poured water over from the electric kettle.

I'll cook, Leyla told her. They bought grape leaves, rice, garlic, ground meat, parsley, onions, carrying the packed blue plastic bags back to Sascha's apartment. Sascha sat on the sofa smoking and watched Leyla fill the grape leaves, stack them in a pot, pour water over them, and cover the pot with a plate, so that they did not spill over, just like her grandmother had taught her. Leyla chopped up garlic, put the garlic in a bowl with olive oil. She put plates on the table, blended water with yogurt and added mint. Most of the time they talked little. Sometimes Leyla asked herself who needed the other one more, Leyla Sascha or Sascha Leyla? She went to Sascha's, stayed at Sascha's, went home, showered, changed her clothes, and rode back to Sascha's.

∼

Uncle Memo called, her father said on the phone. He says that Ahmed called him and said: You all need to leave, I can't protect you anymore. Al-Nusra's power has been weakened, her father said. There are new militias. They are calling themselves Daesh, Islamic State in Iraq and Syria.

Her mother started writing even more emails and letters than usual. As before, she put copies of the letters in thick binders and forwarded the emails to Leyla. Subject: Inquiry regarding admission of family members from Syria—Syria admissions program [ref-nr.: 001929], Syria: Admissions directive of the Federal Ministry of the Interior of 12/23/2013. Her mother wrote to the Federal Office of Migration and Refugees, the Ministry of the Interior, and UNHCR, the United Nations Refugee Agency. She wrote that Leyla's grandmother was elderly, that her feet were tired, that she would not survive fleeing to a reception camp in Turkey or Lebanon or across the Mediterranean or the Balkans. Her mother asked what possibilities existed and wrote that she would vouch for her. Yazidi Kurds are considered infidels, *kuffar*, in the eyes of the militias. Especially now at Christmas, she wrote, imagine what it's like for us and for our family members to live in this fear. The troops loyal to Assad on one side and the Islamist militias on the other. What is possible? What can you do?

In every contact I have with the UNHCR it is explained to me, she wrote, that our relatives have no chance of being accepted into the admission program of the federal government because they are not in Lebanon but in Syria. Nothing remains for me to do but to ask you yet again, in the most polite and emphatic way possible, to open a humane path of solidarity for people menaced by war and fanaticism so that our family members may live in safety and peace.

〜

Were you able to reach them? Leyla asked on the phone.

No, her father said, not for five days. I think the electricity is out again.

Two days later, he called again: I was able to reach them. It was like a game, thought Leyla. She asked, and her father answered. As if they were throwing dice, a game of chance, and her father would answer on the basis of the dice: I was able to reach them, or I was not able to reach them. As if they were playing for their lives, but it wasn't a game.

Sascha breathed softly and regularly next to her while Leyla lay awake. She imagined the village in darkness, longed to be there in that darkness. She imagined she was lying next to Uncle Memo and Mîran on the ground, lighting one cigarette after another in order not to fall asleep. In front of them was the wall of earth that had been raised, behind it the darkness. Here and there noises, wind, a dog barking, silence. She imagined them waiting and hoping that what they were waiting for would not come to pass. How much more she would rather have been waiting with the others in the trench than lying here in the bed next to Sascha's steady breathing. Waiting was lonely when you were the only one waiting.

Over and over there were power outages. I haven't been able to reach them for seven days, her father said. Silence on the other end of the line, then the clearing of his throat. Leyla asked if he was worried. And said, Of course, that's such a dumb question. Leyla lay next to Sascha and stared out at the tree behind the window. Its branches blended with the darkness. What if she never saw her grandmother again? Leyla thought about her grandmother's floral dress and her bent back. About her grandmother sitting in the living room combing her long white hair after showering, then weaving it into braids. Leyla got up, went quietly to the bathroom, and pulled the door shut behind her. She still felt sick. The nausea did not abate, refusing to retreat. Leyla leaned over the toilet bowl and stuck her finger down her throat until she gagged and tears shot out of her eyes. She flushed, washed her hands with soap, rinsed her mouth out, drank some water, and went back into the bedroom to the sleeping Sascha, lying back down next to her.

⌢

They will die. They will not die. They will die. They will not die. The fear and nausea that attacked Leyla had no structure. It overcame her without warning, in bed, in the library, while she was walking over the cracks between the stone slabs. The fear and the nausea were like a possible stumble: with every step and in every moment, the danger of stumbling was hiding.

She stood in the supermarket in front of the dairy case. She didn't know what she was doing there. She walked for a long time with her cloth bag through the endless aisles of shelves, finally going home without buying anything.

Assad's army was laying siege to cities, sealing them off, letting the population starve, and throwing bombs on residential districts and hospitals.

Leyla read about the encirclement of Yarmouk, where the inhabitants melted snow for water and butchered dogs and cats. One mother said: We cooked herbs in water and then drank the water. We ate grass until there was no more grass.

How could she eat? Leyla asked herself. How could she sleep, attend lectures, sit on the steps in front of the library, smoke, drink beer in the evening in Sascha's bar, while at the same time—Leyla did not want to complete this thought.

She couldn't eat anymore. Even the thought of eating sickened her. Although she was not entitled to that. She told herself over and over, I am not entitled to that. How could she have problems eating when she had so much food? Leyla told herself that she was not allowed to feel sorry for herself. It was not about her!

Fear made Leyla superstitious. She formed the names silently with her tongue over and over: Grandma, Uncle Memo, Aunt Havîn, Zozan, Mîran, Welat, Roda. As if she could rectify something with that, as if it were a type of protection.

⌒

When did people stop talking about a revolution and start talking about a war? When the opposition armed itself, when the foreign fighters entered the country—men with combat experience in Afghanistan and Iraq who had written the Islamic confession of faith on their flags—or when the first car bombs exploded, when people buckled explosive belts around their waists, when the regime began bombing cities? Leyla attended her lectures and went grocery shopping afterward, running down her list: milk, bread, cheese. Then she carried the food home.

Leyla filled Sascha's sink with water and dish soap, soaked the sponge, and did the dishes. Sascha said: Let that be, you don't have to do that. But Leyla did the dishes anyhow. Leyla started taking out the trash when it overflowed. She wiped out the garbage can and let it dry in the bathtub. She watered Sascha's plants with the tin watering can that was on the desk. She dusted the plants with a wet towel the way Sascha sometimes did when she remembered to do it.

⌒

Leyla lay next to Sascha on the bed with her face buried in Sascha's red sweater. Sascha stroked Leyla's hair until she fell asleep.

⌒

Sascha said: You're always here. Don't you want to live with me?

Leyla said: I am already living here.

But you still have your room in the shared apartment, said Sascha.

⌒

But every few days Sascha said: I can't do it anymore. This is all too much for me. Then Leyla rode back to her room in the shared apartment, lay on her bed, stared at the ceiling, couldn't sleep, and still went to her lectures the next day.

The way to the seminars, the pigeons that scattered into the air on the square in front of the university, the strong wind that caused her eyes to tear up.

The crowds of people in the cafeteria and next to them Leyla, sitting alone with her tray of food at one of the tables, not hungry but eating anyhow, then leaving the building and seeing on her phone that Sascha had not written to her. Leyla crossed the square again, causing the pigeons to scatter for a second time, got on a streetcar and didn't know where to go. Back in her shared apartment she flung herself on the bed, buried her head in the blanket, and looked at her phone again.

∽

Sascha did not write until days later. They met in the park. Sat on a bench and smoked. Leyla had bought Marlboros for herself. Sascha was already rolling the next cigarette and said: It can't go on like this. It's too much for me. I need space. You don't know how to be alone. Leyla nodded. Sascha said: I don't want to break up, but it's not working. What do you know about anything? said Leyla. Sascha stood up. Leyla stood up. I'm sorry, said Sascha. They walked home in opposite directions through the park.

∽

In the evening, Leyla went to the library; the reading room was already almost empty. Leyla sat at one of the huge wooden tables in the middle of the room. In the black casement windows, you could see the reflection of the library, with its bookshelves, rows of tables, and chairs. Leyla imagined that there was nothing more than this library, an island reflected in the water all around it. The library was the last place in this world. Leyla imagined herself rambling through the aisles for days, through the open access shelves, computer labs, the stacks with their sliding bookcases in the basement. The rough carpet that swallowed her footsteps. The smell of old paper.

At midnight, the library closed. Leyla went past the security men at the entrance. She was tired, but not tired enough. She took detours, side streets, roamed around without knowing where she was going, but then eventually stood at her own door.

She unlocked the door. Are you still awake? Sascha wrote.

Yes, answered Leyla. Can I come over?

Yes, wrote Sascha.

Leyla turned around in the entryway and walked quickly through the park devoid of people.

Sascha opened the door immediately.

Leyla stayed one day with Sascha, went home to shower and change her clothes, and rode to her lecture. She sat in the lecture hall and didn't listen for a single second. She sat there and took notes, but all her sentences were incomplete. What was the professor even talking about? The professor opened her mouth, then closed it again. She gestured with her hands and changed the overhead transparency that was projected onto the screen behind her. Leyla couldn't continue like this, she knew that. She also couldn't stay sitting there, impossible. But where should she go? Should she run out of the lecture hall? But why run? There was no hurry. She could slowly and calmly put her pen and notepad in her bag, put the bag over her shoulder, and walk out of the lecture hall. She would close the door behind her, walk down the stairs, and leave the university building. And then, where to? Leyla stayed in her seat until the lecture was over, slowly put her pen and notepad in her bag, and left with the others.

Sascha was sitting in front of the university building waiting.

~

I have written to everyone, her mother said on the phone. Her voice sounded thin but steady. I can't do anything more, her mother said. I don't know who else I should write to. What on earth am I to do? I wrote to the Federal Office of Migration, to the United Nations Refugee Agency, to our representatives in parliament. I even wrote to the German president!

Threaten that you will go to the press, said Leyla. Write to them that our family is in danger. Say that we will go to the public.

And which public should we go to? her mother asked.

~

If they die, Leyla told herself, I'll take a Kalashnikov, like one of the Kalashnikovs my uncle took with him every year to Newroz and fired into the air and later took with him to the trench to guard the village. I'll take a Kalashnikov like that with me to the Federal Office for Migration and Refugees. The federal office had written—Leyla's mother had taken a picture of it: Please direct your inquiry to the agency responsible for such matters. The agency responsible, however, had already pointed out in the very first letter that the family members would have to have been in Lebanon by 2012 in order to be placed on the list of refugees slated for family reunification in Germany, and since that was not the case, the agency responsible for such matters considered itself not responsible. To this agency responsible for such matters that has declared itself not responsible I will take my Kalashnikov, Uncle Memo's Kalashnikov, Leyla told herself.

⌒

Leyla found a video on YouTube: Drone flight over Aleppo. She watched the video over and over. Streets devoid of people, bombed-out houses, rubble everywhere. Entire apartment blocks had collapsed; only the sky above them remained an undisturbed blue. Over forty percent of Aleppo was destroyed, the entire east side of the city, as it was stated in the video. There were hardly any fruit or vegetables to be bought; the markets were empty. We have less and less fuel; we are using the last reserves. Soon we will be living in complete darkness again.

I was walking in my neighborhood, al-Mashhad, where my office is. I was standing in a shop in our street to buy something to drink when the first barrel bomb hit, just five houses away. I took cover for a few seconds because of the metal pieces flying around. Then I ran out onto the street. Only a few seconds later a second barrel bomb hit. A metal splinter pierced my bag, another one my leg. I ran from the street back to the shop. Seven people who had sought refuge there were dead, crushed by the rubble from the ceiling that had collapsed. They died only because in the few seconds of the explosion they had decided, unlike me, to hide between the shelves, whereas I ran onto the street.

⌒

Sascha didn't want Leyla to pick her up anymore from the café where she worked or to sit at the bar drinking beer and smoking while Sascha stood behind the bar. Sascha said, I can't do this anymore, I need space. Leyla couldn't help but think of this sentence even when Sascha opened the door for her and Leyla came running up the last few steps, slipping out of her shoes, her backpack, and her jacket, when she was burying her hands in Sascha's hair and Sascha was reaching for her, when her lips were looking for Sascha's mouth, her hands opening Sascha's jeans, her tongue opening Sascha's labia while Sascha moaned beneath her, and when they were lying next to one another breathing, just breathing.

Sascha started going more often to her seminars and painting again for the first time in a long while. She always came home late in the evening now and wrote to Leyla that she was tired and just wanted to go to sleep. Sascha went dancing. You should also do something for yourself, Sascha said. So Leyla went dancing too, with her roommates. She and her roommates took the streetcar home. Before Leyla turned on the light, she wrote to Sascha, I'm home. Sleep well. Sascha didn't answer. Leyla looked at her phone at five o'clock in the morning when she woke up. She didn't know what had woken her; she had fallen asleep with her phone in her hand. At nine o'clock and again at eleven, Leyla wrote: Everything okay with you?

Let's talk later, Sascha finally answered.

At three o'clock in the park, Sascha wrote a few hours later. On the benches behind the meadow.

Sascha lit a cigarette. Leyla took the lighter and lit a cigarette for herself too. Soon after that they again went home in opposite directions through the park. Leyla didn't think about anything.

⁓

She saw the two of them together at the opening of an exhibition. She had blond hair; that was almost the only thing that Leyla said to Bernadette about it on the telephone. Blond hair and green glasses with a thick, red border. The people at the opening were beautiful. They had just glanced at the pictures on the white walls and the videos projected next to them. Leyla had been there with her roommates. There had been wine in plastic cups. Leyla told Bernadette that the other woman had water-blue eyes, behind her glasses with the thick lenses. She had stood next to Sascha. Are you sure? asked Bernadette. Yes, Leyla said. I'm sure.

Sascha left the room, returned, and again stood next to the woman with the water-blue eyes and blond hair. Leyla downed her wine in one gulp, told her roommates what was happening, and turned around.

On the way home it rained. At home, Leyla took a long, hot shower until the windows and the mirror were fogged up. What a waste of water, she thought. But she wasn't freezing anymore. She wrapped herself up in a towel and sat on the edge of the bathtub.

It was as if the days were paralyzed. Leyla got dressed, tied her hair back, rode to her lecture. Leyla sat on the streetcar and wrapped her scarf tighter around her neck. What an ugly country it was here. Always gray. It was unbearable.

⁓

Later, Leyla couldn't remember anymore how the day had begun. Presumably, her parents had long since been at work when Leyla got out of bed, went into the kitchen, put the espresso maker on the stove, sat at the table groggy from sleeping so long, and waited for the pot to hiss and the coffee to boil up into the upper part. With her coffee in hand, she sat in the sunshine to smoke.

Her father came home from work earlier than usual. That day, he didn't even change clothes but sat down right away in front of the television. Leyla asked, What's going on? but her father paid no attention to her. On all channels it was the same image. Leyla couldn't say when she had comprehended what was happening. She only remembered that they didn't speak. Her father changed channels without stopping.

He and Leyla stared at the women in the dresses of her grandmother, her aunts, and cousins. Leyla saw a broad, bare plain, dried-out grass and straw. Leyla saw men like her grandfather, her father, her uncle. She saw them all running for their lives with nothing but what they were carrying with them. She saw their steps kicking up the dust. She saw the sun, saw mothers holding their clinging children. Women crying into their white headscarves. People who from pure exhaustion could not cry anymore.

She spent the days in front of the television. It was reported that Sinjar was surrounded. Sinjar was wounded. The newscaster repeated his sentences over and over, only sometimes changing the wording or his facial expression. The images hung in a never-ending loop. The women with their infants in their arms. The dust. The weeping faces. The black flags. On the ground, the body of a man on whose face a circular filter was superimposed so that it looked like he was lying under a pane of milk glass. It is the middle of summer, the voice-over narrative said. Forty-five degrees Celsius in the shade. Little children, old people, sick people are dying of thirst in the mountains. The first refugees reach Duhok. Tens of thousands have not made it here and are stuck in the mountains. A man said: In the mountains there is no water, no electricity, no streets, no bread; there is not even a single green tree. Leyla watched the moderator and the reporter who had joined him on Kurdish television break out in tears as they reported about Sinjar. Leyla saw the videos from the rescue flights of the Iraqi army, the bottles of water that had been dropped from helicopters, bursting apart on the rocks. She saw children crying and screaming, saw crowds rushing for the cargo hold of a single helicopter. She saw the Yazidi representative Vian Dakhil break down during her speech to the Iraqi parliament. There have been seventy-three genocide campaigns against the Yazidis, and now it is being repeated in the twenty-first century. We are being slaughtered. We are being exterminated. An entire religion is being exterminated from the face of the earth. Brothers, I appeal to you in the name of humanity to save us.

Leyla saw videos of mass shootings: the fighters with faces covered, the villagers kneeling in front of them, the shots, the dust rising up.

Leyla saw videos of women and girls walking chained, saw the slave markets of the fighters of the Islamic State. Bearded men, who said to the camera laughing: I want a blue-eyed Yazidi girl. Reports from escaped women who had been sold from fighter to fighter. Thirty-year-olds, seventeen-year-olds, nine-year-olds who had been raped so often that they died from their wounds. Leyla turned off the television.

~

The nausea no longer gave her any respite. The nausea was still there when she bent over the toilet bowl and stuck a finger down her throat. Leyla sat alone during the day on her sofa, digging her bare toes into the living room rug. She watched the light move from place to place, the dust swirling in the rays of sun that fell through the curtains. Outside it was summer.

Leyla only ate when she noticed how long it had been since she had eaten. She only showered when she could smell her own sweat. Sleep almost never came to her, in spite of her exhaustion. She spent her nights in her bedroom in front of her laptop, while her father sat downstairs in front of the television watching the same images. She saw videos of executions, of slave markets, of refugee camps, of men and women her age holding a gun in their hands for the first time.

~

Leyla went to demonstrations in Munich, which were announced for every day of the week, as in Hanover, Bielefeld, Berlin, Hamburg, and Cologne. Her father said, I can't manage it. I have to work. But even on the weekend when he was off, her father didn't go along but stayed at home sitting in front of the television, not getting up, not speaking for hours, eventually uttering sentences like, I don't understand that. Why? He repeated the word: Why? Her mother came along twice but then had to go back to work.

Leyla never went directly home from the demonstrations but always spent time wandering aimlessly through the city. They were also alone on the huge squares or the pedestrian zones. They cried there, they screamed. Sometimes a passerby stopped, observed them for a while, then simply moved on. But once there was a report on the German news about the demonstrations, then another one. Still, it was like they were always just looking into their own faces. In the first news report they showed a crying girl in Bremen who said: My aunt is in Sinjar. I haven't heard from her in a week. Leyla sat next to her parents in front of the TV. Neither of them said anything. As always, the dish of sunflower seeds was on the table, but her father didn't touch them. When Leyla went to bed, she saw that Bernadette had called, but Leyla didn't call back, not then and not the following few days.

~

Later, Leyla tried to arrange the events in a certain order, but she didn't succeed. Just in June, the Iraqi army had ceded Mosul to the Islamic State. They hadn't even fought for it. On the third of August, the Islamic State entered Sinjar and all hell broke loose. Leyla had not looked at the calendar that day; she had only later connected the date August 3, 2014, to the events that she had seen on television, as well as the words genocide and ferman, as they called it. August 3, 2014, was the day when, it seemed later to Leyla, time had been ruptured. Everything that happened afterward, how she exactly spent those weeks, who she had encountered at the demonstrations, how she had gotten back to Leipzig: she could remember nothing. It didn't matter. The Kurdish YPG was able to break through and establish an *escape corridor* from Syria all the way to the plateau of Sinjar. But in September, the Islamic State attacked the city of Kobanê, and in October there was fighting *street by street*. And still, autumn came.

~

Back in Leipzig, Leyla didn't go to the seminars anymore, or to the lectures or the library. She moved, this time to the apartment of one of her roommate's acquaintances who was taking a bicycle tour after completing his bachelor's degree. Eastern Europe, the Balkans, maybe farther; he had all the time in the world.

Leyla spent her nights in front of the kitchen window looking down at the street, as if she were waiting for something. Everything seemed quiet down there. Leyla stared into the yellow light of the street lamps, just staring and staring into space.

At some point she started to go out. She walked around at night, looked up at the windows of apartments in which here and there people were awake and televisions were flickering, contemplated the blank streetcar arrival board. She walked past closed shops and silently blinking neon signs, turned off at empty intersections to go down side streets or follow rail tracks. For hours, she walked past large apartment blocks and playgrounds with dirty sandboxes, walked across stone slabs and dark lawns and asphalt, walked to the parks and the bars where she had been with Sascha, walked even past the row houses in the suburbs with their trimmed hedges, walked for so long that finally exhaustion overtook her.

~

Her father laughed sadly and said on the phone: It's strange, but for the first time the Germans know who we are.

Her mother said: I can't do it anymore. For three years we have been watching that without interruption. And now Sinjar. Who can endure that for four years? her mother asked. It is unbearable.

The worst thing, said Leyla, is watching. I can't watch anymore.

~

Leyla and her old roommate were sitting at the window of a café. Outside, a streetcar drove by. In the café, people were working at their laptops, leafing through magazines, eating cake. Her old roommate was talking about something that Leyla immediately forgot. Leyla nodded, as her old roommate talked; she strained herself to concentrate. Then Leyla talked about Sinjar. Suddenly, she couldn't stop talking. She listed everything that she had read, seen, and heard. She kept talking and talking. She tried to keep her voice under control but her voice started to shake, threatening to fail her when she said that seven thousand women and children were still in captivity with the Islamic State. Leyla wasn't sure if she was the only one who had noticed the faltering of her voice. Her old roommate nodded again and again while Leyla was talking. Only at some point, after several minutes, she interrupted her. She said: That is bad, I know, but bad things happen in the world all the time. Leyla didn't know how to respond to that. She said nothing, and instead talked about something else in her faltering voice, hastily paid for her coffee, said goodbye, and went home. When she had arrived at home, she saw that Sascha had called. But Leyla did not call her back.

In the mornings, Leyla contemplated the hollow in her pillow where her head had lain, the knife from yesterday's breakfast on the kitchen table next to the plate with the breadcrumbs, next to it the half-full cup of coffee that had been sitting there for twenty-four hours. These objects appeared to her like signs that indicated she really did live here, that she was at home in this apartment, this city, and this country. It was *her* towel lying damp on the bathroom floor—she had hung it on the hook, but it had fallen off— and *her* half-full coffee cup that also was sitting there because she, Leyla, had left it there that way. Leyla stood there and contemplated the objects around her. It was hard for her to believe that there was a connection between her and these objects surrounding her in this precise place. If she went away from here, would the objects remain until they gathered dust, until someone came to wipe away their traces, to obliterate them?

⌐⌐

Leyla wished she could leave her name behind, drop it like a cigarette that she put out with the tip of her shoe somewhere outside, and nobody would ever be able to make a connection between her and the stub. She wanted to shed her name and everything connected with it like a snake shedding its skin. So that her name could no longer write her story but she could write the story of her name. To be a blank slate, Leyla thought, a person without a name, without a story.

Her name was the name of martyrs, şehîd. The death of two of them, the captivity of the third—all that was inscribed in her, prescribed for her. Her life, her story were measured against their names. Leyla thought that her name did not belong to her. She belonged to her name.

⌐⌐

Later, Leyla could not say for sure when she made the decision. Perhaps the word decision is also the wrong one for it; maybe she didn't make any decision at all. She read that the first thing the Islamic State fighters did to the Yazidi women was to remove their ribbons. The ribbons that Leyla too had received every year at Çarşema Sor, the festival of the new year, in April, from her Aunt Felek. You were not ever allowed to cut off the ribbons, and if they came loose on their own, you were supposed to tie them around the branch of a tree and could wish for something. She saw crying people living in tents and the photographs of their dead or kidnapped daughters, sons, mothers, fathers, grandmothers, and grandfathers that they held up in the air. Watching this for months was unbearable, but still Leyla could not turn away.

Her father said on the phone that her grandmother's married niece, who was living in the Sinjar region, had gotten into a car with her family when the IS fighters had reached their village. In the car, they made it out of the village. They took nothing with them, her father said, just the car. If they had not had the car, they would no longer be alive.

Leyla thought about how her grandmother's niece's house was still there even though she had fled with her family. The outside walls, the inside walls, the courtyard, the trees in the garden, the cushions and blankets they had slept under, the plates they had sat in front of, the glasses they had drunk out of. Leyla imagined that the tray from dinner was still on the floor in the living room, with the pot of tea on it, sugar residue at the bottom of the glasses.

Leyla read about the Şeşo family, about bakers, political scientists, students leaving Germany to join the Yazidi combat units.

Leyla wrote a message on Facebook, then a second and a third.

Leyla watched videos. The female fighters braided each other's long hair. They wore loose ocher-colored pants and vests, everything in a camouflage pattern. They held Kalashnikovs in their hands, shouting: *Jin jiyan azadî*, women, life, freedom. *Berxwedan jiyan ê*, resistance is life. At night they sang and danced around the campfire. During the day they fired shots; there were videos of that too. They appeared never to sleep.

I joined the female fighters in 2011, one of them said whose name was Nesrin. At that time there were still military academies where we could be trained. We were in the underground and hid our weapons at our friends' families' houses. I am not only responsible for these seven fighters but for the whole battalion.

As a sniper, you have to maintain your composure and keep your eye on the target. I cannot count how many I have killed: there were many.

When the female fighters went into battle in the videos, they let out cries of joy, high piercing trills like those the women normally made at weddings. These women's cries terrified the IS fighters, at least the female fighters said so. If the IS fighters were killed by a woman, they would not enter paradise.

I won't return to my old life in the village, said Nesrin. Not when so many comrades and friends have died. In the beginning, we were still afraid of death. But now we are simply fighting in this war. I am no longer afraid. People are killing other people. Death is nothing now.

If a female fighter died and became a *şehîd*, her body was wrapped in a shroud and put beneath the earth and the photo made especially for her was hung on the living room wall.

~

Leyla, they are coming, her mother said on the phone. We finally received word. She sounded relieved. Leyla packed up her backpack, went to the train station, and boarded the train. Her parents picked her up. On the ride home, her mother said: Thank God, I am so happy. Finally. Leyla said: I can't be glad. They are coming, after all, because they have to flee. Her mother asked her what the alternative was. Leyla didn't say anything. Her father nodded to himself.

Leyla stood next to her mother and father in the arrival hall at the airport. In the crowd, men waited for their wives, mothers for their daughters, everyone for someone. Leyla walked from shop to shop uneasily. More and more people poured out of the door with suitcases and backpacks. Some of them were on vacation. In one of the shops, Leyla bought a pack of chewing gum. How she used to love the airports! The arrival board showed that the plane from Istanbul had landed. Time passed, then more time, then travelers poured out of the exit again, all walking past them. And then suddenly there was a scream. Which of them had screamed first, Leyla or Zozan? They ran toward one another, Zozan hand in hand with their tiny grandmother. Kisses, hugs, more screams, her uncle was alive, her aunt was alive, Zozan was alive, Mîran, Welat, and Roda were alive, her grandmother was alive. Leyla buried her face in her grandmother's headscarf, breathed in her scent, this scent of an old woman and sun and field and summers and the garden. And her grandmother looked at her with wide eyes and picked nervously at her sweater.

～

The others, Leyla found out later from them, had not told her grandmother that they were leaving forever. The others had simply told her: You are going to take a trip, an excursion. You are going to visit your children for a few days in Almanya. Her grandmother had just nodded at that.

They had told her she should pack her things. Uncle Memo had brought her a suitcase. Her grandmother had not known how to do that: pack a suitcase.

As a young woman she had fled from the village where she was born and had grown up, had lived for a few months in the Sinjar region with relatives, and had then come to the village that she never left again. She had lived for many decades in her house with the garden and the chickens, had given birth to her children, held her grandchildren in her arms. Her husband was buried on the hill in the middle of the village. In the village, her days and years followed the rhythm of festivals and harvests, sunrises and sunsets, morning prayers and evening prayers, feeding the chickens and working the fields, baking bread and pickling cabbage, watering the garden and having tea with her neighbors.

The village was all she knew, nothing more than that. The others told Leyla how she had opened Uncle Memo's suitcase and stared into its emptiness. The suitcase was dented, the lining shredded. She stroked it with her bony hands. It was a small suitcase but still too large for everything she owned. She carefully folded her few skirts, aprons, dresses, and floral headscarves, all sewn herself by hand and patched time after time, and stacked them in the suitcase. Then the earth and the dried olive branch from Lalish and the little metal box from the ledge over the door in which she kept a needle and thread, a piece of soap, the green comb for her white hair, and the few photos that were tied together with a string. Before she shut the suitcase she laid a white cloth on top, the burial shroud she had sewn just days before.

~

They departed early in the morning. Her uncle lifted her onto the back of a pickup truck. Her grandmother pulled her headscarf over her face, holding it tight with her hand so that you could still see her eyes, grabbing the rear gate of the truck as if she were afraid of flying away in the wind.

Maybe she looked back at the village one more time. Maybe she just held her hand in front of her eyes to protect herself from the dust in the air.

They drove out of the courtyard down the gravel lane to the paved street, past the garden with its olives and pomegranate tree, the orange trees and lemon trees, the bushes and beds, the beehouse. Once they were on the road, they accelerated. Soon the houses were already blending into the color of the earth; soon they were lost from sight.

They needed five hours to drive the eighty kilometers. They took detours through certain checkpoints where they had heard nobody would cause difficulties for them. They walked the last part on foot. Her grandmother was exhausted. Uncle Memo carried her on his back.

When they tried to cross the border, they became refugees, not for the first time in her grandmother's life. Back then, when she was a child, they had also surrounded her village and wanted to kill them all because they were Yazidis. They had to wait a whole day; the border patrol did not want to let them through, saying that Turkey was not admitting any more refugees.

But they had permissions, and not ones from Turkey, but from Germany, her father said. The border guards did not speak her grandmother's language. Her grandmother didn't understand what they were saying. The soldiers asked her questions, but her grandmother couldn't answer. She reached for her dress with her hand, smoothed it out, stared straight ahead.

They reached Mardin late in the evening.

Their lodgings were in the newer part of the city, in the northern part, and had thin walls. They got a room on the third floor. Because the elevator was broken, Uncle Memo and Aunt Havîn carried the suitcases up the stairs, and Zozan and Mîran held Grandmother's hands and went up with her step by step. They could hear the street noise below, as well as voices and shouting from other rooms. Grandmother was restless and couldn't sleep. When the muezzin recited the evening call to prayer, she panicked. Her shoulders were shaking. There are Muslims here, she cried. The Muslims are coming for us!

Nobody is coming for us, her uncle said.

When he wanted to leave to get something to eat for them all, her grandmother asked from her hotel bed: Where are you going?

To get food, her uncle said, so they told Leyla.

You can't go now, her grandmother said. They are outside. If you go, they will kill you.

~

A few days later, her grandmother boarded an airplane for the first time in her life. She didn't know exactly what that was, an airplane. Uncle Memo fastened her seat belt. Her grandmother kept touching the metal buckles of the seat belt and grabbing hold of the nylon belt when the airplane started moving and then accelerated for takeoff. Then they were above the clouds, the sun shining, a bright glow behind the plastic windows. The seat belt sign above their heads was extinguished. Her grandmother said: The weather is nice, I am going outside now.

With her all-too-thin hands, she stroked the plastic table unfolded in front of her, the armrest, and the croissant wrapped in plastic. She didn't unwrap it, still holding it in her hand when Leyla embraced her.

~

The house they brought her grandmother to had a red tiled roof, wooden shutters painted dark brown, heavy doors. It was huge. Her uncle said: This is the house of your second eldest son, the house of Silo and your granddaughter Leyla. Her grandmother nodded and politely declined the chicken they served her. Thank you, but I'm not hungry, she said, as if she were in a stranger's house.

They kept asking her, almost begging, until she finally started to eat. And even then, she repeatedly laid her fork aside and asked: Have the children eaten already?

Yes, the children have already eaten, they answered.

When her grandmother was finished, she wiped her hands on her apron. Her father gave her a paper napkin. Her grandmother held the napkin for a long time in her hand, then folded it up and stuck it in the pocket of her dress.

Her grandmother sat on a mattress in the corner of the kitchen that they had put there for her since she wasn't used to sitting on chairs.

She sat there and shivered. She wore two jackets, a thin one, a thick one, two pairs of socks, a scarf, and a wool cap over her headscarf. And, still, she said from the start: I am cold.

Her grandmother had become very thin over the last four years, even thinner and smaller than Leyla remembered, and even older: she had deep furrows in her face.

Her grandmother was bored. Already on the second day she asked: When are the neighbors coming over for tea? And then: What kind of a house is this? Why aren't any neighbors coming for tea?

They said to her: You are in Germany. That's the way it is here.

Her grandmother stood at the garden fence and spoke Kurdish to the neighbor who had just come home from work. Leyla said: She doesn't understand you. You are in Germany. Leyla said: Come, Grandma, let's go inside.

Her grandmother said: Leave me be, I want to chat for a bit. She giggled and held her hand in front of her mouth as if it was inappropriate to show her teeth when laughing.

Leyla found her grandmother out front on the street. Her grandmother was walking away bent over, one step after the other, single-mindedly. Where are you going? asked Leyla. Her grandmother said, I am going home: my village is back there. I can see the houses already. She pulled the jacket tighter around her bony body. I'm cold.

Leyla said: You are in Almanya. Her grandmother laughed. Almanya is far away, she said.

Soon, they locked the door at night because her grandmother kept getting up, going to the door and then out onto the street. Now she stood at the door, rattled it, and cried. Where do you want to go? Home, said her grandmother.

You are in Almanya, they said. She sat with them in front of the TV watching Kurdish television. When there was a report about the massacre in Sinjar, her father changed the channel. Your grandma shouldn't see that, he said.

But her grandmother grasped it all. She knew that you always left your village when they came to kill you.

All those years she had never spoken about how her father had been killed and they had been driven out of the village when she was still a little girl, but now she suddenly started to talk.

She said: My father was on the way to Sirte. It was a hot day. He had already been underway for an hour with the others and was tired. It was midday, so they rested. Each of them looked for a place in the shade. They came to him first. They demanded that he recite the Shahada, the Muslim confession of faith. He said, I will not recite the Shahada, so they killed him. Her grandmother told the story a second time, then a third. Leyla sat next to her and nodded. The fourth time, Leyla said, I know. The fifth: You already told me that. But her grandmother started again from the beginning.

She sat on the kitchen floor and sang mourning songs, as if her father had just died. She sang for an hour. Enough, Leyla's father said, but she sang for another hour, and Leyla's father left the house. She kept singing until her voice was just a rasp.

Her grandmother whimpered, buried her head in her hands, sobbed. She hit herself in the chest with her fist, tore at her dress. What's wrong? her father asked.

They killed my father, her grandmother shouted. What did he do that they should have killed him?

Watch out, Leyla's grandmother said to her and reached for her hand. They have set a trap for us. They've surrounded us and want to kill us.

It was a mistake, her father said. She is an old woman. We should not have brought her here.

Leyla bit herself in the lip so that she didn't break into tears. Her father looked away because he noticed that Leyla was fighting tears. Her mother was the only one to keep her composure the way she always kept her composure. At the hospital, even under the greatest pressure when patients were lying half-dead in the emergency room and every second mattered, her mother always remained calm.

Come, Leyla, she said, help me wash your grandmother. Aunt Havîn helped me yesterday. Leyla first tried to get out of it, saying, I don't even know how to do that; I've never washed another person. It's not difficult, her mother just said. They helped her grandmother out of the sweater, pulled her dress over her head, slipped off her white underwear. When Leyla saw the pointed bones of her grandmother's elbows, her protruding ribs with just a thin layer of skin stretched over them, she cringed. She helped her grandmother into the bathtub. Is the water warm enough? her mother asked in her broken Kurdish. Her grandmother nodded. What's up? Are you going to help me? Leyla's mother asked her.

Leyla imagined how they would all wake up one day and the war would be over. How they would all put her grandmother back on an airplane, would all stand together on the gangway after getting off the plane looking out into the landscape shimmering with heat, then ride together with her grandmother from the airport back to the village. They would feed the chickens and bake bread as if nothing had happened.

Leyla went back to Leipzig.

～

Hadia. Leyla read the name on the death certificate when her grandmother died. Leyla read the name for the first time. She helped her mother fill out the forms for the transfer of the body. Hadia, the name was like that of a stranger. As if it weren't her grandmother whose body was being transferred. Of course, that was her name, said her mother; it's on the Syrian documents. Next to the missing birth date, next to the note: nationality ajnabi, foreigner. Hadia was an Arabic name that probably most closely approximated her Kurdish name. It was also the name that the German authorities entered in her documents, that was written on her permission to enter Germany and on the document granting her asylum, the name under which she lived for three more months before she died.

No one ever called her Hadia.

Leyla couldn't help but think of all the names that her father had held over thirty years ago in Turkey, when he was on the bus as Cemil Aslan riding from Nusaybin to Mardin and then registered as Firat Ekinci, ninth child of Majed and Canan Ekinci. In the years that he still wrote for magazines and gave speeches and carried banners at demonstrations, he had called himself Azad, freedom. But freedom had never come, instead the odyssey through the bureaucracy: asylum decision unclear, Hildesheim district court, decision tabled, suspension of deportation, residency requirement, letters, more and more letters to the authorities. Her father had gotten tired. He eventually called himself by his old name again: Silo.

Leyla thought about Leyla and the other women and men in uniform whose photos hung on the walls at Uncle Nûrî and Aunt Felek's and Aunt Pero's homes and whose Kurdish names were different than the names under which they were registered and, in turn, different from the Kurdish names they gave themselves when they went to fight in the mountains, the final names that they died with.

⌒

For three days they gathered in the Yazidi community center in an industrial district of Bielefeld. The parish hall consisted of two large rooms with long rows of tables and chairs, one room for the men and one for the women, between them a large kitchen that connected them. In the kitchen, Aunt Felek and Aunt Havîn stood before huge pots giving instructions. Aunt Felek, the older of the two, clapped her hands together. Time for breakfast, she shouted.

The first guests were already arriving. Leyla had not been among so many people for a long time. She stood somewhat apart from the others, helpless and overwhelmed by all the faces, but just briefly. Aunt Felek clapped her hands once again. Come on, let's go! We have things to do. Leyla carried trays with little glasses and saucers, served black tea to the women in their room. One tea glass got knocked over; Leyla went back into the kitchen to fetch a rag, then went into the room with the men, where her cousins were helping out at a counter. I need more tea, she said, and coffee.

Soon Leyla's hands were moving without her thinking about it. She went back and forth between the kitchen and the two rooms as if she were part of a larger organism that kept working although it had so often been torn apart and put back together.

Leyla rinsed tea glasses, cut bread, cucumbers, and tomatoes, filled little bowls with olives, and waited for the next orders.

Aunt Felek always knew the next thing to do. She carried pots from the stove to the table, lifted them back onto the stove, salted huge amounts of rice, bulgur, trshik. While she stirred the pot, she chatted with her sisters and cousins, laughing, telling stories, gossiping. Leyla carried crates full of tomatoes and cucumbers from the car to the kitchen. They go there, said Aunt Felek, and those go there.

Leyla imagined they would all just keep doing what they were doing, she herself always just running back and forth between the kitchen and the two rooms, following her aunts' directions. She imagined it would never end, that she would be allowed to stay here forever, and the thought comforted her.

~

The two rooms kept filling up more and more. Women Leyla didn't know at all, or only in passing, but to whom she must be related, came into the kitchen to help. More and more guests took their seats at the long tables. The old women gathered around Aunt Pero, who had stood up to greet the newly arrived guests. They all began weeping loudly together, holding each other's shoulders, drying their tears with the corners of their headscarves. Then they all sat down again, drank tea, and ate pastries. But as soon as new guests arrived, Aunt Pero and the others stood up again, weeping and wailing.

Her cousins were there, and the part of her family that lived in northern Germany, but also many others Leyla had seen for the last time in the village, or in Tirbespî, Efrîn, or Aleppo. The neighbors from the village, the nieces who had married and moved to Turkey and their children: they all lived in Germany now. Even the relatives who had fled Sinjar in 2014 were there, at least some of them had made it to Germany since then, and strangers Leyla had never seen before but who all stressed that they were her family. Leyla looked closely at them, the few men with dark jackets and moustaches standing in front of the building smoking, the old woman with a white headscarf and white hair, whose hand she kissed. Zozan, who was a blond since she had started her training at the hair salon, told her the name of the old woman, saying her son had brought her to Germany, and listed the names of the remaining family members who were still in the IDP camps in Iraq waiting until they could be brought to Germany as part of the family reunification program or had saved enough money to pay migrant smugglers. Leyla nodded, wanting to say something, but she was soon forced to move on. The woman whose hand you kissed, Zozan told her later: Her first husband died in the fight against Saddam and two of her sons are fighting now.

~

Leyla stood with the women behind the building and smoked when she noticed that her cell phone was vibrating in her jacket pocket. Leyla let the call go. Back in the kitchen, she saw that Bernadette had tried to call her three times. She had also written messages: Everything okay with you? And ten minutes later: What's going on, why aren't you calling me back? And in fact, Leyla intended to call her back, just not now. She simply didn't know what to tell Bernadette. Bernadette was much too far away. The girls they had once been when they used to steal T-shirts and sunglasses together or lie by the lake were too far away, and besides: Leyla was needed right now in the kitchen. But she didn't call back the following day either, nor the day after that.

~

Leyla recognized her immediately when she entered the kitchen.

Evîn.

Although Evîn had changed, even changed a lot.

Leyla looked at Evîn like a stranger while she stood there waiting until the other women had greeted her, had kissed and embraced her. The longer she waited, the more nervous she became. It had all been so long ago. Leyla had grown up in the meantime. She had moved away from home, had started studying at the university. And four thousand kilometers away, Evîn had also moved away from her parents and her brother, whose children she had taken care of all those years, but unlike Leyla she had married, a widower, and had her own children. That much Leyla had heard, but she didn't even know how many children Evîn had. When during the war the grocery prices had kept going up and up and the attacks of the Islamic State on Rojava were multiplying, she too eventually packed her suitcase and left for Germany with her family.

When Evîn, with her loud laugh and large nose, had finally greeted all the other women and was standing in front of Leyla, she didn't know what to say. They were suddenly the same height; it had never been like that before.

Leyla kissed Evîn's cheeks and didn't know what to do with herself. Evîn carried a chubby baby in her arms who stuck his fist into his mouth and looked at Leyla with big eyes.

Pretty, Leyla said.

My first son, Evîn said and laughed. I was so happy finally to have a son. I have three girls already. My husband is outside with them. Leyla nodded.

Evîn's hair was pulled back and fastened with a tie; there was more gray on her hairline than there used to be. The little wrinkles around her eyes had multiplied, many little wrinkles. She still wore red nail polish, but she looked very tired: that's what had changed so much about her. She was older than Leyla could ever have imagined her to be, but her age was not in her laugh, her wrinkles, the rings around her eyes, or the gray hair.

Evîn still smiled. How are you? she asked.

Good. I'm okay. And you?

I'm fine. Are you married now too? Evîn asked.

No, Leyla said.

Engaged? asked Evîn.

No, Leyla said and quickly added: I'm still in college.

That's good, said Evîn. Then you will first finish college and afterward get married. But do you have a boyfriend?

Leyla shook her head.

You can tell me, Evîn said, laughing, and turned around to greet the next woman.

Leyla took a cutting board from the cupboard and began to prepare pita bread. She was disappointed. It felt the whole time like betrayal that Evîn had married. And it felt like a second betrayal that Evîn's only question for Leyla was if she had also gotten married. She didn't ask about her studies; Evîn, of all people, who had always been the only one in the village to ask Leyla what she was reading.

Evîn had always been the one to have her own opinion, to laugh the loudest, the one who had the biggest mouth and the biggest nose, as people say, who wore neon T-shirts and painted her nails red, who smoked Marlboros. Unlike the other women, Evîn had not talked incessantly about marriage and children. Evîn was the one Leyla thought she wanted one day to be like. But what had she expected? Of course Evîn had gotten married, just like Rengîn had, just like Zozan would, just as all of them expected Leyla to do.

～

Leyla knew that right in this moment, while she was kneeling in the kitchen with the other women rolling grape leaves on the floor, stuffing peppers and eggplant, putting kûlîçe and *meschebek* on plates, her mother and Aunt Havîn were still at home washing her grandmother's body, sprinkling it with water from the sacred spring at Zimzim.

～

Leyla was standing at the stove filling a pot with grape leaves when two of her aunts called on her cell phone.

Your father is not answering his phone, Aunt Havîn said; she sounded upset. Your uncle isn't either. We can't find Grandma's burial shroud. We simply can't find it, she said. Take the phone to your father, please. Leyla stuck the phone between her shoulder and ear, washed the bulgur and ground meat off her hands, and went into the room where the men were.

She scanned each table, all the old and middle-aged men with their moustaches, entangled in endless conversations. The room was full. Mîran, Welat, Roda, and a few of the younger ones walked back and forth in their jeans and white sneakers between the rows of tables serving tea and coffee.

It took a while for her to find her father. He sat at the end of one of the tables between five other men he had introduced to Leyla as his cousins; two of them had been, like him, members of the communist party decades ago. Naturally, they were talking about politics.

Aunt Havîn can't find Grandma's burial shroud at home, said Leyla.

How should I know where it is? her father said, seeming irritated. Tell them that. They should simply use a different shroud.

Leyla went back to the kitchen. In the meantime, the women were finished with the grape leaves. Leyla joined them and dried dishes. Rohat appeared in the kitchen door, long since a head taller than Leyla but still just as serious as he had always been since his arrival in Germany. Your father is calling for you, Leyla.

～

Her father poured tea for himself and stirred the sugar. There were even more men there now, and the room was bursting at the seams. The clinking of the spoons in the tea glasses was swallowed by the conversations, and the air was stifling. Leyla squeezed onto a chair at the edge of the table. Are you hungry? her father asked. Leyla shook her head.

Her father took a sip of tea.

When your grandmother arrived at our house, he said across the whir of voices, I saw what she had packed in her suitcase. Her comb, her soap, her apron, her few dresses and socks. And the white cloth, the burial shroud. I couldn't bear to see the shroud, he said. I have endured everything. But not the thought that she clearly knew when she left her village she would never see it again alive, that she would never go home again.

He took a drink.

I threw it away, he said. As if I believed she would make it home again to die if she didn't have a shroud.

He emptied his glass in one gulp and then said, without looking at Leyla, You all must have a lot to do in the kitchen. Leyla nodded.

～

Her cousins carried the casket on their shoulders into the hall. The wood, Leyla thought, is heavier than the body inside it. The shaykh stood at the head of the casket and said the prayer for the dead, but Leyla didn't hear his words, for hardly had he begun when a tumult broke loose, shrill weeping and screams from the women. They tore at their clothes and their hair, hit themselves with full force on their chests with their fists. Leyla was distraught, even though she knew the old women were wailing for her grandmother. Still, their outburst was so sudden and violent, so distant from everything here, from Bielefeld, from Germany. A while ago she had wanted to stay here forever with the others, but now she would have liked more than anything to leave the parish hall, walk on and on all by herself in any direction until her feet couldn't carry her anymore and she had to sit down. But Rengîn grabbed her hand and lay her arm around Leyla's shoulder. It was good to be held by Rengîn. It was good to stand here with the others. And it was as if the women's wailing burst a dam inside Leyla that had held back her tears for a long, long time, like a river. She had served tea, washed dishes, sliced tomatoes and cucumbers, pursed her lips together, swallowed, inhaled, exhaled. But now her tears burst forth, flowing down her cheeks, dripping from her chin onto her blouse. Next to Leyla stood Zozan, next to Zozan her father, next to her father Uncle Memo, next to her uncle her grandmother's niece, next to her grandmother's niece her husband.

All the people around Leyla floated away before her eyes. Zozan reached for her arm; she too was weeping silently like Leyla. The old women wailed and moaned. The men did not cry, just stared onto the ground in front of them, at the casket, or past the wailing women into space. And finally, at some point, her father shouted hysterically: That's enough! The casket was carried out of the hall accompanied by the loud weeping of the women.

～

Three days later, Siyabend and Rohat brought the casket to Turkey, to Nusaybin on the Syrian border. The last people who had stayed in the village assumed responsibility for the casket, and Siyabend and Rohat flew back to Germany.

The villagers sent photographs, taken from a car that drove behind the pickup where the casket was tied down to the truck bed. It looked like a procession, like the ones Leyla had seen at weddings. To the left and right of the casket a man and a woman squatted in the wind, protecting their faces from the dust, the cold, and the wind with kerchiefs. Leyla zoomed in on them, but the more she zoomed in, the blurrier the picture became.

Leyla looked at the villagers' photos of the transfer of her grandmother's body to her burial place again and again. The green island in the middle of the road, the boulevards in the city. On the sidewalk a mother with a child holding her hand. You could only see her back. Houses, and between the houses a vacant lot where sheep were grazing. The color of the houses, the color of the earth. The dust covering the red paint of the pickup truck, the dust in the wool of the sheep.

The only people who had stayed in the village were those who had no money to pay migrant smugglers or were too old or sick to leave. Refugees from Sinjar had moved into the empty houses; they made food and distributed it to everyone.

The villagers sent a new video that they recorded on the hill in the middle of the village. Her father watched it and said that when he died, he wanted to be buried in Kurdistan.

In the video you could see the villagers burying her grandmother next to her grandfather. Around the grave, the other graves. All around the hill the plain, in the north the mountains, the Turkish border.

They lowered the casket into the ground.

They piled stones on the casket, a blanket of stones. Then the large headstone. Her father said there was a story that the dead wanted to follow the living, wanted to go back with them in the evening to the village. The dead hit their foreheads on the headstone and remembered then that they were dead.

~

Leyla sat with her parents in front of the television. It was late already and she was tired, but none of them managed to get up. On television came one video clip after the other. All three ate salted sunflower seeds, the hulls cracking between their teeth. On TV there were bare trees, an autumn landscape. Under the trees sat Şivan Perwer playing his saz, his hands gliding over the long neck of the instrument. Şivan wore şal u şapîk, the loose pants and the loose shirt, the long kerchief knotted around his waist. His shirt had epaulettes and looked like a uniform. Suddenly you could hear shots, machine guns, so loud that they tore through the music. Now Şivan was standing in a trench behind a bulwark of sandbags, soldiers next to him. He sang: I am a young Kurd.

The soldiers held their machine guns in firing position. They shot into the vast barren landscape, where no people could be seen. Leyla had seen these images so often: the vast land, the scattered houses.

Şivan sang: You carry bomb and gun.

In the next image there was a living room with a television in it. On the television naked mountains, midsummer—Leyla had seen these recordings from Sinjar over and over: the people running for their lives, mothers with infants in their arms, children, fathers, grandfathers, grandmothers, the dust and the exhaustion on their faces.

A young man sat in the living room in front of the television and contemplated the mountains and the faces of the fleeing people on television. I am a young Kurd, sang Şivan.

The young man ran his left hand over his face as if he were wiping tears from his eyes.

Şivan stood at the sandbags again and sang.

A woman appeared, presumably the mother of the young man. She sat behind him on a foam mattress like the ones that had been in her grandparents' living room, wore a white-and-blue floral headscarf, a floor-length dress from the same material, over it a red sweater.

The young man—Leyla only now saw how tender he was, how slender and wispy—jolted up, as if nothing could have stopped him. His mother looked at him, horrified.

The young man stood in front of a wardrobe. He opened both doors, took out a pair of camouflage pants and a camouflage jacket.

I am going to war, sang Şivan.

~

The young man kneeled before his mother, kissing her hand and her hair. When I am killed, mother, don't cry, sang Şivan. I am going to war, I am going to battle.

All right, enough, said her father and turned off the television. I am tired: I'm going to bed. He got up and left the living room. Leyla's mother stroked her hair, then followed her father to bed.

Leyla just kept sitting there staring at the black screen. Then she put on a jacket and went outside to the garden. She rummaged around in her jacket pocket until she found tobacco, filters, and rolling papers. She suddenly felt light. Her decision had long since been made, she thought; she just hadn't been aware of it. She lit her cigarette, sucked in the smoke, and blew it into the air.

~

When she was back in Leipzig, she went the very first day to the association building. She had to look for the address in her Facebook messages. There was only a group of old men sitting there drinking tea at a table. News from Ronahî TV was playing on the television on the wall.

The men looked at Leyla in amazement when she told them that an acquaintance had told her that every Tuesday a group of Kurdish students met there. Yes, that's true, one of the men said finally, except that the group now meets every Thursday. Leyla nodded and was about to leave when the man asked who the acquaintance was who told her about the group. Leyla said his name. The man then wanted to know if she was a Kurd. Leyla nodded. What's your name? he asked. Leyla said her name. The man told her to wait a moment while he called his daughter on the phone who lived nearby. It's best for you to talk to my daughter, the man said. I don't want to cause any inconvenience, said Leyla. The man asked if she would like a çay; his daughter would be there shortly. Leyla nodded, took off her jacket, and sat down at one of the tables. The man brought her the tea. Leyla took two spoonfuls of sugar, stirred, and waited.

Soon thereafter the man said: Ah, here's Rûken finally. How nice, said Rûken, who took off her foggy glasses, cap, scarf, and jacket and greeted Leyla with a kiss on each cheek. She smiled. How nice that you have come.

⁓

It was not yet morning. Leyla sat at her kitchen table and lit a cigarette with the butt of one that was still burning. Over the houses the sky turned gray. Leyla brushed her teeth, packed her toothbrush in the backpack she had bought back then with Bernadette. Heat off, windows closed. Lights out. The sky turned gray. Perhaps it would rain.

To leave is first and foremost a succession of steps. Leyla got up, slung her backpack over her shoulder, took a step through the room, then a second one, walked into the entryway, opened the apartment door, stood in the stairwell, locked the door behind her, went down the stairs, threw the key in the mailbox, pulled open the door of the building, stepped over the threshold, and took the first steps.

AUTHOR'S ACKNOWLEDGMENTS

I thank my father for the stories and my family, above all my sister, Nesrin, my brothers, Dilovan and Jindi; and my friends, especially Julia, Judith, Luna, Cemile, Sakî, Svenja, Eser, Beliban, Düzen, and Isabel. I thank my community, my mentors, and all the others who supported me and who I learned from; my agent, Elisabeth Botros; and my copyeditor, Florian Kessler.

I thank the Lukas Artists' House for the residency grant, the Lüneburg Literature Office for the Heinrich Heine grant, and the city of Munich for a literary grant.

GLOSSARY

Abitur—A German secondary school diploma qualifying the recipient to study at a university

agha—A title of honor given in the Ottoman Empire to civilian and military officials

ajnabi—A designation for a foreign noncitizen in Syrian Arabic applied to Yazidis and other Kurds

Hafez al-Assad—Former president of Syria and father of the current Syrian president, Bashar al-Assad

Almanya—Kurdish word for Germany used by Leyla's cousin Zozan as a pejorative nickname for her

aprax—Kurdish word for stuffed grape leaves, known more widely elsewhere as dolma

Baathism—An Arab nationalist ideology espoused by the former leader of Iraq Saddam Hussein and by the Syrian president Bashar al-Assad and his father, Hafez al-Assad

Mustafa Barzani—Highly prominent Kurdish political figure who became leader of the Kurdistan Democratic Party in 1946 and led the Peshmerga in a revolt against the Iraqi regime in the late 1960s

çay—Kurdish word for tea

Christian Social Union—Conservative political party in the German federal state of Bavaria that forms a faction in parliament with the Christian Democrats

dengbêj—A genre of Kurdish music or the singer-storyteller who performs such music

dew—A nonalcoholic drink made from water, yogurt, and mint that is popular in Kurdish cuisine *ferman*—Term used by Yazidis to refer to specific instances of persecution in their history, including massacres and forced expulsions

Garachi—A Muslim Romani people living in Turkey and Azerbaijan

Germanistik—German term for the study and scholarship of German language and literature at the university level

"The Internationale"—An anthem associated with the socialist movement since the late nineteenth century whose lyrics were originally written in French but have been translated into many languages

JITEM—Gendarmerie Intelligence and Counter-Terrorism, the unofficial intelligence agency of the Turkish police that has been active in operations against the PKK

kemençe—a stringed bowed musical instrument of the lute family originating in the Eastern Mediterranean and used, for example, for the performance of Turkish ceremonial and folk music

kutilk—A Kurdish meat dish

Lalish—A valley in northern Iraq that is holy for Yazidis and houses the tomb of Shayk ʿAdī ibn Musafir

maultaschen—A specialty of the German region of Swabia, a pasta shaped like ravioli that is stuffed with meat, spinach, onion, and spices

mîr—Kurdish title of nobility meaning roughly chief or prince

murids—Lowest of the three Yazidi castes, it denotes "commoners"

Newroz—The celebration of spring and the new year in Kurdish culture

Palmyra—An ancient city in Syria and UNESCO World Heritage Site that was taken control of by Islamic State forces between May 2015 and March 2016

Şivan Perwer—A Kurdish poet, writer, singer, and performer who fled Turkey due to persecution as a Kurdish nationalist and whose songs were banned in Iraq, Syria, and Turkey

Peshmerga—Kurdish military that helped overthrow Saddam Hussein in 2003 and is responsible for the security of the Kurdish autonomous region in northern Iraq

pîr—One of the three castes of Yazidi society, it is found on the hierarchy beneath *shaykh* and above *murid*

PKK—Kurdistan Workers' Party, a political organization and armed guerilla movement based primarily in Eastern Turkey and Northern Iraq

qewals—Yazidi religious singers who preserve and pass down traditional religious knowledge through their performances whose function is particularly important given the historical prohibition of writing down religious teachings among the Yazidis

raki—An alcoholic drink popular in Turkey and other Mediterranean regions made from twice-distilled grapes and anise

şal û şapik—Two items of traditional Kurdish dress worn by men consisting of wide and loose pants tied by a scarf and an open jacket and vest worn over the jacket

saz—A stringed instrument used to perform Kurdish music

schupfnudeln—A southern German and Austrian specialty, a kind of dumpling or thick noodle made from egg and flour and/or potatoes, often served with sauerkraut

şehîd—Northern Kurdish (Kurmanji) word for martyr

Shabiha—State-sponsored Syrian militias accused of committing atrocities against the Syrian opposition

shaykh—Term used in pre-Islamic and Islamic times to refer to an elder, tribal leader, or religious leader; in Yazidi society it refers to a hereditary caste of leaders

Shaykh Adî ('Adī ibn Musafir)—A twelfth-century Sufi mystic who is an important religious figure for Yazidis and whose mausoleum is in Lalish

Shaykh Mend Fekhra—A Yazidi religious figure believed to have had the ability to cure snake bites and considered to be the founder of the Mend order of snake charmers

Sinjar—A region and town in northern Iraq inhabited predominantly by Yazidis

Der Spiegel—A weekly German-language news magazine published in Hamburg

suq—Arab market or bazaar, often covered

trshik—A Kurdish food consisting of water, salt, meat, rice, and other ingredients

za'atar—A spice mixture including herbs, toasted sesame seeds, and spices used in the Eastern Mediterranean region

zurna—A double-reed wind instrument used to play folk music in many Middle Eastern, Central Asian, and Mediterranean countries